MAMMOTH

Douglas Perry

Amberjack Publishing
New York, New York

Amberjack Publishing
228 Park Avenue S #89611
New York, NY 10003-1502
http://amberjackpublishing.com

Publisher's Cataloging-in-Publication data

Names: Perry, Douglas, 1968-, author.
Title: Mammoth / by Douglas Perry.
Description: First edition | New York [New York] : Amberjack Publishing, 2016.
Identifiers: ISBN 978-0-9972377-1-9 (pbk.) | ISBN 978-0-9972377-2-6 (ebook) | LCCN 2016931183
Subjects: LCSH Murder—Fiction | Camps--California--Fiction. | California--Fiction. | BISAC FICTION / Crime.
Classification: LCC PS3616.E79289 M36 2016 | DDC 813.6--dc23

Cover Design: Red Couch Creative, Inc.

Printed in the United States of America

PROLOGUE

Toby Berenson tapped the gun with his hand. "Ever seen something like this before?"

Chief Kenneth Hicks leaned forward for a better look. He pressed his tongue against the top of his mouth and made a clucking noise, the sound of serious pondering. "No. Can't say that I have."

"Pretty impressive," Berenson said. The fat man massaged the gun's scope, patted the handguard. He was the town's dry cleaner, but he loved Robert Ludlum's books. He thought he knew weaponry.

Hicks nodded. It was impressive. An HK33 assault rifle. A West German gun with a Soviet cartridge. Certainly unusual around these parts.

"Well, the day just got interesting, didn't it?" Hicks picked the cartridge up from the desk, felt the weight of it, then placed it on the blotter. He sat back and put his feet on the desk. The heel of his right boot clipped the gun's barrel, which rocked like a seesaw. The Mammoth View police chief hooked his hands behind his head, watching Berenson watch him, pleased with Toby's expression. Hicks knew he didn't look like a man who'd had a heart attack five weeks ago. Lloyd had found the chief on the floor of the john, his belt unbuckled. It made Hicks furious to think what he must have looked like. How he had to be carried like a child to the cot in the cell. Thinking about it now, his pride in his recovery capsized into despondency. He dropped his feet to the floor with a thump. Over the past month he had become a man of emotional extremes, a stranger to himself. He mindlessly grabbed his hat from the desk and put it on, just to give himself something to do. He had been indestructible once, he thought. A marine with a swagger in his walk and a tattoo of a bathing beauty on his arm. At least he still had the bathing beauty.

He let his gaze lose focus, turning Toby Berenson's face into oatmeal. "You really found it on the side of the road?"

Berenson nodded, shrugged. "Fully loaded and ready to go."

The front door swung open and a bolt of sunlight hit Hicks dead in the eyes. He squinted, sending deep creases down his cheeks. He had an out-on-the-range face, someone had once said, trying to compliment him. Hicks remembered that and smiled to himself. No one here knew that he'd never been on a horse.

Lieutenant Lloyd closed the door and stepped over to the desk. He pressed two fingers to the assault rifle's barrel and whistled. "Nice toy."

"Yeah," Hicks said. "Ain't it?"

Lloyd took off his hat and wiped his forehead, grinning at the gun. He was about to ask where the weapon came from, but the chief cut him off with a look. Hicks nodded toward the holding pen in the back. It was time to check on their prisoner. The chief watched Lloyd step past him and disappear around the corner. Otis had been yelping about something back there just a minute ago, but Hicks had ignored him. That's what he had a staff for.

The chief picked up the gun and held it like an appraiser at Christie's. It looked brand spanking new.

"What do you think?" Berenson ventured. "Coyotes?"

Hicks cocked an eyebrow at him, amused by the dry cleaner's use of slang. "In Mammoth?" He shook his head. They had illegals pass through town here and there, taking the long way north from the Weedpatch migrant camp, but human smugglers? This far off the beaten path? "Could just be a collector," he said, not believing it.

"Yeah. Could be."

Berenson jerked, frightened by a sudden noise. The steel door in the back banged again, and Hicks turned around to look for the sound.

"Hey! Hey!" Lloyd yelled.

The chief put the gun on the desk and stood up. Surely Jimmy Jamison wasn't trying a jailbreak. Jimmy wasn't as harmless as Andy Griffith's town drunk—that's why they called him Otis, after the character in the TV show—but he was definitely sober by now. He was always as timid as a kitten when he was dry. "Stay here," he told Berenson.

Hicks stepped through the tight hallway and hustled into the back room. In the cell, Jamison was sprawled on the floor, flailing like a dropped goldfish. His wrists leaked thin globs of blood onto the concrete floor. A knife, to butter the morning biscuit Hicks had brought in for him, glinted in the overhead light. Hicks stared in disbelief, his head fizzing.

"Chief?"

Hicks found Lloyd kneeling next to their writhing prisoner. The officer had wound toilet paper around his own hands, and now he grabbed Jamison's wrists with them. Hicks crouched, felt himself blink hard and fast. The wounds didn't look deep, but what did he know? They had to get Jimmy to the clinic.

"Something's happened," Lloyd said, looking up as he squeezed Jamison's wrists.

"I can see that."

Lloyd's eyes followed his boss's, landed on Jamison's contorted face. "Right," he said. "But, I mean . . . out there. In the world." His gaze again flicked to his patient. "What he was listening to."

Hicks noticed the black Japanese radio sitting on the cell's cot, the same cot where the chief had been placed for safekeeping just a few weeks ago after his heart seized up. Some kind of explosion crackled from the receiver. Hicks moved closer. A man's excited voice pushed through the static gauze. ". . . It's spreading everywhere. It's coming this way. About twenty yards to my right—" The speaker's microphone screeched, then nothing, as if the radio had keeled over, just like its listener.

"Where is this?" Hicks asked.

"I think he said out by the mill."

The fizzing in Hicks's head had become crashing waves. "We'd better get out there," he said.

The chief turned toward the hall. He prided himself on his stoic demeanor, but he was sure Lloyd had clocked his fear. He didn't much care. He was thinking about whether he should take the HK33.

CHAPTER ONE

Tori woke with a ringing in her ears. She wondered if she was getting a cold.

She rolled to her feet anyway and pulled on a pair of shorts. She shook out her limbs in the dark, squeezed her fingers into fists. Like always in the morning, she felt boneless and fuzzy, lost somewhere inside her body. A floorboard burped under her step. Liesel, in the bed next to hers, shifted like an old fishing boat. Tori tiptoed past her, slipped into her shoes. She eased open the cabin door and was off, running down the gravel embankment with quick, scissoring strides, disappearing into the woods.

The rush of air into her lungs shocked her. At first she thought she was going to gag, but then something inside her adjusted, something mysterious, and her breathing eased. She looked up. The night still grabbed at her arms and chest, but beyond the treetops, way out in space, the horizon shimmered like tinsel.

Tori wanted to love this early morning ritual. She wanted it to give her spiritual insights, open her up to nature, her body, and endless possibility. Instead, she felt lonesome. She felt small.

The morning dug deeper into Tori's lungs, a familiar, annoying burn. She picked up her pace. She shot between two trees and into an opening in the forest. All the other kids in camp stuck strictly to the program. They didn't work any harder than the coaches made them, which was plenty hard enough. But Tori knew she was behind the curve. She'd become serious about running only in the past year, and she was sixteen already. Her father had secured a spot for her in this girls' training camp outside Mammoth View, up in the Sierra Nevadas, about two hundred miles from their home in Bakersfield. It was the only running camp in the country for girls, and she'd been stunned when her father proposed it. She'd wanted to go to camp, just normal summer camp, since she was twelve, and her dad had never even considered it. He expected her to work during the summers. Slinging pizza. Hawking newspapers. Anything. Got to do your part for the family fund, he said. Now, out of nowhere, he wanted her to do this special, two-week sleep-away program, and insisted on driving her up there himself.

When she asked why he'd changed his mind about camp, he said he recognized her potential, that was all. Thought she could be good enough for a college scholarship. Good enough for the Olympics one day. With her dad's sudden enthusiasm, she had started to believe it really was possible. She couldn't be ready in time for the Moscow Games—she'd be just nineteen, and that was going to be Mary Decker's Olympics—but by 1984 she would be for sure. Decker, the little pigtailed teen who'd become famous a couple of years ago after winning the 800-meters race at a U.S.-Soviet meet in Minsk, fascinated Tori. If Decker could outrun those big Russian women, maybe Tori could too. She would work hard at Spritle's Racers, she'd promised her father, harder than she'd ever worked in her life. But hard work was only part of it; she knew that much. Did she have enough of that special sauce, enough *extra* red blood cells, to be really good? Good like the Kalenjin, whose bone marrow could send a rocket to the moon? She didn't know. No one knew yet even if Mary Decker could run with the Kalenjin.

Tori slowed as she moved into the center of the clearing, gazing skyward at an array of stars being blanked out by the morning. She thought about how everyone loved her father. People lit up when they saw Billy Lane coming. Slapped him on the back, ready for a quip, ready to laugh. But he was rarely Happy Billy for her. He gave her this hard, disapproving look all the time, like he was a hungry hawk ready to swoop down, and she was just this small, scrawny mouse, an unworthy snack. Tori thought she heard something—a hawk or a mouse, some kind of animal—and she picked up her pace again. Still in the clearing, still looking up at the sky, she thought how the world seemed too big out here, bigger than it should be. Her ears pulsed, the pressure jostling about inside her, thumping against the sides of her head. She stumbled, turning her foot awkwardly. She caught herself, but it didn't matter. She kept stumbling and turning, finally dropping to the ground with a bang. She held on tight.

By the time Tori made it back to the camp, she had calmed down. They'd all been told on the first day that the Mammoth Mountain area was geologically active and that an earthquake was always a possibility. This one hadn't lasted very long. Thirty seconds, maybe a little more. No big deal.

There was no damage at the camp. No trees or buildings had fallen down. Tori stepped into her cabin and looked around. Her book—Jane Austen's *Persuasion*—had slid to the end of her bed. That was about it. Her lump of dirty clothes on the floor had been undisturbed by the tectonic ruckus.

Everyone was in the dining hall having breakfast. Tori sat at a large table with her training group. No one moved over for her, so she teetered on the end of the bench, one buttock floating free in space. "You're all still alive," she joked.

"Not for much longer," Liesel said, dramatically holding her nose. "Go take a shower, Tor!"

Everyone laughed, the sound exploding over the table and bouncing off the windows. Tori had grown accustomed to the teasing. She was the new girl. Almost all of the others had been in the camp last summer. Tori didn't mind the teasing that much, but her face and neck still flared into a crimson rash every time. She hated that she was so transparent. She reached across the table, grabbed Liesel's cup of orange juice, and hawked a loogie up from her toes.

The quake had knocked out the phone line to the camp, though no one had noticed yet. The coaches discouraged parents from calling. Isolation was a powerful motivator. That's how it was in Kenya and Ethiopia, after all. Coach Prinzano, like Tori's high school coach, said that if you were going to be a real competitive runner, you had to think and act and live like an East African, like a member of the Kalenjin tribe. You had to force your body to rewire itself, if it could. That's why Spritle's Racers was at high altitude, more than seven thousand feet up the mountain.

After breakfast and a round of stretching, the seventeen teenaged runners broke up into their training cliques. Tori, Sofia, and Summer would spend the afternoon together doing 800-meter repeats on the track, synchronizing their strides and pushing themselves to the brink. But first they would head off on an eight-mile run along the outer bank with Mary Bowen and her group. Tori enjoyed the slow group runs more than anything else in the program. They provided a sense of community, rather than competition, among the girls. When their various warm-ups were done, seven of them headed out along the nature path, keeping their elbows in tight but letting their legs casually swing like hammocks. It was a challenge—alternately frustrating and satisfying—to hold themselves back, to keep their form while lazing along like old ladies.

The girls chatted during these runs—Liesel, for one, babbled constantly, about the University of Oregon's interest in her, about the hair on her boyfriend's back, about her favorite pair of short-shorts and what she wanted to eat for dinner—but Tori preferred to keep to herself, her head slightly down, watching the dirt path unrolling before her. She liked the way her insides felt when she ran. She liked how her body knew exactly what to do—her left knee springing up just as her right heel rolled forward and the toes pushed off—without her brain having anything to do with it. It was a relief, she thought, to not think at all. She had worked herself into a pleasant, numb state when Sofia nudged her.

"Look at that," she said. "What is that?"

Tori squinted into the sun. She didn't see anything and shrugged.

Sofia pointed again. The girl was a wispy thing even for this crowd, Tori thought. Sofia's black hair bounced. Her thin, coppery arm refracted the sun as she strained to maintain the alignment of her outstretched finger. More than any of them, Sofia seemed to love to run, just the pure act of it. Mile after mile. Liesel had commented on it one night while lying in bed. She joked that it was because Sofia's mother had run across the border when she was pregnant with her.

Tori followed the finger, squinting at the trees, the sky-glare, the precipitous drop beyond the edge of the path. This time a blob also caught her eye, something across the ravine. It was moving with them.

"Do you see it?" Sofia asked.

"Yeah."

"Is it a coyote?"

Tori stared across the gulch. She'd never seen a coyote, not in real life. She thought it looked like a bear . . . but it couldn't be, right?

She tried to squeeze more focus out of her gaze, but no dice. It was too far away. It was just a blob. A blob moving along with them, like a speck in the corner of your eye.

"I don't know," she said. "But I'm glad it's over there."

Sofia didn't like that answer. "Hey—" she said, reaching out and tapping the shoulder jouncing ahead of her.

The back of a hand whacked Sofia's wrist, causing her to jump in fright.

The shoulder and the hand belonged to Mary Bowen—Coach

P. always used her full name when talking to or about her, no one knew why. What everyone did know was that Mary Bowen was the queen of the camp, a junior trainer after two summers as the coach's star pupil. Except she didn't really care about helping the other girls train. Keen to start her freshman year at the University of Arizona, she cared about her splits. She cared about her regimen. She cared about her long, perfect legs, which she carefully shaved in the shower every morning until there was no hot water for anyone else. She cared about herself.

All the girls admired her anyway. Mary Bowen was a jock through and through, with the rolling stride of a cocky drunk and the broad, indecent shoulders of a mannequin. She would chat now and again during slow runs, agreeing with or *Hmmm*ing at whatever Liesel was saying, but she was disciplined about her form. She did not want to be touched or bumped.

"Mary . . ." Sofia said, her quiet voice now a little ragged. "Mary, what is that?"

"What?" Mary Bowen said. She was looking straight ahead, concentrating on her feet gobbling up the path.

"Over there."

Everyone followed Sofia's finger across the ravine.

"There," Sofia said.

The blob was still moving along with them, flashing in the sunlight. Tori strained to put it in perspective with its surroundings. It was big, she knew that much.

"What is that?" Liesel parroted.

"Is it a bear?" Tori asked, daring to offer her opinion.

The girls had unconsciously picked up their pace. Tori's jaw rattled with every footfall. This wasn't a slow run anymore. They had to be doing a five-minute mile all of a sudden—while craning their necks, looking over and around each other. Mary watched the blob just like the rest of them, her eyes like gun slits. The others repeatedly turned to look at Mary, waiting for a sign. Should they run faster? Should they dash into the woods?

Mary hooked her thumbs on her hips and broke stride. Sofia

spun to avoid a collision. The girl in the lead, Robin, flapped her arms like a goony bird to arrest her momentum. As the younger girls caught their breath and gathered together, resting on each other's shoulders and backs, Mary stepped to the edge of the path, squinting across the ravine. The blob had stopped too. It wavered like a mirage. All at once, it disappeared.

Mary Bowen waited, chewing on her lower lip, her teeth worrying into a small tear in the fleshy center. "It's nothing," she finally said. "A local. There's a lot of rednecks around here. The idiot just fell over. He's drunk." She looked at her stopwatch. "Now our time is ruined."

CHAPTER TWO

"How's it look out there?" Billy called.

Sam, peering through the glass in the front door, grinned. "Not many cars left on the street. People are getting out of Dodge."

Billy Lane couldn't believe their luck. The diversions—especially the big one, the one they'd all laughed about—had worked better than they possibly could have imagined. And the earthquake—well, that was just pure serendipity. A nice little kick-start to the plan. He checked his watch: he'd cleaned out the vault in four minutes flat.

He tripped over the bank manager on the way out. The banker kept his hands on his head, his face pressed into the floor. Billy noticed that the man had balled up his necktie into a little pillow for his ear. He considered what to do with him. The man had seen his face. But after Billy shaved and cut his hair, would the old guy be able to recognize him, if it came to that? Would there be even a flicker?

The whole thing had gone so easy—too easy. The public panic had started before they even reached Second Avenue. When the first bomb went off, three blocks from the bank, people really got moving. Cars jerked away from the curb and screeched around corners. People ran. All headed out of the little downtown. Jackson had been able to park right in front of the bank; he wouldn't have to circle the block. By the time Billy and Sam walked in, only the manager and one teller were still in the place. The guard had already run into the street. The teller smiled when they came in, which seemed odd. Sam, wearing his big fake nose and badger-hair mustache, walked right up to her and punched her in the face. She hit the floor as if she'd fallen from a plane, her nose lying across her cheek like roadkill. Sam hit her again with his rifle as she lay sprawled on the floor. She wasn't going to remember the past month, let alone the man who'd decked her. Seeing this, the manager threw his hands in the air like a football referee. He opened up the cash drawers without complaint, whispering *please please* over and over as if wooing a lover. All Billy could think was: it wasn't supposed to be this easy.

Billy hadn't done a bank job since Seattle. Little T was, what, four years old? Five? Becky's sister had driven in from Tucson to look after the kid for the week. Becks wouldn't leave her with just anybody. They headed to LAX dressed for the Yukon. What did they know? They had lived in the Southwest their whole lives; they had no idea what to expect in Seattle. Billy could still picture Becks on the street outside the First National, wearing that white sweater that showed off her shape. She was the only diversion they'd needed. They would have gotten away free and clear if he'd offed the guard, but of course he hadn't. He'd tied him up instead. The man had somehow pulled himself loose from the chair and stumbled outside right when Becky was running for the car. The guard plugged her with a single shot in the back. Pure luck. They had to leave her there, bleeding out in the street, screaming, the sound of sirens in the distance. When Wilson swung into a turn half a block away, Billy vomited all over himself.

All these years later, he still didn't know how he managed to brazen it out when he showed up at the hospital later, how he convinced the cops that Becks had simply been in the wrong place at the wrong time, a tourist out looking for the Space Needle while her useless husband was taking a piss in the park. Maybe the coppers had bought the story because they wanted to believe they lived in a city that was a tourist destination. He went straight from the hospital to the airport, hopped the next flight back to LA. He never talked to Wilson again: Wilson, who had the old school chum working at the bank; Wilson, who assured them it would be a piece of cake.

Billy put his Browning Hi-Power to the manager's head. His hand shook as if it were taking control of its own destiny. The bank manager, recognizing what was happening, also came to life. He choked on a sob, twisted his head to look at Billy and plead his case. "No, please," he tried to say, but he swallowed the words. Snot fell out of the man's nose. Billy closed his eyes, put his left hand on top of the right one, and pulled the trigger. The report threw the gun toward the ceiling, wrenching Billy's shoulder. Brain matter sprayed across the floor. Billy refused to look. He stood and turned away before opening his eyes. First time for everything, he thought. Better safe than sorry. He'd learned that the hard way.

Sam sauntered to the stolen Buick Skyhawk and ducked into the backseat. Hefting the money-stuffed plastic bag over his shoulder, Billy kneeled at the bank's front door and locked it. He jammed the keys through a storm drain, tossed the bag in the trunk of the car, and climbed in the front passenger seat. A fire was raging in a dumpster down the street, the last of their diversions. Billy thought he could hear a fire truck's siren, far away, as Jackson eased the car from the curb. There were a few people on the street, but they weren't looking at the bank or the Buick. One old man wearing suspenders was crouched in an alley, covering his head. A middle-aged woman and a teen boy were running for a side street, away from the fire.

This, right here, this scene: it made Billy smile. The thrills in his line of work were few, if he was honest, but they were real. And however few they were, the assembly line would have offered far fewer. His father—Big Bill—had built bombers during the war, and he'd kept doing so after the war. Billy could have done the same; his father could have punched his ticket with the union, no problem. But Billy had other ideas. He was sure he could be the next Elvis. He was in the mailroom at RCA, his second year there, when he met Becky. She worked as a secretary at a flooring company—laminates and whatnot—while trying to be an actress. They immediately bonded over their frustration at being unknown. Billy's voice was true and clear, after all. Becky could bring forth tears on command. And they were beautiful. He was tall and long, with a gorgeous sweep of dark hair. A young Robert Wagner, Becky called him. She was blue-eyed, apple-cheeked, and lithe. She could be the next Eva Marie Saint, she said. So why hadn't they been discovered? They did their first job together—hitting a clothing store—after seeing *Ocean's Eleven*, for the excitement of it, and they ended up finding their true calling. By the time they had relocated to low-profile Bakersfield, they were full-time burglars, though Becky still did community theater to feed her soul.

In the years since her death, Billy had convinced himself that the Seattle bank guard's lucky shot had been an assassination—just one more in the series: President Kennedy, Sharon Tate, Fred Hampton, Sal Mineo, and Christa Helm. He knew Becky could have made it in Hollywood if she had really wanted to. If she had played the game like Tate and Helm. Hollywood was as corrupt as Washington, D.C.—that was what you had to remember. Joe Kennedy had run whores for RKO before the war. That was no secret. Becks received offers after she did that lingerie ad for Macy's but she'd refused them. Maybe before she met Billy, she would have taken those offers, gone down the rabbit hole. But after Billy, and then the baby, she didn't want it, not like that. She was better off in Bakersfield; she was happy. Billy was sure of it. Her performances at the playhouse had a purity they never could have had in Lotusland. Her portrayal of Alison in *Look Back in Anger* was unbelievable. As for himself, Billy had given up singing without any trouble at all. He enjoyed belting out a song, absolutely, but he'd always felt it wasn't really all that masculine. That was his father talking, but that didn't mean it was wrong. Big Bill understood what man's work was. And Billy never had any doubts about the decision. A man needed a real profession. Besides, Elvis had gone out of fashion by then, and Billy had no intention of being the next Bob Dylan. *Money doesn't talk, it swears,* Dylan sang. Which just proved the guy was an asshole. Money was the only thing a man could count on. Money made the world go 'round. Who wrote that?

The Buick jolted to a stop. The access road to Highway 395 was backed up—backed *way* up. All along the road and down the highway as far as they could see: nothing moved. Some people had climbed out of their cars and were talking to other motorists. Billy glanced in the rear-view mirror, saw vehicles piling up behind him. Sam had turned around in the back seat, keeping an eye out for the fuzz. The hunting rifle, tucked under a blanket, sat lightly in his arms.

He was going to have to consider working with Sam again, Billy thought. He had been pleasantly surprised at how calm the little guy had been throughout the operation. Robberies were the lowest-margin part of Billy's business—because he was careful, steering clear of potential big scores, the ones that drew heat. He didn't do heists in Bakersfield, either. They had to be at least fifty miles from home. He really looked for excuses not to do them at all. So much could go wrong. He had nodded all the way through the opening scene of *All the President's Men*, his armpits prickling. He had warned Sam about what this job would be like, what he would feel as it was happening, but the guy wanted to do it. "Hell, if a spoiled rich bitch can pull off a bank job, anyone can," Sam said. Patty Hearst had made everyone see the possibilities of the criminal life.

Billy sat back, a hot fear boring into his stomach. He had to think of the bank manager as an object, not a person. If you have to turn a screw, you turn a screw. The screw exists for your benefit. It doesn't have a family; it doesn't have any other purpose but to fit perfectly against your screwdriver. The car inched forward, jolted to a stop again. They had to get out of town, before the cops found the mess in the bank and the lockdown began. The highway should have been wide open at this time of day; there should have been no traffic at all. They hadn't counted on this level of mass panic. Billy closed his eyes, counted: one Mississippi, two Mississippi, three Mississippi.

On their second or third job, back in the winter of '61, he'd been forced to smack a store clerk when the man wouldn't do as instructed. Becky had been shocked. She made him go to Mass with her the next Sunday. "Do you have any faith at all?" she'd asked as she watched him chewing gum and zoning out on the bench next to her. She was kneeling in the pew, her shoulders rolled forward like a beggar. "I have faith in us," he responded. The remark had pleased him as he said it, but her expression made him change his mind. He shook himself. He didn't know why he was remembering that now.

He reached into his pocket, mindlessly massaged the Browning as if it were a rabbit's foot. He had to get rid of the thing. He began to rethink making Sam a partner. There was the lost assault rifle, for one thing. No matter that Sam bought it under a false name. Losing track of it showed a dangerous carelessness. And as cool as Sam might be under pressure, it could never be the same as with Becky. He and Becks had done it for love, to be together on their own terms. Why was he pulling a bank heist now, after all these years? The money? That's what he told himself, but he knew that by the time you factored in prep costs and laundering the cash and splitting it up four ways, you had to go back to work. No, he did it for sentiment, which was never a good reason. You couldn't rely on your judgment when you were doing something to bring back what might have been. If a crook doesn't have sound judgment, what does he have? That was why, until this job, he'd worked alone for the past dozen years. Bookmaking. Low-risk residential break-ins. Pushing a little coke. A living. But now it was time to ratchet up his earning. Inflation was eating away at every dollar, even if he didn't declare most of it. There was another reason as well, one he didn't let himself consciously think about. Billy had to figure out a way to send Tori to college. She was starting to look so much like her mother. He wanted her out of the house.

Billy opened his eyes. "Turn around," he said.

"What?"

"Come on, do it."

"We can't get around this," Jackson said. "There must be an accident up there."

"I know. We're not going to get around it. We're going to go back."

Sam wheeled around in his seat, interested. He peered into the front of the car.

"I'm not turning myself in," Jackson said. "I've already done five years in the can."

"I haven't done *any* time in the can, and I'm not going to start now," Billy said. "Now let's go. We have to get through downtown again while there's still time."

"What are you talking about? Where are we going?"

"We're going up the mountain. There's a camp up there for girls. Good place to hide out for a few days."

Sam barked out a laugh. "Yeah! Girls! Let's do it."

Billy cut him with a look. "They're teenagers, goddamn it!"

"Teenage girls," Jackson said, angling the car into the median and turning it around. "It doesn't get any better than that."

CHAPTER THREE

"You feel that trembler this morning?"

"Nah," Hicks said. "Slept right through it."

Lloyd drove with purpose, guiding the Bronco along the dirt road that led into the hills above Meridian Fields. Mammoth Mountain shimmered in the distance to the north. Now that they were higher up, Hicks fiddled with the police radio, with no luck. It had been popping in and out for weeks. The push-to-talk button kept sticking, allowing only transmission, usually on some unknown channel. Lloyd should have gotten the thing fixed while Hicks was laid up, but he didn't think he had the authority to approve the expenditure. Which was true enough. The chief sat back, frustrated.

"Temblor," he said.

"What?"

"Temblor's the word. Not trembler."

"Temblor?" said Lloyd, trying the word like an exotic new dish. "I don't think so."

Hicks didn't want to argue about it. Lloyd was the one with the associate's degree.

They'd rushed Jamison to the clinic—"Not life threatening," the admitting nurse had assured them—but they couldn't reach

Jimmy's wife on the phone and the chief quickly decided they couldn't wait. Hicks's stomach hurt thinking about it. Sure, this thing on the radio, whatever it was, could be a real clusterfuck, and, yes, Marco would track her down after he had a cup of coffee and got dressed. None of which changed the fact that the real reason he and Lloyd didn't go find Pamela Jamison themselves was that Hicks felt responsible. He didn't know what to say to her. Jimmy could get pretty mean when he was drinking. He knocked Pamela out cold once, which was why they picked him up whenever he went on a tear. But Pamela was devoted to him. Hicks could understand that. He liked the guy, too. Probably the smartest man in Mammoth View. Jimmy was always interesting to talk to. He'd been all over the world. He knew about things like ocean currents and astronomy. He'd talk to you for hours, drunk or sober, about black holes, the Big Dipper, Ursa Minor.

Hicks wondered what Ursa Andress was doing these days. He let himself picture the actress, the smoky hair in her face, the severe look in her eyes that foretold emotional and probably physical domination of the next man she met. She had to be about forty by now. He couldn't imagine that. Was she still making movies? *Ursula*—that was it. Not Ursa. She was a Swedish girl, not a Martian. Watching her walk out of the ocean in that Bond flick, that was the first time Hicks ever realized he was capable of cheating on Sarah. His wife was sitting right there beside him in the theater, but he'd wanted to climb up on that screen, throw Andress down in the surf and do a *From Here to Eternity* on her. He'd had to go get a bucket of popcorn to settle himself down.

"Come on," he said to Lloyd. "Step on it, will you? You drive like my mother."

Lloyd stepped on it. Behind them, Lake Crowley made its appearance again, jerking into the rearview mirror as if being moved by a crank. So far they hadn't seen anything. The sawmill property was empty, like always. The surrounding woods were empty. There was nobody at the lake. Nobody at the campsite. Hicks had searched the landscape with binoculars until he began to question his own perception, until nature began to seem unnatural. The tall grass looked mechanical, the hills like movie sets.

"Why do you think Tom Singer will know something?" Lloyd asked.

"Tom's place has a panoramic view of the lake and the old sawmill," Hicks said. "The whole valley, almost. If something happened out here, he would have seen it."

"If he was standing at the window."

"Yeah."

The bland, brown grassland gave way to woods as they climbed. The road here was barely large enough for the Bronco, but there was no way to accidentally drive off the side. Trees, one after the other, pressed right up against the road. On and on the trees went, seemingly into infinity. They had the windows down on both doors, and the cool air swept through and around them.

"You know, the sun causes earthquakes," Lloyd said.

"How's that now?"

"It pulls Earth toward it. Makes the tectonic plates shift."

Hicks considered trying the radio again. Static could be very soothing. "Mmm," he said.

"There's this push-pull thing going on between the sun and Earth. If Earth wasn't moving, it would fall into the sun. Ever think about that?"

"Tell me more," Hicks said, closing his eyes and dropping his chin to his chest. He chunked out a loud fake snore.

Lloyd pressed his foot down harder on the accelerator. "Just trying to make conversation."

About a mile in, Hicks spotted the mailbox and directed Lloyd to take the gravel driveway that jabbed up further into the hills. Finally they came to a stop in front of a low aluminum gate attached to wire fencing. Lloyd stepped out, leaving the engine running. He squinted toward the property cut out of the woods. A house sat near the back of it. Lloyd pushed on the car horn.

A terrible sound came back at them: a howling, high and

excited, followed by a collective yipping whine. Dogs, of course. Tom Singer was a breeder. One of the best on the West Coast—at least according to Tom. The horn had kicked off a frenzy, and the noise grew, the piercing, goosebump-raising noise of penned-up animals, marching back and forth in their own feces, desperate for freedom and attention, panicked that something was not right.

"Huskies," Lloyd said. "Great dogs." Last year, Lloyd had been forced to put down his elderly black lab, Einstein. He'd agonized over it, and he mourned the loss for weeks afterward. He wanted to get another dog—he felt they provided a valuable companionship that even a loving spouse couldn't offer—but he hadn't. He'd had Einstein for fifteen years, and he just couldn't bring himself to replace him.

Hicks and Lloyd waited for two or three minutes, and still the huskies barked and yowled and whimpered. No one came out of the building to quiet them or to walk down the drive to the men responsible for the racket. Hicks was a patient man, and he was loath to trespass, but enough was enough. They were possibly dealing with an emergency situation. He lifted the latch, walked the gate out of the road, and put it back in place after Lloyd had driven the truck through. Hicks climbed back into the Bronco, and they bumped down to the house. It was a small, single-story cottage. Bags of leaves leaned into one another at the porch railing, directly under the reason for them, an oak tree that twisted out of the house's way so that it could loom over the roofline. A rake stood against the tree's base, looking cowed. No truck, Hicks noted. Tom drove an old Chevy, parked it right in the front. As the officers rolled up, they saw that the front door to the house was open. They looked at each other, and Hicks nodded. Lloyd climbed out and unholstered his Beretta 92. Hicks did the same.

They were small-town cops, but there was enough domestic violence in Mammoth that they knew how to play this scene without strategizing it. Lloyd went first, skittering like a Texas two-step champion until he pressed himself against the house, one boot tipping into the doorframe. Hicks came along behind him, loping with staggering steps, annoyed at the feel of flab shaking in his middle. The vain, irrelevant thought embarrassed him, but he couldn't help it. He nodded at Lloyd, waited for acknowledgment, and then dropped low and turned into the house. Lloyd wheeled into the doorway a moment later, staying upright.

A thick torpor hung over the front room. The drapes were closed, which, along with the shade from the oak out front, gave the air a brackish quality. A ragged orange couch lazed against a wall. Across the room sat an old black-and-white television. The shag carpet had walking paths worn into it. Hicks and Lloyd moved through to the back, poking their heads into the kitchen, the dining room, a bedroom. Hicks felt himself judging what he saw and chastised himself. The place could use some freshening, but no more than any other house without a woman. Tom kept it tidy enough.

"Hello?" Hicks called out. "Tom, you here? It's Chief Hicks."

This caused the dogs outside to ratchet up their mewling and barking. Hicks and Lloyd checked every room, peered into closets. Nothing seemed out of the ordinary. Hicks stood in the kitchen for a minute, taking in the space. He flipped through the butts in an ashtray on the counter, looking for a spark.

"He hasn't been gone long," he said.

Lloyd, reading the plate on a trophy he'd found, didn't hear him.

Heading back outside, they walked around the side of the house. The kennels—large, four-foot-tall wire cages with wooden flooring—stretched length-wise down the right side of the house and wrapped around the back. The dogs banged against the enclosures, biting at the holes in the mesh. A half-empty, forty-pound bag of dog food lay on the ground in front of the first cage, a smattering of spilled kibble lingering around the unsecured flap.

"What do you think?" Lloyd asked.

"I don't know. He could be running an errand. The wind could have blown the door open."

"No. I mean," he indicated the dogs, "should we feed them?"

CHAPTER FOUR

Tori, propped on an elbow, tried to read, but she couldn't concentrate. The blob that had followed them along the running path, the drunken redneck, had unnerved her. They had told the coaches about him when they returned to camp, and Coach P. went to call the Mammoth View Police Department. That hadn't been the response any of them wanted. They wanted to hear that it was nothing to worry about, that it was their imaginations running wild. An incredulous snort would have been nice. Mary Bowen didn't help matters when she later said that Coach P. couldn't get through to the police. The phone was out. Tori had just reread the same sentence for a fifth time—"She had been forced into prudence in her youth, she learned romance as she grew older: the natural sequence of an unnatural beginning"— when Robin banged into the cabin. "Where's Liesel?" she barked, her eyes jumping around the room.

Tori swung her legs off the bed. "Bathroom," she said. "What's going on?"

"An attack. An invasion. Come on." She dashed out of the cabin, and Tori, barefoot, raced after her. They ran into Robin and Adrienne's cabin, where half a dozen girls were pushed together on Robin's bed, leaning into a clock radio. The radio crackled and sputtered, searching vainly for a signal and then suddenly finding one.

"... seen anything like ..."

Static ate the rest of the sentence, but then the signal caught again.

"... at least forty people, including six state troopers, lie dead in a field ..."

Robin turned to Tori. *See,* her look said.

The radio continued: "... will aid in the evacuation of homes within the range of military operations ..."

They caught a few more half-sentences and snatches of words—"Eyes!" the announcer seemed to say more than once—before the static took over completely.

"What does this mean?" one of the girls finally said. Tori couldn't tell who it was.

Everyone started to chatter about what it meant, about making phone calls to their parents, about bomb shelters. Alice, the girl who lived half a mile from Disneyland, started to cry. She jammed the back of her wrist into an eye to stanch the flow. Somebody patted her on the back, harder than was necessary.

Adrienne broke away from the babble. On the camp's first day, Tori thought the pimply girl might be her friend, but Adrienne was desperate to be part of Mary Bowen's coterie. With her frizzed black hair and general gormlessness, she had no idea how to go about it, except to make a fool of herself. She was still trying. "Bad, bad, *Leroy* Brown," Adrienne sang at the top of her lungs. "The baddest man in the whole *damn* town." She leaped onto her bed, bounced, and yanked her shirt up to flash the group. "Ahhgh!" Robin screeched, covering her eyes as if she'd been tricked into looking at the sun. Tori couldn't take it, either. What was wrong with Adrienne?

Tori walked out of the cabin, slammed the door behind her, and sat at a picnic table. But there was no escape. Girls were spilling into the courtyard from other cabins; they were hurrying from the rec room. None of them seemed to notice Tori. They lingered in the open space: one with a foot on her knee like a pink flamingo garden ornament, another stretching her arms over her head as if warming up for ballet class. Summer, the redheaded girl who had the cabin next to Tori's, appeared to be holding her breath. Her name was actually Dana, but everyone called her Summer, short for Summer Peach, her father's nickname for her—because she was "so soft." It was not a compliment, she said, her father also being her high school cross-country coach. The girls—there were ten of them standing around by now—looked like they were getting ready to do a Monty Python skit. After a moment, Summer ruined the tableau. She backed up slowly in a series of unsteady stutter-steps. Tori could see that she was crying, her breathing hard and scattered.

Tori thought about the first time she had noticed Summer, early in the camp's first week. The girl was out on the track, white legs pumping with awkward, mechanical efficiency, a human Newton's cradle. Now, once again, Tori found herself unable to take her eyes off the knobby-kneed girl. Until, with a sudden scrabbling of feet, Summer ducked inside her cabin and shut the door.

The sound of the door crashing against the frame set off a panic. Girls screamed and ran, looking over their shoulders. Liesel appeared on the path, her legs gleaming in the sun. She dropped her toiletries bag. It landed on the stone path with a *thwock*, the lid contorting into a silent scream. A plastic bottle fell out and rolled. Liesel made no effort to retrieve it. Tori followed her roommate's eyes until she found the cause of the scene.

The dog stood at the gap between two cabins. Tori smiled. It hadn't been a redneck or a bear across the ravine from the nature path, she realized. It was just a lost dog. A big German shepherd. The dog's yellow eyes flicked there and there and there, marking the girls. It was panting heavily, like a pig snuffling in slop. The animal's incisors flashed, but Tori noticed something else as well. She stood up without realizing it and moved around the side of the table to get a better look.

A small voice stopped her. Sofia was crouched at the edge of the courtyard, about twenty feet from the dog. She wore a plush red tracksuit that made her resemble a swaddled baby. A lumberjack cap, pulled down low, framed her face like a bowl cut. Her brown head was as round as Charlie Brown's. "Tori—no," she said. "You cannot save it." Tori nodded. She liked Sofia so much. She was so sweet and sad, just like Charlie Brown. Tori held up her palm, indicating that everything was fine—and started moving again. When she made it to the side of the table and realized what she was seeing, she gasped.

There wasn't much left of the dog: a steady stream of blood rolled out behind it, establishing its path. The wound was located high up in its midsection. The dog's back legs seemed to be attached by little more than a smeared strand of vertebrae. The poor thing obviously had gotten out of its house and been attacked by a wolf—or maybe a bear. Tori's mind jumped to Orangey, she couldn't help it. Her dad had found the orange tabby under his car when Tori was eight years old. That very first night the cat jumped onto Tori's bed, kneaded her stomach and settled in to sleep. When Tori got up in the morning, the cat followed her. That lasted for two weeks, two weeks of bliss for Tori, who spent so much of her time outside of school alone. Then Tori came home and found Orangey sitting on the front step as usual, but she had a subdued, cockeyed air about her. When Tori picked her up she discovered that the cat was bloody and whimpering. Her father wasn't around so Tori ran three doors down with Orangey in her arms, because Mrs. Riley was always home. But on this day Mrs. Riley wasn't home, or wouldn't answer the door, and by that time Orangey wasn't breathing anymore.

Tori stifled a sob. She remembered Orangey's wounds vividly, and, looking at the heaving dog, she changed her mind about her diagnosis. It didn't look like another animal had mauled it. It looked like a gunshot wound.

"Get back!"

Tori, startled, tripped, tumbling away from the dog.

That wasn't Sofia, Tori realized. Sofia had probably never yelled in her life. Swinging around, Tori saw Coach Clancy easing into the courtyard, crouched low. The coach held out her left arm and made a long sweeping motion. Some of the girls, their eyes swiveling between Coach Clancy and the dog, moved out of the way. The coach was cradling a rifle in her right arm. She jerked upright all at once, aimed and fired.

The dog twisted out of the smoke and noise. Pieces of the animal burst in the air like firecrackers. The torso landed with a wet, grotesque thump on the steps of a cabin. Tori stared at it on the ground, the smell of burned hair sticking to her nasal cavities.

"It's OK. It's OK," Coach Clancy said.

Tori held her hands to her ears. The ringing—buzzing—was back, worse than ever.

"Everything's fine now," the coach said. "Don't worry."

Liesel—outgoing, self-confident Liesel—crumpled in on herself. She cried extravagantly into her hands and wiped them on her cheeks, a tragedian's game of peek-a-boo. Adrienne rushed to her, kneeled, and hugged the curve of Liesel's back. She vigorously rubbed Liesel's arms, as if trying to warm her up.

"What's going to happen?"

Tori swung her head around, but, like in Robin and Adrienne's cabin, she couldn't tell who said it.

"It's dead," Coach Clancy said. "It can't hurt you."

"Not the dog. The *world*. What's happening?"

Tori finally located the speaker. It was Eileen Blum, one of the older campers. Eileen stood at the edge of the path that led to the showers, her eyes like open manholes. She drew rasping breaths through an equally black, depthless mouth. Tori had never spoken to Eileen; she was too afraid. Rumor was, her boyfriend broke up with her on the last day of school and she gained twenty pounds in the three weeks before camp started. Liesel mocked her behind her back, saying Eileen's Indian name was I Not Lean. But Tori found her fascinating. She liked to watch the other girls warm up every morning before she got started herself, and she always made sure to watch Eileen, marveling at her round belly rolling beneath her shirt, the seam of her short-shorts disappearing under her doughy thigh and then popping free, over and over, as she pumped her legs. Eileen was a *woman*, not a girl like the rest of them. And even with the extra weight, she was still fast—three days ago she ran 220 yards in twenty-four seconds. The problem, of course, was her endurance. She didn't have any. Eileen hadn't finished a slow run in the nearly two weeks they'd been there. She told Coach P. it was because she wasn't dull enough to be a long-distance runner; she needed constant stimulation. Coach P. pointed out that she'd been invited to the camp because she won the CIF cross-country championship for the San Francisco section last year. Eileen just shrugged at that.

Coach Clancy looked away from Eileen and scanned the rest of the girls. She took a step back, as if she feared they might charge at her. "I know you're all scared about what you're hearing on the radio," she said, her voice a little wobbly at first. "None of us is entirely sure what we heard. But this much we know for sure; you're safe here."

Tori glanced at Eileen, who had let her eyes drop to her shoes. Tori knew what Eileen was thinking. They weren't safe anywhere. They never had been.

CHAPTER FIVE

Downtown Mammoth View was two blocks of two-story red brick. There was a barbershop and a grocery, a little Italian restaurant and a clothier's, a ski shop, a five-and-dime, a diner and a combination book-and-record store. The centerpiece, of course, was the Greek Revival bank, built during California's gold-rush days, though in the Mammoth area it had been a short-lived silver rush. The bank's soaring granite columns gave the business district some ambition, and, more important, made the wealthy skiers who arrived every winter feel at home. Around the corner on Second Avenue were the Moose lodge, a small one-story office building, a single-pump gas station—and the police department.

Jackson rolled the Buick down Main Street, making sure he abided by the fifteen-miles-per-hour speed limit. The little downtown was still empty. More than that: it was abandoned. Billy had begun to figure out what had happened. He surveyed the gaping buildings, second thoughts percolating. This was the kind of thing—this panic—that brought out the state police, maybe even the National Guard. This was something that would make the evening news. Then what?

Billy noticed the wrenched-open doors of the grocery. A head of lettuce, a torn bag of chips, and squashed candy bars littered the sidewalk. Through the door he could see a row of shelves, but he couldn't make out the items arranged on them, just the colors: orange, yellow, blue—a lot of blue. "Stop for a minute," he said.

"What?"

"Stop the car."

Billy stepped out of the Buick as it was easing to the curb.

Jackson leaned across the passenger seat. "What are you doing? You gonna hitchhike?"

"We need to eat something."

"Sonuvabitch," Jackson snapped. "What the hell is wrong with you? I should just leave you here."

Billy leaned down to make eye contact. "We need to be able to think straight, and we need calories for that. Come on. Five minutes and we'll be gone. Three minutes. When's the last time you ate? You have breakfast this morning?"

Sam, ignoring Jackson's glare, clambered over the seat and onto the sidewalk. He raced into the store. "Goddamn it," Jackson said. He turned the car off.

The three men walked through the grocery. It was a small, rectangular room, but the overhead lights gave it the illusion of depth. Billy and Sam started grabbing wrapped sandwiches, bags of chips, Ho Hos and Ring Dings. Sam opened a bottle of Miller High Life and gulped it. Jackson picked through the bananas in search of one without brown spots. Billy felt a strangeness inch up on him. He couldn't believe the store's owner, or the hired help, or whoever, had just walked out and left the place wide open.

"Let's get a move on," Jackson whined. "We have to get out of here." He'd found a good banana.

Billy whacked Sam on the shoulder to put a stop to his beer guzzling. When Jackson was right, he was right. The town made Billy uncomfortable, too. It had nothing to do with the fact that he'd left a dead man in the bank down the street, though that didn't help. It just felt creepy. The town was what snobs called picturesque, and what he called fake. Even the grocery seemed more like a gingerbread house. He wouldn't be surprised if he peered behind the row of soda bottles in the refrigerated aisle and found elves back there stocking the shelves and cackling. Billy hit the sidewalk, with Jackson and Sam right on his heels. They glanced around at the barren street, and climbed into the car. Jackson turned the ignition. The Buick jumped forward and accelerated. Billy looked at his watch: they'd been in there less than five minutes, just as he'd said, and now here they were leaving the town behind, no one the wiser. The squat brick commercial buildings had been replaced by modest, one-story homes, and then those quickly fell away, replaced by greenery, trees. Billy sighed audibly.

"This is crazy, man," Jackson said in response.

"Yeah."

"No, I mean, fucked up. We've fucked up."

Billy kept looking out the windshield, tried to keep his voice blank. "Why's that?"

Jackson looked at Billy with popped-out eyes. "You and the two of us show up at a girl's summer camp? A floppy-haired hick and two black dudes? Shit. You think they're going to ask us to roast marshmallows with them? Have a pillow fight?"

"What are a bunch of kids going to do?" This was Sam, chiming in from the back.

"You don't think there are adults with 'em?" Jackson barked, looking at him in the rear-view mirror. "Dumbass."

They were ascending Minaret Road now, the Buick's engine growling. Billy remembered it from when he took Tori to the camp; it felt strange to go up and up and up like this. He reflexively torqued his jaw to make his ears pop. Without leveling off, they came to a break in the road, with Minaret continuing along the side of the mountain while three smaller tributaries headed straight up to the ski lifts. Jackson pounded on the steering wheel. He was scared. He couldn't hide it.

"Which way do I go, goddamn it?"

"That way." Billy pointed.

"So what are we going to do?" Sam asked, leaning forward.

"We gonna kill the people?"

Billy twisted around in his seat. "We're not going to hurt *anyone*, you got that? Jesus!"

"All right, all right. No need to take the Lord's name in vain," Sam said, smiling and putting his palms up. "You're the one who discharged his weapon in the bank, man."

Billy faced forward again. Discharged his weapon? What was that, army-speak? He was beginning to wonder if he'd discharged his weapon at the wrong man.

"So what are we going to do?" Jackson asked.

Billy kept staring out the windshield. He wasn't thinking straight when he made the decision to go up the mountain. Jackson was right. He had fucked up. He didn't want to tell them about Tori, which was the reason he'd thought of hiding out at the camp in the first place. What had he been thinking? He didn't want Jackson and Sam to know about his daughter. He didn't want them to know anything pertinent about him or his life. It was safer that way.

He turned to Jackson. "Look, they've probably heard about what's happening in the town, right? The panic, I mean. They had to have felt the earthquake."

"Yeah, probably."

"So as far as they know, it was the Big One. And we're showing up to save the day. We're their saviors."

"Praise Jesus," said Sam.

"Their saviors?" Jackson ground his mouth into a grimace.

"Good Samaritans," Billy insisted, warming to the idea, trying to actually sell it now. "We're there to protect them. We're concerned citizens. We spend the night, and in the morning, with the panic and the jam-up over, we convoy out of there. We lead the way. They must have some cars up there. When we get to the highway, we ditch 'em. Put the pedal to the metal. Easy-peasy."

"Right," Sam said, enthusiastic. "Easy fucking peasy."

Jackson's skin prickled from anger and frustration. Why hadn't he realized Billy Lane was a moron? "They're going to *see* us, man," he said. "They'll be able to *identify* us. You didn't think of that?"

Billy pressed a thumb to his temple. Jackson was a worrier. Worse than an old lady. "We're not bank robbers, for crying out loud. We're Good Samaritans. Just remember to use your operational name, and we'll be fine. Nobody's going to be questioning these girls about the bank."

Jackson let it go. What else could they do at this point? He pushed the Buick up the mountain, taking the engine to a stuttering whine before easing off the accelerator. Damn, he thought. This was a big fucking mountain. Had to be as big as Everest. Why hadn't he ever heard of it? A big mountain like this just four hours from Los Angeles? A four-foot-wide wooden sign appeared on the side of the road, attached to two two-by-fours that had been pounded into the ground. "Spritle's Racers, Est. 1975," it said. The words were carved into the wood in a faux cursive script: that must've taken someone hours and hours of whittling, Jackson thought. He wondered if Spritle—whoever the hell that was—had done it himself. He quickly discarded the thought. Spritle sounded like a Jewish name, and they weren't really whittlers.

The car turned into the property and followed the driveway around a dumpster and a storage shed. Billy craned his neck, hoping to see Tori right off, scared at the thought of seeing her. There were times when he'd thought—fleetingly—about bringing her into the business. Some street cons were easier to pull off with an innocent-looking girl. Tori had the smarts for it, and she was tough—Billy had noticed. She'd be better at the life than Becky ever was. She'd been brought up in it, even if she didn't realize exactly what was going on. And God wouldn't get in the way, like He had with Becky. That would be a bonus. Billy had never taken Tori to church. As the car pulled up to the turnaround in front of the main building, he spotted a middle-aged woman hustling toward them. He didn't see any girls around. "Who are you?" the woman asked, peering into the driver's side window at Jackson.

Billy leaned across Jackson and into the sunlight so the woman could see he was a white man. He put on a reassuring smile. "We're here to help. You know what's going on?"

The woman nodded warily. "Coach P—the head of the camp—just got back from Mammoth View. He says there's no one anywhere. He's going to go looking for the police or the sheriff."

Billy didn't like the sound of that. He'd hoped they wouldn't be so pro-active. "The police are pretty busy, Ma'am." He recalculated his plan on the fly. "You should all go," he said to her. "Right now. There are evacuation spots, away from the trouble. Plenty of protection there. We can lead you."

Fear washed over the woman's face like a toxin. "What's happened? What's going on?"

"Lot of conflicting information, Ma'am, but we have to do what the authorities tell us. For the good of everyone. How many people do you have here?"

The woman stepped back, staggered for a moment and caught herself. She looked around, then back to the car. "Is it the Russians?"

Billy cocked his head, surprised by the question.

"We haven't seen any Russians," Jackson piped in, fearful of dead air. "It's probably just precautionary. You know, the earthquake."

"*Who* are you?" the woman asked again.

Billy made eye contact, smiled. "Just people, Ma'am. Citizens. I'm Curtis. Curtis Jones. We're trying to do the right thing. We've kind of been deputized. How many people do you have up here?"

The woman looked into the distance, as if she would be able to see all the mysteries of life if she just squinted hard enough. "Okay. Okay. There's twenty-one of us. Seventeen kids. Teens. This is a camp for runners."

"Rumors?" Jackson asked.

"*Runners*. Like Jim Fixx."

"Right," Jackson said, confused.

"I see you have some cars over there," Billy said, tilting his head toward the side of the building, where the back ends of a '74 Monte Carlo and another vehicle were visible. "Can you fit everyone in them?"

"I think so, yes. There are four cars. One of them's a station wagon. One's a van."

"All right, let's get moving."

The woman nodded. Billy noticed that tears had filled her eyes. She headed back the way she came.

Billy had rethought the whole plan. They couldn't just take off on their own now—that would be suspicious. The woman would remember every line and mole on their faces. But the headmaster, or whoever the guy was who'd gone into town, had already gotten everyone spooked, so they couldn't stay the night, either. The headmaster clearly wanted to take the initiative. So they'd take it for him. They'd lead all of them north, higher into the mountains. During the planning for the job, Billy had studied a map for just this reason. There was a little road, Route 120, up there. It was the long way around—more than twice as long, switchbacking through the mountains—but it eventually would dump them into Stockton. Once they made it to the city, they could easily lose the campers, "accidentally." The group would be so grateful to have survived the crisis, everyone calling parents and spouses from pay phones, that they wouldn't even notice that their saviors were gone. Now he just had to catch Tori's eye, give her the sign before she said something. He knew he could count on her.

Tori kept her eyes down. She focused on the wooden floor, on the nail heads and the gaps between the slats. She could hear Coach P., that was enough. She didn't want to see him. She knew that look, had seen it on her father's face more than once. There was nothing worse than an adult trying to disguise his fear with a mask of calm.

The running trails were off-limits, he was saying. Same with the pond. The lights had suddenly gone out about an hour before, and it appeared the blackout was affecting much of the area. Obviously the earthquake had been bigger than they could tell here at the camp. There might be aftershocks, Coach P. said, so everyone should stay in the camp, where the coaches could keep an eye on them. Just hunker down until they got some answers.

"I'm going to go back into town to coordinate with the authorities," he said, pulling mindlessly on the bill of his cap. "I'll bring back supplies, and we'll have a plan of action. All right?" He marched out of the dining hall without waiting for an answer.

Silence followed his exit. He forgot to say that everything was going to be fine, Tori thought. That was rule number one when talking to kids during a crisis. You're announcing you're divorcing mom, that the cops are at the door, whatever—you always end by saying everything's going to be all right. Tori stewed over what it meant that he'd forgotten to say it. One of the girls—Eileen—stood and headed for the walk-in pantry behind the tray-table rack. Others began to follow. Within a few minutes, a dozen girls were rummaging through the canned goods and elbowing each other. Girls returned to their tables with cold cereal and Graham crackers and warm 7-Up. The fruit and veggies were gone—a delivery hadn't arrived as scheduled that morning. "I'm getting fat just looking at this crap," Mary Bowen said as she settled again at the back table where she always sat. "I can feel my butt squish when I sit down."

"At Princeton, the freshmen have to run around the campus naked the first time it snows," Robin said, leaning in to make eye contact with Mary. "They call it the Nude Olympics."

"They *have* to?"

Robin shrugged. "I think the seniors make them."

Mary Bowen looked dubious. "Does Princeton even have a track program?"

Robin shrugged again and dumped a pile of powdered milk on her bowl of Wheaties. She shoveled a spoonful into her mouth. "It doesn't taste like milk at all," she said, forcing herself to swallow.

Liesel laughed with such force that a glob of whatever she was chewing shot across the table, clopping onto Mary Bowen's tray.

"Dammit!" Mary barked, abruptly standing up. She grabbed the tray with both hands and banged it on the table in frustration. She left it there and stormed off.

"You're supposed to add water to it," Tori said, tapping the directions on the powdered milk container.

Robin flushed, her cheeks and forehead darkening to a crimson glow. She started to laugh. She pushed another spoonful of cereal into her mouth.

"I don't think that's good for you," one of the girls said.

Robin opened her mouth to show the girl the masticated bran puttied to her teeth and tongue. It looked like vomit.

Sitting there, watching Robin gross everyone out, Tori knew she needed to get away from these people. From *all* people. Things had become too tense. She would sneak out of the camp and go swimming, she decided. Along with a desire to be alone, she feared that she stank. With the electricity out, the showers didn't work. There were backup batteries for the pumps, but no one seemed to know how to connect them. That meant Tori had been on two runs without washing. She was tired of being hot and itchy. Leaving the cafeteria, she headed for the track and, after looking around for the coaches, casually dropped off the side of the path.

Ten minutes later she was kicking away her shirt, shorts, and flip-flops, and walking into the pond in her underwear and bra. She dunked her head under and hung herself, arms out, feet swinging. The dead man's float. Her legs felt like sandbags, wonderfully heavy and useless. She'd been so relieved when the coaches said they didn't have to train anymore today. She'd decided right then and there that she didn't want to know if she had the makings of a Kalenjin. Maybe because she was sure that she didn't. She was sure she would be found lacking: inherently, biologically ordinary. She was good at this one thing—running—but with no chance to be great. Story of her life.

When she surfaced, Tori discovered she had drifted at a forty-five degree angle more than halfway across the pond. And she wasn't alone anymore. At the edge of her sightline, she could make out Mary Bowen standing thigh-deep in the water under the big granite outcropping. She had pulled her blond hair into a ponytail, and she was vigorously lathering her pits with a bar of soap. Her glistening white swimsuit made her shine in the sun like a decommissioned missile in a Fourth of July parade. Up on the rocks, Robin, who'd become Mary's devoted pet, stared at the sky. There'd been a lot of smoke in the air all morning. A wildfire, probably. Robin cupped a hand at her forehead to block the sun. Her paisley bikini top floated on her concave chest. The coaches had said the smoke was nothing to worry about, that whatever it was, it was far in the distance. Robin looked worried anyway.

Tori saw that Summer was there, too, trying to be brave now to make up for her embarrassing crying jag during the wolf attack. (That's what they were calling it, The Wolf Attack.) She appeared to be doing calisthenics. Ally, Madison, and Adrienne were stretched out on the rocks across from Robin, no doubt burning the undersides of their arms and legs and enjoying the pain.

Robin inched down the rocks and into the water. She said something to Mary Bowen, who turned and looked up the path. Someone was there at the top of the trail, calling to them, waving. Tori didn't want to be around Mary and Robin—*Batman and Robin*, as Liesel had started calling them, a slap at Robin, not Mary Bowen. Tori had been out here enough times, sitting in the shade and watching Mary Bowen . . . and Robin, Ally and Madison, her Girl Wonders. They were always laughing among themselves, confident in the purity of their characters because the subject of their derision—self-conscious, pathetic Summer or maybe even dorky Tori herself—could never say with absolute certainty that the sniggering was directed at her. Tori slipped under the water, pinched her eyes shut, and kicked for the little alcove where Batman and the others wouldn't be able to see her surface. She sneaked out of the water and, dripping wet, bounded into the woods. She immediately realized her mistake. Not only had she left her clothes, flip-flops, and towel behind, but the trail as well.

She refused to consider going back in the pond and doing a walk of shame out of the water in front of Mary Bowen and the others, who would know she'd tried to get away unseen. She wondered what jokes they'd make about her soggy, old-lady underwear. She stepped gingerly through the pine needles and grit along the hillside that led around to the back of the camp. A shiver bolted through her, sudden and mean. She felt gooseflesh fluff along her arms.

After about a hundred yards, she hopped over some brush and noticed a patchy, makeshift path, barely wide enough for a person. Thanking the gods, she followed it. The path came and went; she wasn't entirely certain it was a path. It could have been created by stampeding animals—ducks or wild boar or lemmings, rather than humans. Twice she lost the thread and thought that was it, only to again find bare ground that approximated footfalls.

Fifteen minutes later she came upon a surprise: a small hot spring squeezed between a clutch of trees. Steam wafted from the pool like the aftermath of a magic trick. It was a beautiful sight: a watery black hole, shrouded in mist and full of promise. She knew she shouldn't go in, that it was too tucked away, too isolated, but she also felt like she had to. There was a hot spring right in camp, but she'd never been in it. Unless you went at two in the morning, there were always other girls in there already. And it was always the obnoxious ones.

Tori dipped her toe in the water and immediately jerked it away with a grunt of surprise. The water was really *hot*. She'd never even heard of a hot spring until she'd arrived at the camp. She didn't believe at first that it was a natural thing. It sounded like a miracle, one of the wonders of the world. She plunked her foot into the water and gritted her teeth. She worked her way into the spring slowly, section by section, sucking in her breath when she submerged her torso. It hurt, and it was perfect. Finally, she lay back, allowed her feet to float, and watched the forest telescope into the sky. She let herself relax, really relax.

Other than her predawn runs, she hadn't been alone since arriving at camp. It'd been almost two weeks of communal living, of bumping around inside a hive of busy, super-competitive bees. She wasn't used to it. She'd never been away from home before. She'd never even done a sleepover with school friends. Shyness had gripped her forever. She could recall backing up a lot as a child, turning away from people to inspect the corner of a wall or the arm of a chair. Her father had always indulged her shyness— Tori suspected he blamed himself for it, because she didn't have a mother in her life. Tori waggled her limbs in the murk and closed her eyes. The buzzing in her head rose up, resisting the quiet, hurtling her toward a black tunnel in her mind. She sloshed around some, until she felt once again like she really was there, even if no one else was.

A long, low, whine brought her out of her daydream. She opened her eyes and watched the water swirling around her in small concentric waves. Another sound hit, this one like a long, distant thunderclap. A car horn. Probably a truck. Tori sat up, but the sound was already dissipating. The water settled into its brackish languor again. Tori felt overheated. Forcing her limbs to respond, she climbed out of the hot spring, looked up. The sun hovered directly overhead. The morning was gone.

Tori shook off as much of the water as she could, then used her hands to squeegee her stomach and legs. That done, the day's warmth began to work its way into her muscles. She thought she could feel her goosebumps slip into satisfied nothingness. She set off toward the camp. Coming down onto a hiking trail, she noticed a strangeness in the air: the crackle of rocks and twigs under her feet, the *huck-huck* of her breath, and . . . nothing else. The complete absence of sound beyond whatever she made herself. Tori let out a little warrior yelp and listened to it stretch out into the world and fade away. She felt powerful—as if she controlled sound itself. It was how she wanted to feel when she went running in the morning. She luxuriated in it until the trees pulled back and she stepped down into the camp courtyard.

The rows of cabins gaped. The door of each one stood open. Perplexed, Tori watched the scene for a minute. She walked to the first cabin and peered inside. It was Robin's cabin, Robin and Adrienne. Clothes were strewn across the floor. One of the mattresses had tipped off the bedframe. Nothing unusual, Tori thought. Tori moved on to the next cabin, where she found a similar scatter of belongings. She pushed out of the cabin and stood in the middle of the courtyard. She noticed blood on the paving stones, big splotches of it. She tried to remember where the dog had fallen; she squeezed her eyes shut to picture it. A worm of bile worked its way into her throat.

She ran to the dining hall. After that, she went over to the coaches' lounge, and on to the coaches' lodgings. Empty. Everybody was gone.

CHAPTER SIX

The reality finally settled on King about fifteen minutes after he left the station. He was a goner.

He drove in silence, not daring to turn on the radio. The earthquake that morning had knocked him out of bed at about six. In retrospect, it seemed like an appropriate way to be woken up, a perfect introduction to his new life. He'd padded into the kitchen, ready to tell Janice to be sure and listen to the show today, but she had already left, out the door without a word.

How did it come to this? He deserved the silent treatment for passing out in the middle of it last night? Like that had never happened to her while they were in the sack—though of course she'd chalk that up to his performance rather than her drinking. There'd been a "heart to heart" a few days before when she got home from work and found him whacked out on the floor of the bedroom. He'd waved her off. It's not the grass, he'd told her as she shrugged off her suit jacket and stepped out of her skirt. He was just working hard on this project, and as soon as he was done with it, he'd be focused on her like a laser. As he said this, a look of disgust crossed Janice's face as if she suspected he had silently cut one. That look had stayed with him, burrowed into his brain.

King wasn't exceptional. That was the nub of it. That was what she couldn't abide. Janice had fallen for the King of the Afternoon, a title he'd given himself in San Diego when he reached the top of the ratings in his time slot. He'd made sure the name stuck even though he only stayed on top for one ratings period. Janice had been a high school girl in La Mesa listening to him on KLRD. She'd sprawled on her bed after school every day, driven to a hot, squirming state by his cooing baritone. But that was years ago, and it was clear now that he'd simply caught the zeitgeist in San Day-Glo. Now every station had someone talking about sex in between the songs, and a lot of them were more entertaining—and certainly more knowledgeable—than Oscar "King" Desario. And King couldn't disagree. He never wanted to be a DJ. He wanted to be an actor. A stage actor. An actor/director/all-around theater impresario. A modern-day George Abbott, but one with a social conscience.

King stopped his Dodge Dart at the intersection of Chester Avenue and 4th Street. The traffic signal pulsed yellow in all four directions. King could feel the pulsing inside him. *Big*, he thought. That imperative had been the impetus for his radio project, even with the ulterior motives involved. Thinking big again. He stared out the windshield at the brown sky. He was going to get his New York money. He just needed a little bit of luck today. His stomach did a flip, and he gripped the steering wheel. You had to do what you had to do, he reminded himself. You had to think big—you had to take chances—if you were going to change your life. He thumped the wheel like a drum. Ba-dum-dum! *Shouldn't the weed be more help with the big thoughts?* The pot had helped him with his voices, the sounds, the pauses. But would it pay off? Maybe he should try something with a bit more kick. Acid or coke or even heroin. Think what his inspiration would be like then? He looked both ways and saw nothing, then pressed down on the accelerator. The Dart jolted forward.

He wasn't going to achieve his goals in Mammoth View, he understood that much. San Diego to Bakersfield to Stockton to this little pokey town. Clearly, he'd run out his string in radio. He had to get back to acting, to *real* performing. He'd almost made it his first time around. He needed to keep reminding himself of that. In '68 he'd landed a spot in the Los Angeles production of *Hair*. It didn't matter that it was the chorus. No small parts. He was right there, backstage at the Aquarius Theatre, *on* stage at the Aquarius. With Ben Vereen! With Jimmy Rado! With it all hanging out! He had *life*, mother. He had *laughs*, sister. He had *freedom*, brother. He had good times, man.

He had to go to New York. That was the goal. The Big Apple. The City That Never Sleeps. He should have gone in '69, when it was there for the taking. When he was young and—well, not beautiful, but at least interesting-looking. It wasn't too late now. He wasn't too old. For Hollywood, sure. Hollywood only wanted the next Shaun Cassidy, the next John Travolta. But Broadway was different. Even from the front row, no one could see the crow's feet around your eyes. Broadway was open to different kinds of looks: on Broadway, Gwen Verdon was a sex symbol. In Hollywood she was nothing.

King blinked hard to make himself focus on the road. He should have expected to lose his job, he thought. He knew about history repeating itself. When he had realized what was going on out there in Mammoth View, that it really was happening, he had panicked. Just walked out of the booth and out of the station. He got in his car, fired up a joint, inhaled deeply, and left—in the middle of his show. "2X2L calling CQ. Isn't there anyone on the air? Isn't there *anyone*?" the recorded voice heaved behind him as he slammed the door shut and ran into the parking lot. He sure as hell wasn't going to wait for the police to show up.

As he cruised along Chester, his brain pulled up Kristi Sasaki. She was the only one still at the station when he bolted. Sitting there in the sales room, reading *People*, oblivious to his show. It was a one-man operation there for every on-air personality. What would she tell the authorities if they came calling? He had no idea. He pictured her talking to Chief Hicks, words spilling out into the atmosphere like factory exhaust. Though he didn't actually see her mouth: just the little belly pooch that always peeked out from the bottom of the tops she wore. She sold a lot of air space with that slip of flesh. He felt himself swell, and, annoyed, he squirmed in his seat. Middle-aged men buy air space, and so sexy young things like Kristi Sasaki sell it. He was quite sure she enjoyed playing on those old pervs until they pulled out the checkbook. Mr. Franklin at the fertilizer company, Johansson the contractor, the jokers who ran the resorts. Yet the first time he met Kristi, he had been certain she was a dyke. The short hair, the cheap turquoise-bead necklace she wore, the love of jogging—it just seemed so obvious.

But then, after he'd been at the station for a few months, something changed. She started to recognize him. Whenever she saw him coming, she'd smile and say, "Hey, man." Sometimes she'd flash him the peace sign. There was just something . . . *inviting* . . . about the way she looked at him. He hadn't known how to follow up, though. Did she really like him or was she just being "on," keeping in practice for her next sales call? Should he ask her out? Take her to the Orpheum in Bakersfield when Janice was away? Invite her to the next United Farm Workers rally, which he knew Janice had no interest in? He'd queried Kristi on her musical tastes, joked with her about Nixon's exile in San Clemente down the coast, asked about her jogging rituals, but he never did anything . . . not really. His lack of courage haunted him.

He punched down harder on the accelerator. If he was going to make a run for it, he might as well get going. He swung onto Brundage Lane; he was going to go around downtown and take County Line Road all the way out of the county. Straightening the car out, he blitzed down to Lake Road and jerked into another turn. Slowing, he turned the wipers on, then, unsatisfied, he flipped on the defroster. He pulled over when he couldn't see anymore.

King stubbed out the joint in the ashtray and stepped from the car. He put his hands on his head.

"Jesus Christ!" he said. "Jeeesus Christ!"

Up ahead, orange flames jumped into the sky. The long, low building at the corner—the town's storage facility—was engulfed. Spectral embers zipped through the air like bees. This had to be part of it, he thought. King started to walk toward the flames—until he realized something had emerged from the conflagration and was headed his way. The thing was shaking and twisting, throwing off bursts of color. King bit down on his lip, but he didn't even feel it. He was transfixed, like he was watching a laser light show. Then he realized what he was looking at. It was a person. A person on fire.

King backed up. The flaming figure kept coming toward him—faster now—and King swung back to the car. He climbed in and slammed the door just in time. The man crashed into the side panel, causing the car to rock like an inflatable raft in a pool. King jammed his key into the ignition . . . his house key. The car jolted again, and he felt his stomach float for a moment before bouncing down on his bladder. Was the guy trying to pound out the flames against the car? A quiver of nausea tickled his throat. He feared he might pass out. He identified the right key and thrust it forward. It clicked and scratched, finding every unintended crevice along the steering column. At last the key dropped into place and turned. A shudder rolled through him, an incredible, enervating release—did he piss himself?—and he threw the Dart into reverse. He jerked backward, switched to Drive, torqued the car around, and pushed his foot down. In his rear-view mirror, he could see the Fire Man rolling on the ground. Was that Alton, the town's maintenance man?

King felt tears fill his eyes. *I couldn't do anything*, he told himself. *There was no way to save him.* He wiped at his eyes with a sleeve. Getting his breathing under control, he turned back onto Main and sped up. Now, finally, he began to notice the world around him. For starters, there were no other vehicles on the road. He blasted past parked cars on the shoulder here and there, but he saw none moving up ahead of him, none moving behind him. Coming up on the intersection of Chester and 4th, he accelerated past a group of men in a parking lot who seemed to be kicking something on the ground. A moment later, a police car appeared in the oncoming lane. The siren's lights were flashing but the car was moving slowly, as if the driver was looking for someone. For *him*! King swung onto 4th before the copper could get a look at his license plate, and as soon as he straightened the Dart out he saw it and braked.

A roadblock. A big black car right in the middle of the road. A man standing there watching him pull on the steering wheel as if it were a ripcord.

The car came to a halt. King looked at the man about thirty yards in the distance. The man waved for him to pull the car to the side of the road. He imitated an airline ground crewman, indicating with robotic arms where he wanted the vehicle.

What would Stokely do? King wondered. He turned the Dart off, pocketed his keys, and stepped out. Would Stokely Carmichael—would Huey Newton or Eldridge Cleaver or any serious radical—just get out of the car and do as he was told? King noticed that the roadblock man wasn't wearing a uniform. This wasn't the police. Could it be the FBI? The CIA?

"Hey," the man called to him. "Thank God . . ."

King moved around to the front of the car.

"Listen, ah—" the man said, but now King started to run, breaking for the open field that stretched out next to the road. It was a G-man—King had never been so sure of anything in his life.

"Hey!" the man called after him. "Hold up!"

King didn't hold up. He had wanted to be a part of the underground for years. All the foxiest chicks were radicals: Bernardine Dohrn, Kathleen Cleaver. Even Squeaky Fromme had a certain waif-like appeal. King bounded down the embankment, humped it across the field. His breath scraped at his throat, the keys in his pocket banged against his thigh. He hadn't sprinted like this in almost twenty years, since he anchored his high school track team, but he still had it in him. He stayed fit, ate well. He ducked into the sickly woods behind the Union 76 station, dodged some brush, and kept going.

When King realized there was no one coming up behind him—that he had gotten away—he started to laugh. He was on the lam! He coughed, losing his balance for a moment. He slowed, and finally stopped, hands on knees, hacking and gurgling. He spat a long, thin tube of saliva at the ground. He trotted for another hundred yards or so and then walked the rest of the way, but still he made it to the house in little more than half an hour. He fell into a squat against the inside of the front door. He laughed again, hard and loud. He'd outsmarted the FBI. He'd never felt so alive. He reached up and locked the door.

CHAPTER SEVEN

Hicks and Lloyd returned to a ghost town. The Bronco rolled along Main Street, the men peering through the windshield at desolate sidewalks and buildings. A bag of trash lurched down the street in front of them, the breeze carrying it this way and that, frustrating Lloyd's attempts to avoid it. The door to Billie's Travel Shoppe creaked open on its own. Hicks forced himself not to gape or say anything. The chief, stunned by what he was seeing, had nothing useful to say. He figured his lieutenant wouldn't express surprise or anxiety if the boss didn't, and that was the best he could hope for until they got some information.

Hicks rolled down his window to let in the late summer smells: charcoal smoke and ripe garbage and pine needles. Nobody liked this time of year. With all its quaintness—the brick facades and curlicue store signs—Mammoth View didn't feel like a real place when there wasn't snow on the ground. It felt like a mistake, a town removed from its proper time. No one knew what to do with themselves. Lloyd turned onto 3rd Avenue, toward the office, and as the vehicle swung around Hicks spotted Frank Lundstrum running toward them, a shotgun cradled in his arms. Hicks put a hand on Lloyd's shoulder, nodded at the rearview. The chief leaned out the window as Lloyd pulled to the curb. Lundstrum grabbed onto the passenger-side door.

"Thank God, Chief. Thank God you came back."

"Frank, what's going on here?"

"I should have gone with everyone else. I wanted to protect my business, but my gun's not working. Toby's got a goddamn Gatling gun, and all I have is this damn thing."

"Frank, slow down," Hicks said. "Where has everyone gone?"

"What do you mean? You don't know?"

"Know what?"

"About the evacuation."

Hicks looked at Lloyd, who shrugged, then back at Lundstrum. "There was an evacuation order?"

Lundstrum sputtered, confused. "Well . . . ain't that right?"

"You seen Marco?"

"What?"

"Officer Barea."

"No—no, haven't seen him. Doesn't he do night patrol?"

"Frank, just tell us what's happening. What you've heard. Exactly."

"I don't know. I didn't hear the announcement. It was on the radio. John Cranston told me. Billie Travers. I don't know."

"What did the radio say?"

Lundstrum banged the side of the Bronco in disbelief. "The invasion, Chief!"

Invasion? Invasion of what—locusts? He had guessed the thing on the radio this morning was some kind of hunting-party mishap that was being misreported, but now . . . he just couldn't guess. Did Lundstrum mean the Russians? Could that really be possible? Hicks looked out the windshield for something to indicate they were in the middle of a national emergency. He smelled the air for something . . . different. *Anything.* What would an invasion smell like? Police work was all about gut feelings, and ever since the heart attack, his gut had been on the fritz.

"Is the military in charge, Chief?" Lundstrum asked. "NASA?"

Hicks picked up the police radio's hand microphone, pressed

the button. Still nothing. He thumped the transceiver down. NASA? Hicks began to wonder if Lundstrum had lost his marbles. Had everyone but he and Lloyd gone nuts? "Get in the back, all right, Frank? You'll be safe with us."

Lundstrum, as thankful as a rescued puppy, pulled open the back door and climbed in.

"And give me that gun," Hicks said.

"Chief . . ."

"Come on, hand it over."

Lundstrum passed the gun forward. Hicks popped the shells out and tucked it between his legs, barrel down.

Lloyd revved the engine like a nervous tic. "Chief," he said. "Winnie's at home."

Hicks let out a breath, nodded. "Yes, of course. Let's go."

The vehicle jumped forward and Lloyd turned onto Custer Avenue. The needle on the speedometer swung to forty miles per hour. Forty-five. Two weeks ago, Winnie would have been downtown at this hour, but she left her bookkeeping job when she learned she was pregnant. Lloyd insisted on it, even though she wasn't even showing yet. It hadn't been very long since she'd quit, but Hicks knew Winnie just well enough to know she must be going stir-crazy at home.

Hicks held onto the door handle as Lloyd threw the Bronco into another turn. Now that Lloyd had expressed concern for his pregnant wife, Hicks thought of Sarah. Who wasn't waiting for him at home. She'd hated it here from the first day. The Great Nowhere, she called it. She didn't care that he wanted to be the boss for once in his life. He was fifty years old when the offer came. It was only going to happen in a small pond. A very small pond. She should have understood how much he needed this— to be called chief, to make decisions and sign off on payroll—but she didn't. She'd never had a job. She'd never taken orders from anyone but her father and her husband. He had figured she would come around, take up hiking and enjoy the views, maybe even try skiing, but she loved Fresno too much. She loved the city life, their friends, their place in the world. Not that he believed it was her fault. At this late date he could hardly blame her unhappiness on the town. He hadn't even tried to convince her to stay.

Lloyd slammed the vehicle to a stop, bounded out. "Honey! Honey!" he called.

Hicks snapped out of his reverie, climbed down from the cab. "Stay here," he told Lundstrum, who was leaning between the seats, trying to see into the house.

Hicks stepped into the foyer behind Lloyd. Something didn't feel right here, either. He put his hand on his holster, nervously drummed his fingers on the leather. He glanced to his left: the living room. A sagging couch, a loveseat, two leather chairs. The styles and wear suggested they were all hand-me-downs from dead relatives. He looked to his right: a small alcove—a mismatched desk and chair—leading to the dining room, then a hallway and the bedrooms. On the wall hung a framed poster from the 1974 Spokane Expo featuring the fair's Mobius strip logo.

"Winnie?" Lloyd said quietly, soothingly. "It's Johnny." A sound tinkled from the back, and he bolted for it.

Hicks followed, carefully, peering into each room until he reached the kitchen. The afternoon breeze was banging the back door's screen against the frame. Lloyd was on the porch gazing out at a fenced-in yard.

The officer looked over his shoulder as Hicks joined him outside.

"The house is empty," the chief said.

Lloyd nodded, which turned into a shake of the head. "She's gone. Just like old Tom Singer. Maybe they ran off together." The lieutenant regretted the joke as soon as he said it. It was inconsiderate. He pulled the visor of his hat low on his forehead and dropped his eyes to the railing. "Sorry, Chief," he said.

CHAPTER EIGHT

Ten seconds, she thought. That's how close she was. So close and yet so far away. Just like her mother.

Tori never knew Rebecca Holland Lane. Her mom died of cancer when Tori was four years old. Tori knew only photographs of her, not the real thing. She knew only that her mother would have been a movie star if she'd survived, that she was on the verge of stardom when she became sick. Tori always wondered about that. She wondered why she hadn't been in any movies at all, not even small parts. Something about the story sounded bogus. Her mother didn't really look like a movie star. TV, maybe. A sitcom actress. Tori sometimes thought the snapshots on the walls could be anyone. Like maybe Dad found them at a garage sale and decided the toothy blonde looked like the kind of girl he would fall for. The living room featured a big, framed image of Mom at twenty, Dad's favorite photo. Tori understood why he liked it: the lively round face, the sun-bleached hair as straight as a two-by-four. She's looking right at the camera, beaming a smile of absolute confidence. Tori couldn't see herself in that woman at all.

Her father wasn't nearly so perfect. He was a handsome man—all her friends said so, with his bent nose and even more bent smile, his thick black hair and intricately defined arms. But that wasn't the only way he was different from the other dads. He did some kind of shady business, something to do with gambling. She was only guessing about the gambling, but she thought it was a good guess. He watched the Indianapolis 500 on TV every year even though he had no interest in motor sports. He cared about football, but he didn't actually get to watch much of the Super Bowl. People called him on the phone throughout the game, and the conversations sometimes became heated.

Tori looked up, distracted by a sparkle of light. She'd been staring at her shoes clapping along the asphalt, and so now the sudden rush of stimuli—the greenery and water and sun dazzle—made her head pound. She stopped, shielded her eyes with a hand. There was a pond pushed up against the road. It stretched out to the forest, level and still. It seemed like a strange place for a pond. Growing up in a city, she was accustomed to clear delineations between the urban and natural landscapes. There should be a fence or something, she thought. She stared at her reflection etched along the surface of the water: a skinny, shapeless girl with bad hair—Olive Oyl in a T-shirt and running shorts. She couldn't really see her face in the water but that didn't matter: she'd memorized it long ago. Bland, gray eyes; thin, pointy nose. The cheekbones were okay, but then the lower half of her face couldn't finish the job; it kind of collapsed in on itself, narrowing sharply down to a baby's chin. She wondered all the time how she could fail to get either of her parents' looks. She wasn't beautiful. She wasn't cute. She was just . . . there.

Dad loved her anyway. She believed that. He didn't say the words, and he could be mean, telling her to shut up for no reason or to stay in her room for the night. But he trusted her to get his gun when someone rang the bell. He took her shopping for clothes sometimes, without her asking, and let her pick out whatever she wanted. He didn't punish her the time she ditched study hall. She started counting again. One Mississippi, two Mississippi. By the time she reached ten, a car was going to come around the side of the mountain, see her, and pull over. This time.

She was her father's daughter, that was for sure. She was a Lane. But was she a Holland? Her mother's parents had wanted her after their daughter's death, but it hadn't worked out. They then disappeared completely from Tori and her dad's lives. If she had any aunts or uncles or cousins on her mother's side, she wasn't aware of them. She had the sense that they were better people. Maybe they thought her mother was slumming with her father. This was just a guess, but it felt right.

Tori put her head down and marched on. She shivered. The sweat-suit top over her Spritle's Racers T-shirt wasn't enough, despite the 70-degree day. A mink coat might not have been enough. Fear, or something like it, bubbled in her stomach, sending spikes of ice through her veins. She felt abandoned, even though it was her own fault they all left without her. She didn't think she was in danger, though. Not really. Whatever was happening in the world, whatever that news report was about, had nothing to do with her or Mammoth Mountain. She'd get to town, find a phone, and her dad would come and get her. By nightfall, they'd be back in Bakersfield, where they'd be safe. The Russians wouldn't bother invading Bakersfield. It was too boring there.

She looked down the road. Ten more seconds, she thought. Ten more seconds and everything will be all right. On Monday she'd clocked nine minutes and fifty-seven seconds over three thousand meters, the first time she'd broken the ten-minute barrier. If she could lop ten more seconds off this new personal best she'd break the state high school girls' record for the distance. She'd get the attention of college coaches for sure if she did that. Ten seconds is a lot, Coach P. had reminded her when he saw the smile on her face. It's a hundred yards—if you're fresh and going flat-out. You're still a whole football field away from your goal, he'd said. *A football field.* But Tori refused to think like that. Ten seconds wasn't a football field. Ten seconds was nothing.

She wondered what Polly Jean Colson was doing right now. PJ had graduated in June. Her best time was also nine-fifty-seven—Tori had been there to see it. PJ had encouraged Tori after that race, told her if she—PJ—could get under ten minutes, then so could Tori with her super long legs and her high tolerance for pain. She asked Tori to stay with her after practice broke up, to run one more set of splits. "That's the only way to get what you want," she said. "You have to want it more than everyone else. You have to go for it." She smiled when she said things like this; she had one of those big, the-world-is-wonderful smiles that radiated outward like a force field. It was the smile of a girl in a travel poster: Visit Switzerland! Tori's mood darkened at the memory of it. She remembered walking to algebra class with Jenny Brown in April and mentioning that PJ had invited her over to watch *Saturday Night Live* and spend the night.

"You can't do that," Jenny said.

"What do you mean?"

"She's a lesbian. Everybody knows that."

"She is *not*," Tori said, feeling her face get hot.

"Come on, Tor, she's a total jock."

"I'm on the cross-country team."

Jenny waved that away. "She does all the sports. Be ready, Tor. She's totally going to molest you."

Tori didn't believe her—but she knew she couldn't be sure. She had wondered why a senior wanted to be her friend. She came up with an excuse to stay home that Saturday. She would never go over to PJ's house. She stopped staying after practice with her, stopped making eye contact and smiling when passing her in the hall. Thinking about it now, Tori wanted to cry. She spat into the pond, causing her reflection to explode into a series of ripples. She'd run a nine-fifty-seven, but so what? She'd never get her time ten seconds lower. PJ couldn't do it, and she was a total jock.

CHAPTER NINE

Their third date changed everything. They saw *Splendor in the Grass* at the Village Theatre in Westwood. It was Becky's idea. Billy had suggested *Wild in the Country*, at the Landmark up on Hollywood Boulevard, but inevitably he'd given in to her wishes. A mistake. Warren Beatty's smug face, all sleepy eyes and girly lips, had really pissed him off. He'd refused to hold Becky's hand as they walked up the aisle to the lobby.

Becks grabbed onto Billy's arm and hugged it. A group of sorority girls ahead of them pranced toward the doors, their voices popping and cackling. One girl had a purple bow on the top of her head like she should be in an Archie comic. She bounced on the balls of her feet and suddenly did a twirl, as neat as could be. It made Becky grin. She wanted to do the same thing. She wanted to be that girl—a college student without a care in the world. She snagged Billy's hand, forced his fingers to fold over hers. She clearly didn't realize he was in a mood. She felt as happy as the dancing girl in front of them. Probably happier. Billy couldn't believe how oblivious she was to his signals. But that was Becky. Always happy, all the time, Warren Beatty or no Warren Beatty. Sporting half a grin, she exaggerated the sway of her hips as she moved through the lobby with her boyfriend, proud to show herself off to all these college kids she didn't know. She and Billy stepped out of the theater and turned south, toward the parking lot. She held his arm again, this time with both hands, like a fireman going down a pole.

They crossed the street, their hips bumping, neither of them speaking. That was one of the things Billy liked about being with her; neither of them felt the need to talk all the time. They were comfortable with one another. Becky flung her feet out in front of her like a racehorse begging for the whip. She wanted to skip. She wanted to do-si-do. It was that kind of night: warm and lively, with a breeze just strong enough to slip playfully under her skirt without making her worry that it could send the thing shooting skyward *à la* Marilyn Monroe. They walked past the two men in dungarees standing at Weyburn and Gayley. Becky smiled blandly to be polite.

The men pushed themselves away from the building and fell in behind the couple. Billy, still stewing over the movie, didn't notice them. The commercial district disappeared to the east as Billy, Becks, and their pursuers crossed an empty lot. Up ahead, Los Angeles National Cemetery rose into view. Becky realized what was happening first. Looking back on it, Billy would count this as a mark against her. She always paid attention to men on the street, how they looked at her—or didn't. She tugged at Billy's shirt, whispered. He reacted immediately, but it was too late. Becky screamed as she saw Billy's face shudder and go slack. He fell forward, cracking his head on the pavement. Becky dropped to the ground right after him, needing only a shove to lose her legs. When Billy turned over, he was surrounded. Becky sat next to him, sobbing into her hands. Her knees were raw; blood bubbled down her right leg. A dozen or so of their fellow moviegoers were crowded around, unsure what to do. "Was it jigaboos?" one of them asked. Billy didn't know, but that sounded right. A policeman pushed through the crowd a couple of minutes later, but by then it hardly mattered. The men were long gone with Billy's wallet and Becky's purse.

Humiliation swept over Billy as he answered the officer's questions. It was right there on the cop's face: disgust that Billy had let this happen, that he hadn't been able to protect his own girl. Becky's concern about the lump on his head only made matters worse. Lying on the bed in his apartment an hour later, an ice pack on his head, he told her he'd get her money back, with interest. He even told her how he was going to do it; he wanted her to know he was no coward. Becky could tell he was serious, more serious than he'd ever been about anything. "I'm going with you," she told him.

Billy still thought about that moment all the time. He looked in the rearview mirror at the station wagon behind them, all those unformed teenage faces, their mouths grim and unmoving. He could see a bit of the blond girl's shoulder and arm in the mirror. She was sitting in the backseat of the wagon, against the door. She had taken a liking to Billy the moment she saw him standing there next to the Skyhawk. She walked right over with her backpack as the camp counselors organized who went where. She asked him who he was and what he was doing there. She told him her name twice, even though he hadn't asked. She was his daughter's age—she might be Tori's friend—but he'd flirted in return anyway. An old habit. *Mary, eh? A good Irish name. Maybe we're distant cousins from back in the old country.* Not that long ago he might have done more than that. He might have told her to come along in their car. Given her the ride of her life.

Did it all go back to Westwood? Billy wondered. It had taken him a long time to get over the shame of that night. That shame had caused him to take all kinds of risks in the years since. Was it responsible for the turn his life took? Had it led him down through the years to this dingy green car, driving on this barely-on-the-map road with two black men and a sack of stolen money in the trunk? Would he be a respectable member of society if he just hadn't been jealous of Warren Beatty?

He let the thought peter out. I am who I am, and there's nothing wrong with that, he told himself. Americans love criminals—at least the crooks who have style, whose actions have something to say about the world. The Wild Bunch, Bonnie and Clyde, John Dillinger. They were as famous as any movie star or rock singer. The Lovely Lanes could have joined the rolls of the country's famous outlaws. That was the name Becky came up with after their first job. The newspapers would never use a nickname like that, Billy told her, laughing. It was too girly. Becky didn't care. The Lovely Lanes it was.

Except Becks was long gone, wasn't she? No one had ever heard of the Lanes, lovely or otherwise. And now Billy had crossed a line, one his wife never would have crossed. He'd killed a man. Shot him in cold blood. Billy had gotten caught up in his own past, in what might have been, and he'd lost his way. For what is a man profited, if he shall gain the whole world and lose his own soul? Becky came up with that, too, after their first robbery. Moses wrote it in the Bible. A warning, Becky said, down through the ages. God was watching.

Tori, Becky's daughter—with Becky's eyes and her smile and her little knobby chin—rose up in Billy's mind, and he wiped her away. He'd failed to spot her at the camp, but he told himself there was a reason for that. He'd tried to stay in the background, to not draw attention to himself. And all those teenage girls looked the same, with their long pink legs and big frog eyes. Tori was in one of those cars back there, safe and sound. He imagined them singing camp songs as the coaches drove. Michael, row the boat ashore. Ninety-nine bottles of beer on the wall. All the classics. She was with friends. Probably thought this was all a reaction to the earthquake, an overreaction for safety's sake. Most important, she didn't know any of it had anything to do with her old man.

Jackson issued an expletive under his breath. Billy shook himself and glanced at the road ahead. They'd come up on a logging truck with a full load. The thing was massive: at least sixty tons, with a towering winch bouncing over the cab, and dozens of logs stacked in offset rows. The vibration from the road gave the impression that the logs were rotating, like wheels upon wheels. A rolling factory.

"Damn it," Jackson said. The truck rumbled impressively, but it appeared to be on a treadmill. Jackson looked at the Buick's speedometer. Fifteen miles per hour. This wasn't acceptable. It would be next week before they made it to Stockton and ditched their followers. "Look at this," he said, gesturing at the truck.

"Pass him," Billy said.

Jackson leaned his head out the window. "There ain't much room."

"I thought you were a professional getaway driver. It doesn't seem to me that we're getting away."

"Oh, I see." For the first time today Jackson's voice had some lift to it. "You want some Mario Andretti action."

"Yeah, baby," said Sam, lounging in the back like a satyr.

Jackson swung the Buick into the opposite lane, surveyed the situation. He could make it, but it would be tight—which was how he liked his women. Smiling at his joke, he pushed the car up to the truck's rear axle. Then a little bit further. The vortex between the two vehicles made the Buick shake like a belly dancer. The dashboard popped out of alignment, gibbered incoherently. Jackson decided it was time to put both hands on the steering wheel. He could definitely do this, he told himself. No problem. He held the car steady, his brow knitted in concentration. He increased the speed slowly—thirty, thirty-five, forty—inching up alongside the truck as if getting into position for a movie stunt. He was ready to punch through with a final, powerful burst, but he hesitated. Something wasn't right. The truck banged next to him like a blast furnace, the load clinging to the steel catches. Jackson pinpointed the problem. He wasn't gaining on it anymore. The truck was matching his speed. Worse, the cab was angling into the oncoming lane, closing off the open space.

"Shit!" Jackson yelled. He pumped the brake. The tires on the driver's side stuttered on the edge of the asphalt. The car slipped back, and Billy pressed his palms against the dashboard. One of the truck's axles was right there beside him, as big as a crane. The side window rattled; he felt certain one of the clanging chains on the truck's carrier was going to crash through and brain him. Jackson slowed the car still more, and they slipped back further. The truck's wake flung the Buick into place in the appropriate lane. The truck slowed again. Thirty. Twenty-five. Twenty.

Jackson cursed as if having a sneezing fit. "That mother could have killed us!" he added.

Sam pushed his head between the seats, his eyes as round as ice-cream scoops. "What the *hell*?"

Jackson glanced at Billy. "You don't expect me to take that, do you?"

"No," Billy said. He was sweating, but, like Jackson, his fear had quickly turned over to anger.

Sam, worried, pulled on his ear. "What are you saying?"

"I'm saying, hold onto something, motherfucker. This is an 'E ticket' ride." Jackson slowed the Buick to a crawl, took his foot off the pedal and left the car only to its momentum. The logging truck extended its lead, rumbling and gurgling.

"What are you doing?" Sam asked.

"Be patient. Watch the master work."

Billy turned in his seat, spotted the station wagon coming up behind them. Coach Prinzano waved from the driver's seat. A collage of girls melded together in the back seat.

Up ahead, the logging truck eased into a turn. The cab disappeared around the side of the mountain, the load wagging like a dinosaur's tail. Jackson didn't let himself hesitate; he punched down on the accelerator. Sam toppled backward, cracking his head against the rear window. Billy gripped the side handle. The back of the truck rushed into their frame of vision, as big as life, blotting out the road and the sky and the mountain. Jackson jerked as if having a spasm, and the car hopped into the oncoming lane. He couldn't see around the curve or the truck; he had to hope no vehicle was coming in the opposite direction. He certainly wasn't going to wait around to find out. The Buick exploded past the truck while still in the midst of the turn, the engine roaring, the spoiler shaking. Jackson didn't dare take his eyes off the road to glance at the speedometer. His right foot, stomped down on the gas pedal, began to cramp. It was going to seize up at any moment. He clenched the foot, marveled at the numbness there, and eased it off the pedal. He blinked hard. Nothing but empty road ahead of them. Safely out front now and back on a straightaway, he skidded the Buick into the correct lane, holding the wheel in a bear hug to keep the car from going into a spin.

"Yes!" Sam screamed. "Sonuvabitch! Yes!"

Jackson smiled at the sight of the truck driver in the rear-view mirror. The man was screaming bloody murder, pounding his fist. A redneck, naturally. That was one redneck who'd go to bed tonight knowing a black man had showed him up.

CHAPTER TEN

Melvin Johnson had seen this before. In a movie. Clint Eastwood straggles into a dusty little town on a donkey. The bell's ringing and there's no one on the street, no one anywhere. The place appears to be abandoned . . . until, here and there, he spots scared eyes peering from curtained windows.

Melvin, standing in the middle of Main Street, surveyed the emptiness a second time, just to be sure. He didn't have a donkey, but his brother Gordon was an ass. Heh-heh. Now he just had to find the one pair of eyes that weren't scared. In the movie they belonged to a Mexican girl with big wahwahs. Big enough to suffocate in. That would be just fine with him. Everyone had to go one way or another.

"What do you think's going on?" Gordon asked.

Melvin put his hand up for silence. Gordon never could enjoy a moment. He always had to ask why. Melvin started down the middle of the street. He'd seen downtown Mammoth View empty like this many times before, but that was in the dead of night. In the morning there were always people around. *Always*. He reached 3rd Avenue and peered around the corner. Even Benny wasn't sitting in front of the diner. The silence lengthened; it began to make a noise of its own, a buzzing. About now was when the bell was supposed to ring. Then the crazy bell-ringer runs into the street and tells Clint that he rings the bell when somebody's been killed. That in this town everybody's either rich or dead. Well, Melvin wasn't dead. It looked like he and Gordon were the only ones still breathing.

He headed for the diner, Gordon right behind him. He didn't see anyone in there, but the door was open, and so he walked right in. Food sat uneaten on the tables. Drinks poured but untouched. He had a bite of Eggs Benedict and spat it out. Sour. He sipped an iced tea. Gordon, seeing Melvin eating, snatched a slice of bacon from a plate and swallowed it without chewing.

Melvin sat at the bar and tucked into a half-eaten sausage-and-egg sandwich. Gordon joined him, spinning on the next stool. Melvin's little brother snagged a French fry from the plate and popped it into his mouth.

"Good," Gordon said. "Cold."

Melvin threw a hand in the air and snapped his fingers. He looked around, mugging for his brother. "Jesus, service here sure is slow." He cackled, snapping his fingers again and again for emphasis.

Gordon guffawed. The fry fell out of his mouth. "Seriously, Melvin, where do you think everybody went?"

"Don't know, don't care." Melvin had returned to the sandwich, biting down vigorously. The sausage oozed oil from its pores, filling Melvin's mouth.

"Everybody run because of the quake? We've had bigger ones before. Lots bigger."

"Maybe the bourgeoisie scare easy."

Gordon allowed for the possibility. The French were known to be cowards. "Maybe," he said.

Melvin finished the sandwich and slid off the stool. He walked around the counter and pushed through the kitchen's swinging door. The grill had been turned off, but the food hadn't been put away. A mound of meat sat at the back of the grill, the bottom layer flattened out and stiff from overcooking. Uncracked eggs still patiently queued on the side table. There was a bowl of diced tomatoes. A block of cheese. Butter. Cooked fries sat in their baskets above the oil vat. The makings of a feast.

Melvin wasn't hungry anymore. The sausage sandwich shifted in his stomach, and he burped. He stepped back through the swinging door and moved over to the cash register. He hit a few buttons. He crouched and eyed the lid of the cash drawer. It looked pretty solid. He pushed on it, hoping it would pop out. No luck.

He straightened up, cracked his neck, and stretched like a cat. "All right, time to make hay," he announced. He rounded the counter and swaggered out the door. He stepped into the street. He turned to confirm that Gordon had followed him. Melvin let out a cowboy holler. "Yeee-haaaaaaa!" Cupping his hands to his mouth, he called out: "Listen up, Mammoth! There's a new sheriff in town! Melvin Johnson is in charge!"

"Yeeehaaa!" Gordon joined in.

Melvin waited, his head swiveling, eyes darting. No one. Nothing. He raised his arms in triumph. A gunshot had woken him up this morning. A single shotgun blast, and then, a few seconds later, another short burst. He didn't think anything of it at the time—everybody liked shooting their guns—but now he figured there might be a connection. He wondered if some desperado had swept through town, led the police on a chase out into the Meridian. Maybe everyone had gone to watch the showdown.

Melvin had wanted to be a cop when he was a kid. Like Pat Garrett or Buffalo Bob. He remembered jumping out at little Gordo, blasting away with his Fanner 50 cap gun. Gordon bawling—he hated being killed. Melvin screaming at him to fall down; those were the rules. You got shot, you fell down. He always stopped screaming whenever he heard the groan of the bedsprings in the master bedroom, but it was always too late. Daddy, tying his robe, would push into the room and slap Gordon in the head, sending him crashing to the floor. Daddy made him play right.

You didn't cry when you got shot. There was never any excuse for crying. You got shot, you fell down.

Melvin walked along the row of shops on 3rd, Gordon trailing behind. Popping into the stores, they grabbed shoes, candy bars, brochures for European travel packages, two handguns and a box of ammo. They stuffed everything in an extra-large yard bag they found behind the counter at the five-and-dime. In the liquor store, they opened a couple of Johnnie Walkers and the most expensive Paul Masson, guzzled them right there in the aisle. They moved on to the good stuff: beer.

The brothers rounded the corner on Main and headed for the dry cleaner—Gordon wanted to see how fast he could make the clothes go around on the carousel—when Melvin stopped. The bank. Why hadn't he thought of the bank right off? Everybody's rich or dead, he reminded himself. He peered in the glass front door, squinted like Clint. The lights were on, but nobody was home. He pulled on the handle—locked. He squinted through the glass again. Still no sign of life . . . and something else.

The vault door stood open.

Melvin was pretty sure the vault was supposed to be closed after hours, that he'd looked in there during some of their nighttime wanderings and seen it closed. Except this wasn't after hours.

Melvin stepped back, looked left, concentrating hard. He looked right for a long time. He didn't think this was a trick. There really was no one around. He turned back to the bank. He could feel the blood racing through his veins. He clenched his fists in an effort to control his breathing. He hopped toward the door, jerked his knee skyward, and kicked. A small, veiny crack appeared in the lower half of the glass where the heel of his boot had made contact. He tried again, causing the door's hinges to rattle against the frame. He kicked again and again, really working up a sweat—until, shocking himself, he felt the glass pop under his foot. The door rained shards on his boot and pant leg. He'd done it! He reached in and felt around for the deadbolt, couldn't find it. He shook the door—still locked. He looked to his left and right again. Now he and Gordon started kicking in unison. Glass fragments tumbled and skittered in the lobby like pennies from heaven.

"Okay, okay, enough already." Melvin was tall but lean, Gordon a little taller and thicker. Still, he thought they could make it. He kicked away the jagged edges on the door, dropped into a ball, and squeezed into and through the opening. No problem. Gordon, hugging the yard bag to his stomach, pushed into the bank right behind him. They hustled to the teller counter and swung themselves over. They pulled on the cash drawers, meeting unmovable resistance with each one. Melvin couldn't believe it. The vault's open but the teller drawers are soldered shut? He punched randomly at one of the keypads, just like at the diner. Infuriated, he hefted a chair to smash it into a drawer, but stopped himself. He looked at the floor, his heart thumping. He put down the chair, kneeled.

Gordon came up behind him. "Oh, shit, Melvin, what did you do?"

Melvin whipped his head up. "Shut up, goddamn it. I didn't do nothing."

The woman in the blue blouse and short skirt lay on her back with her arms and legs splayed, ready to make snow angels. Melvin studied her bony left arm, which was locked awkwardly in a full stretch. Her boobs had flattened out and slid into her armpits. It was Alice Krendel, he realized. She looked different being dead. Prettier.

Melvin stood up. He noticed that one of Alice's patent-leather shoes had broken. It clung to her foot by half a strap. He kicked at it, and the shoe spun away, clonking into the base of the counter. Alice's foot wavered for a moment, died again.

"What are we going to do?" Gordon was breathing heavy.

"Nothing. We didn't do anything wrong."

Melvin, suddenly in pain, limped around the counter toward the vault. "Goddamn it," he said, wincing. He sat on the floor and pulled off his right boot. His foot came out smeared in blood.

Gordon watched his brother on the floor, gaped at the bloody foot. "What happened? Did you step on her?"

"Goddamn glass." Melvin turned the boot upside down and banged it.

"Here," Gordon said. He reached into the yard bag, extracted a pair of new red Spot-Bilt sneakers.

Melvin wiped the bottom of his foot, felt around in there for glass. He pulled off the other boot and slipped the shoes on. He stood slowly. The right foot throbbed, the bongo beat going all the way up his leg. He kicked at one of his boots—it lifted into the air, turned over, and thumped onto a well-dressed man sprawled on the floor.

Melvin froze. Where did this guy come from? There was no way they had missed him when they came in.

Gordon followed Melvin's gaze. "Oh, *shit*."

Melvin inched over to the body, looked at the face. Never seen him before.

"Is he dead?" Gordon asked.

"Well, he ain't sleeping."

"What do you think happened?"

Melvin tested putting weight on his wounded foot. "Must be murder-suicide," he said.

"Shit, that's heavy, man."

Melvin turned to his brother. "Don't be a zip. Somebody robbed the place."

"Yeah?"

"Yeah."

"You think they took everything?"

Melvin spun toward the front door; Gordon, startled, ducked. A car on the street finished screeching into a turn. Melvin couldn't tell from the sound of the engine if it was getting closer or farther away.

"We've got to get out of here," Melvin said. The brothers ran to the door, squeezed through it, and took off down the street.

CHAPTER ELEVEN

Janice Littlepaugh hyperventilated as she drove. Just another mile, she told herself, swallowing a hiccup. She zapped through the flashing yellow light at the school crosswalk and turned on Custer, ignoring the stop sign. *Just three more blocks*, she rasped out loud, her throat raw, her nose completely M.I.A. She made another turn, and the stucco two-flat finally snapped into view, causing a shudder to roll through her. *There it is*. She could see her asthma inhaler in her mind, sitting there on the dresser next to her jewelry tray. She only needed the damn thing once every blue moon, but of course the one time she forgot to take it with her was the day the Apocalypse arrived. The gold Camaro Sport Coupe, the love of her life, banged into the curb, sending a tiny burp of puke up Janice's throat. She swallowed hard, threw herself onto her feet and raced for the side door. She flung her purse at the kitchen chair and lunged for the arm support, air stuck in her lungs like tar. Redd Foxx flashed through her mind. "This is the big one, Elizabeth. I'm comin' to join ya!" Janice pushed the chair away, made for the bedroom. Jesus Christ, she thought. If she was going to drop dead, she didn't want the last thing on her mind to be goddamn *Sanford and Son*.

She grabbed the inhaler, primed it, and sucked as hard as she could. The epinephrine crashed into her like Dick Butkus. For a moment she felt like she had lifted off the ground. Her knees buckled, and she exhaled gloriously, but only enough so she could reverse course and pull air into her chest, a deep gulp. She sucked on the canister again, just to be sure, just for kicks. She sat on the bed, huffing, sweat leaking down her sides. "Mother*fucker*," she whispered to herself. She wiped a string of drool from her mouth and looked up to find King in the doorway.

"What are you doing here?" she said, annoyed. "Where's your car?"

King bit at his lip. He didn't seem to know what to do with himself, like a priest who'd just heard an especially disturbing confession. "I had to abandon it on the side of the road," he said. "By the gas station. I was waiting for you. So we could go together."

"Go where?" She felt the sweat on her forehead now and became conscious of how she must look. She swiped her sleeve across her mouth.

"Doesn't matter. Out of here. All hell is breaking loose."

"No kidding." Janice shook herself, tried to direct the rolling shiver to her extremities. "We're going to have to hunker down. The highway is packed. Bumper to bumper."

King shook his head vigorously. "No, we can't do that. We'll drive over the mountain. To Stockton. Come on, let's go. Right now."

Janice studied her boyfriend's face. She wondered, for the umpteenth time, how she ever fell for this guy. Her parents, clearly, had done a number on her. "Do you even know what's going on?" she said. "This is serious shit."

"I know—that's why we have to go. Come on." He motioned for her stand up.

Janice realized his plan did make sense. She acquiesced with a nod, but she couldn't let him think she believed he was actually right. She insisted on washing her face first, changing her clothes. "No," he said, "there's no time." He tried to guide her toward the front door, and she pushed him away with both hands, resisting the urge to really sock him one. Once in the bathroom, she let out a long, slow breath. God, she could really use a rolf. She thought about Johanna, her massage therapist, about the strength in the woman's hands. A good rolf was better than sex. Who was she kidding? It *was* sex. She splashed water on her face as King made noises in another room, banging cabinet doors, dropping things. She stared at her sharp, foxlike features in the mirror. She needed to grow her hair out, she decided. Soften up her look. Guys dig chicks with long hair.

"Come on, let's go," King mewled, appearing in the mirror behind her. "We need to leave right now."

Janice dried her face and dropped the towel into the sink. "All right, I'm just going to put something comfortable on." She pulled her stockings down to her ankles, leaned against the doorframe and yanked them off.

"We don't have time, Jan. We have to *motor*."

She spotted his oversized Swiss army backpack by the door, stuffed to the gunwales. She looked around for another bag, maybe the small pink suitcase she used for overnight trips. Nope. Infuriated, she grabbed the backpack, pulled it open. She pawed through his T-shirts, underwear, Levi's. A toothbrush. A packet of those disgusting peanut-butter-flavored Space Food Sticks he wolfed down every day. A fucking Fritz the Cat comic book.

"And what about me?" she said, wheeling on him. "Do I get a change of clothes? Do I get any reading material for this 'round-the-world trip we're taking?"

"I—" he stammered. "I . . ." Janice could see the gears shifting behind his eyes, first this way and then that. What an idiot her boyfriend was.

"I thought . . . you know . . . you'd want to pack your own things."

"Let's just go, Oscar," she barked. "I don't need anything. I'll read about Fritz's scintillating adventures while you're driving."

Janice grabbed her purse and stormed down the driveway, her

nose still pulsing from the epinephrine. At least she wasn't scared anymore. She was too pissed off. She stepped into the driver's seat, started the car. King leaned in through the open passenger-side window.

"I thought I was driving."

"You want me to leave you here?"

King climbed in, and Janice steered the Camaro into the street. "Here," King said. "You forgot this." He dropped the inhaler in her lap. Janice ignored it and instead concentrated on pushing the car hard. She careened into turns and punched the accelerator. Heading east, up the mountain, they were the only ones on the road. It was eerie, this emptiness. It had all happened so fast, with no warning. She'd come out of the bathroom at her office, still sniffling from her morning crying jag, and found her secretary gone. Tania had marched down the hall to get Janice a cup of coffee twenty minutes before and apparently never returned. Janice sat at her desk for a while, first trying to get her boss on the phone, then just sitting. She had started to sift through her index cards—her own unique way of keeping track of projects—when Veronica ran past the door. Actually ran. A full-out sprint. Janice made it outside in time to see Veronica disappear inside her Ford Pinto and screech into the street. There were only four cars left in the lot, including her own. Janice felt she was always the last to know—and she didn't know anything.

King gabbled at her non-stop as she drove. Something about the feds taking over the town, about how he'd escaped with some quick thinking and a head fake, about how this would make a great movie. Typical King nonsense. She peered down side roads cut into the mountain, searching for signs of life. She spotted empty gravel driveways, looming trees that seemed to be trying to tell her something. All the while King kept talking: more about the feds, a fire somewhere, his radio show. They made it to the turn-off for Route 120 in less than twenty minutes, which was long enough for Janice to make a decision. A long-overdue decision.

"You want a bite?" King said, snapping a peanut-butter stick in half with his front teeth.

"King, listen, this isn't going to work."

"No, this is right," he said. "I drove this once with Charlie. It's beautiful up here. Don't you think?"

Janice kept her eyes straight ahead. "I mean, us. You and me. This hasn't worked for a long time."

King stopped chewing, swallowed.

"King, you hear me?" She dared to glance his way.

"You can't break up with me, Jan."

"I do believe this is still America."

"No, I mean. It's not us. We're fine. It's the situation." He put his hand on Janice's leg, kneaded her flesh. "We're going to be okay."

"We're not. You know this." His hand burned her leg. It was going to leave an impression. She pried his fingers off of her. "This is for the best."

King rolled his head against the back of the seat. "It's this *place*, Jan. It's Mammoth View. If we go to New York everything will be better."

"You know that's not true."

"I can make it," he said. "I know I can. I've put it off too long. I've been saying that for years. This thing—this thing that's happening—it's just what I needed, to give me a push, to force me to get on with my life."

"You think you can make it," Janice said, shaking her head. She was talking to herself, or maybe to the Fates, not to King. She realized she was pressing down on the accelerator harder than she meant to. She rolled the car into a turn on the tight mountain road, felt her stomach lift and float.

King's eyes bulged in outrage. "You should have seen me when I was starting out, before I settled for a safe life," he responded, his voice breaking. "My Jimmy Porter in *Look Back in Anger*? That production could have gone to Broadway."

Janice snorted. She couldn't help herself. "I doubt it. You need to get a grip."

"*I* need to get a grip? You didn't see the show."

"I don't even know what you're talking about."

"That's exactly my point!"

Janice laughed, short and angry like a karate chop. How was she supposed to reason with him? She shook her head. "So off to New York, then," she said. "I'm all for it."

King clapped his hands. That was easy. "Right on. Fantastic. All right." He let out a long breath. "I was looking at Variety the other day. Lots of shows, lots of parts. Look, you'll love it. We can find an affordable place on the Upper East Side—"

"I meant for you, not me. King, I *like* Mammoth. Assuming it doesn't blow up today."

King bent forward in his seat. He gaped at her. "You *like* Mammoth? You do marketing for a ski resort. You go to travel-industry conferences. You write brochures."

"Yeah, and I like it. I like Mammoth View." She glanced at her leg. The finger burns were still visible, a dull pink against her white skin. If she touched it she would be able to feel indentations.

The back of a station wagon reared into her peripheral vision. Wood-paneled. She looked up and hit the brake. The wheels locked and slid, and King threw his left arm against her chest as the car shuddered to a stop.

"You okay?" King asked.

Janice ignored him. She should have worn a bra today. That's the last time you get to cop a feel, she thought. She checked the rear-view mirror, then pushed the door open and climbed into the road. A clutch of teenage girls, folded over one another like origami, peered at her through the station wagon's windows. She felt another attack coming on, that familiar tingly tightening in her throat, like a gulp of Pepsi had gone down the wrong way. A middle-aged man in a T-shirt and gym shorts approached. He had a tragic face—cratered cheeks and basset-hound eyes—beneath a sweat-stained baseball cap. His legs were hairy and thick, with bulging calf muscles like cancerous growths. A rust-brown Monte Carlo idled in front of the station wagon; the tragic man had been talking to the driver, a stocky woman, until the screaming brakes distracted him. Ahead of the Monte Carlo sat another car, a red sedan.

"Hello, there," the man said. "That was a little too close for comfort."

"Yeah." Janice looked at her car—and at the foot or so between her front bumper and the back of the station wagon.

"You know what's going on?"

Janice nodded, struggled to swallow. "That's why we're out here," she gasped.

The man leaned in close. "We're trying not to get the girls too worried." He nodded toward the station wagon. "I'm sure you understand."

"Right. Of course."

King appeared at her side. "What's going on here? Everybody all right?"

"I think so, yes," the man said. "We're headed for Stockton, but our lead car got away from us."

"Well, you really can't get lost. This road will take you all the way in."

The man pulled on the bill of his cap as if giving a secret sign. "Understood. We were just reevaluating, is all. Wondered if maybe we were overreacting. It's a long haul to Stockton. Especially with a carload of girls."

"I don't know," King said. "I can tell you that I'm glad to get out of Mammoth."

Now the man took the cap off and rubbed it like a lantern. The bald patch on the top of his head gleamed in the sun. "What exactly did you see?"

"Well, there wasn't much at first—" King paused, enjoying that dreamy feeling that always came over him when he made up a story on the fly. "But once the explosions started to go off, you know? All around town? People went crazy. It was every man for himself."

"Explosions? From the earthquake?"

"No. No, this was different—" King heard a door close, and glanced over his shoulder. Janice had returned to the car. The engine turned over, and the Camaro jolted into the street. Janice pulled hard on the wheel to avoid hitting King and his new friend.

"Janice!" King yelled. "What are you doing?"

Janice jammed the inhaler into her left nostril and set the epinephrine free again. The medicine lit her up, filling her with confidence and a sense of her own power. For the life of her, she couldn't remember why she had been so stingy with this stuff. She gunned the engine and, as King reached for the door handle, roared away, past the other vehicles and into the horizon. The cars disappeared behind her in a matter of seconds.

CHAPTER TWELVE

"Hello?" Tori called out. "Is anybody there?"

She wiped at her face with both hands. Her stomach was spinning, her fingers tingling. It was inevitable that she would cry, and so she didn't even try to hold it back. Why bother? Everybody had been rescued but her. Everybody in the camp. Everybody in this town. Everybody everywhere.

The thought of it made her double over. She put her hands on her knees and spat. Something unnatural shifted in her gut. She was going to throw up. It was coming. She'd always believed the worst feeling in the world was being spurned by the love of your life. She'd been preparing for it since she was thirteen. But this—being left behind, being the last person in the world—had to be worse. So much worse.

She straightened up. The vomit didn't come. Her nasal passages opened. She forced herself to stop sobbing. She snorted hard, sucking a wad of snot up and away, like her brain was a vacuum cleaner. She couldn't just give up, she decided. What would her dad think if she did that? She started walking again. Teachers thought she was a loner because she didn't talk much, but she liked people. She liked being a part of the group. She simply liked someone else to speak first, to let her know it was okay to join in, that her friendship or opinion was welcome. Then she could talk until the cows came home. Being here in this empty town by herself, with no one to judge herself against: it was a very good approximation of Hell. She lengthened her stride, hoping that the real world and all its people were right around the next corner.

There had to be an explanation for this, she thought. Maybe this wasn't a real town. She didn't remember driving through it on the way to Spritle's. She could have been dozing or listening to the radio, but she didn't think so. It could be a movie set, like the place in Arizona where *The Gunfight at the O.K. Corral* was filmed. That was one of her dad's favorite movies, and they'd driven out there when she was twelve, stayed a night in a motel. They'd had a photo taken in old-time Western outfits—she'd been shocked when he suggested it. It was so unlike him. The black-and-white picture was still on the refrigerator, her dad glowering from under a bulbous cowboy hat, a fake six-shooter in each hand, his preteen daughter pressed against him wearing a fancy "Saloon Sweetie" dress and a garter. She was squishing her lips into an exaggerated smooch, because that was what the woman in line ahead of them had done.

Tori stopped walking. She shook out her legs, first the left one and then the right. No, this was real. Nobody could mistake Old Tucson for a real town, and nobody could mistake this place for a fake one. So where was everyone? There was no earthquake damage that she could see. Lights shone in some of the buildings, and she could make out a low humming sound: probably an air conditioner. Someone had to be here somewhere. She figured there must a lot of good places to hide, basements and backrooms and under porches. But why were people hiding?

"Hello? Is anyone there?" she called out again. "Please answer!"

Tori felt the creeps roll through her. Once the echo from her voice died out, the returning silence hit hard. The quiet seemed so complete this time—she couldn't even make out the air conditioner anymore. Had she ever heard it, or was that in her mind? She found herself turning all the way around, carefully eyeing every inch of the street and alleys and buildings within the radius of her sight. Her stomach plummeted once more, landing in the center of her groin. She buckled, and had to catch herself with her hands on her knees. There was no denying it. The town really, truly was empty, as empty as the camp.

She swallowed but it got stuck halfway down. Acceptance of reality was good. Then you could solve whatever the problem was. Miss Dawkins, her math teacher, had told her that when she was having trouble with her homework. Except this time Tori didn't have the equation that would lead to the answer. She had accepted reality, but she couldn't do anything with it. Or at least she didn't know what to do with it. She took a deep breath, but it was too late. Panic hit like a sneaker wave. This time she wasn't strong enough to fight it off. Her limbs went numb and then seemed to liquefy. She fell to her knees. Tears rushed down her face, harder than before, and she heaved. Her stomach muscles, already sore from her attempts to control her breathing, trembled through a long spasm. She recognized that she was out of control, finally, and let it take her away. "Daddy!" she called out between racking sobs. "Daaadddyy!"

She stopped only when she noticed the car about half a block ahead, the driver's side door wide open. The vehicle had apparently tried to take the corner too fast and ended up halfway on the sidewalk. She swiped at her face with her arms, snorted at a new round of snot in her nose. She had her driver's permit. She'd circled the school parking lot in her dad's car on three evenings, her father offering obscure instructions about the side mirrors and the brake. She could drive out of this place, drive and drive until she found the rest of humanity. She jerked around, suddenly realizing that somebody could be watching. She scuttled to the car—a Chrysler—and climbed in. The keys weren't in the ignition. She slammed her hand on the steering wheel. Pain rocketed through her arm and into her chest. The palm of her hand throbbed. "Shit!" she said. "Owww!" She sat back in the seat and squeezed her eyes shut. She didn't want to cry anymore. She wanted to be in control. She wanted to think her way out of this situation. She wanted to be logical. She was about to press down on the car's horn—to blow that horn until she woke up the dead, it was the only thing she could think of—when she heard a sound. A hard, faraway *tuck, tuck, tuck*, regular but not consistent. She popped her head out of the car and stood. She turned to her right, tracking it. *Tuck, tuck, tuck. Tuck, tuck, tuck.* She stepped down to the sidewalk, still trying to identify what it was and where it was coming from.

Tori moved around the car and started to jog. Her head swiveled this way and that, desperate not to miss it, whatever it was. She reached the end of the street, sniffed the air, and headed east. The buildings were smaller here, nondescript. A single-pump service station was on her right. The bay door stood open, and inside it a mud-spattered white Jeep hung in the air. The other direction offered a small road that twisted into a line of trees. She assumed it was houses back there. At last it hit her. A basketball. That was the noise. Somebody was dribbling a basketball. A person, obviously.

The world *hadn't* ended.

She continued to follow the sound, down a side street and through the covered outdoor eating area of a school. She looked out over a large lawn and spotted him. The basketball player, wearing only a pair of brown corduroy shorts, was across the field in the middle of a rectangular asphalt court. A basket loomed on each of the four sides. The ball banged against the farthest backboard, clanged out of the rim, and fell to the ground.

The boy gathered it in, twirled, and juked an imaginary defender. He lofted a skyhook that banged and clanged again. Tori guessed the boy was a little older than her. Seventeen or eighteen. Crouching, she rounded the edge of the lawn, staying near a line of trees, and sneaked to within about fifty yards of him. She settled behind an old sycamore whose exhausted branches nearly touched the ground. She watched, fascinated and relieved. If this boy was here playing basketball without a care in the world, then everything was all right. She had nothing to worry about. She had been afraid for no reason. She took a deep breath and let it out. She suddenly felt silly for all the blubbering and panic. She liked to think she was grown-up, that she could take care of herself. How many of her friends cooked for themselves, did their own laundry, and made it to school every day without parental badgering? She did it all the time. Her father's confidence in her made her feel important, like an adult. But she wasn't. She'd just proven that. When the going got tough, the tough got going, her father said. When the going got tough for her, she'd cried like a baby.

She leaned forward, following the boy's movements. He was tall and slim, with a thick wad of black hair like the Bob's Big Boy mascot. He moved with a natural athleticism, the crook of his arm uncoiling, his feet leaving the ground in near-perfect symmetry. The ball went up, clanged on the rim, fell. The boy snared it with his right hand. Long muscles stretched along his arm; more muscles studded his stomach. Tori bit her tongue.

She thought about Brian Lonzer. She wanted Brian to ask her out, but at the same time she'd spent the entire school year comforted by the knowledge that he wouldn't. The last time she had a boyfriend—Danny Shapiro, in eighth grade—had been a disaster. He'd stepped into her path one day as she came out of the locker cage and asked her to go steady, just like that. They'd never spoken before except in social-studies class. When she said yes, he took her hand and walked her through the school to the parking lot. He waved when she got on the bus. It ended two weeks later with someone leaving a note in her locker that said, "Will you please die so we can all have some piece?" Tori assumed it was from another girl who also liked Danny, and that she had meant to write "peace," but then she spent days wondering if the spelling was correct and the girl was talking about sharing Danny. After all, Danny knew everybody in school; he was one of those unusual kids who transcended cliques. He was in band and was also on the wrestling team. Maybe he could have two girlfriends in school—

or three or four—and they'd never meet each other. She never got to ask him about the note because he never talked to her again.

Even from this distance she could tell that the basketball boy was better looking than Danny Shapiro—and even Brian Lonzer. He definitely had a better body. She could date someone who lived in Mammoth View, she thought. It was only a couple of hours from Bakersfield. Dad might let her take the car up on Saturdays. She noticed the gelatinous dampness on the inside arm of her sweat-suit top, where she'd wiped her nose. God—*gross!* She rubbed it with the other arm. She really wished she hadn't bawled so much. Her eyes were probably swollen into little pellets. She could have a booger hanging out of her nose. She rubbed her face with her hands, sniffed her armpits. She smelled musty, like an old dog. Well, she thought, nothing she could do about it now. She shrugged off the top, dropped it on the ground, and pondered how to approach the boy. *Hi, I'm Victoria Lane,* she imagined herself saying. *Come here often?*

What was wrong with her? Why was she thinking like this, like everything was normal? And why would she say her *last* name, like it was a job interview? She had no idea how to handle the situation. She'd never approached a boy before, never even considered it. But these were extraordinary times. To calm herself, she ran through every stupid pick-up line she knew.

Do you have any raisins? No? Then how about a date?

I hope you know CPR, because you take my breath away.

Do you know karate? Because your body is really kickin'.

Is that a mirror in your pants, because I can see myself in them.

Excuse me, but I'm new in town. Can I have directions to your place?

That last one actually wasn't bad. The boy's parents would know how to reach her father, even if the phones weren't working. There had to be a way. They'd give her something to eat and let her watch TV until her dad arrived.

Tori stood and adjusted her underwear through her shorts. She stretched her legs, listening to the joints pop, one by one, like buttons on a too-small shirt. Her knees ached; it had been a long walk from the camp, most of it downhill. She stepped out from behind the tree. As the sun hit her, a spot danced in her eye. She blinked it away but immediately found it again. It wasn't a spot. It was two men—a tall one and a normal-sized one. They were running together toward the playground. She watched them bound through the school's walkway and across the lawn. There was something about them, something . . . unsavory. Like the men who'd call on Dad late at night, whispering on the front step as Dad wrote in his little notebook.

Tori started to call out to the boy, but something stopped her. She didn't know him. She knew only her fantasy of him, made up right here on the spot. Maybe he was related to the two men. The men had reached the hardtop and jumped the low fence that circled the playing area. The boy jerked around at the sound of the fence screeching. He stuck the ball in the crook of his arm and watched them approach. He looked confused—but Tori wasn't. She understood exactly what was going to happen. Tori instinctively closed her eyes against the sight, but she couldn't shut her ears. She heard the boy hit the pavement with a *thwock*, like a dropped cantaloupe. A groan followed, long and deep, an unmistakable sound of sudden, unexpected pain. Tori opened her eyes to see the men landing on top of him, their arms pumping.

Tori dove behind the tree, missed, and—out of control—rolled. Panicked, she scrambled on her hands and knees, ending up on her side, grimacing from the pain of something jagged—a hundred somethings—digging into her flesh. She righted herself and saw she was on a narrow road that led to a maintenance shed. A *gravel* road. She grabbed a rock, squeezed it tight in her hand, and rose. Should she do this? She watched the men pummeling the boy, who writhed on the ground like an eel. Yes, she told herself. She had to. They could kill him. She bent her left knee like Catfish Hunter and heaved her arm forward. The rock bounced and skittered, way off target. She grabbed up another rock. She squinted, really concentrating this time. She kicked and threw. It bounced about three feet short but otherwise was perfect. The rock caromed off the asphalt and thumped against the shorter man as he reached back to throw a punch. The man's head popped up like a gopher. He spotted Tori standing on the maintenance road. Now the other man's head jerked around and his eyes landed on her too.

Tori turned and ran.

CHAPTER THIRTEEN

Winnie Lloyd shook the doorknob at the police station. Locked. She pressed her nose to the window and peered inside. Usually one of them was in there during normal business hours, unless they were having lunch together at Benny's.

Winnie headed toward Main Street and the diner. She could go for some eggs and bacon. The recognition of her hunger surprised her. It made her feel better, actually, to understand the queasy feeling she had. She stretched her arms above her head and blew out a blot of air, trying to expel her anxiety. She crossed the street, passed the travel office—not open yet—and the ski shop, which of course was closed for the summer. She examined last year's skiwear in the window, and when she turned she spotted Toby Berenson jogging between buildings at the end of the street, disappearing into the narrow alley next to the five-and-dime.

She suddenly realized the real reason she was feeling weird. There was no one else around. Not even old Benny, who'd been lounging in the wooden chair outside the diner every time she'd ever been downtown in the daylight hours. Benny's daughter Terry ran the diner now, and she served her father as if he were Henry the Eighth.

Hustling to catch up to Toby, Winnie came around the corner

of the alley and bumped into a tall man, her head bouncing off his chest. The man's shirt was damp, and he reeked of B.O. "Sorry, excuse me," she said, reflexively throwing her hands up in apology and twirling to get around him. His fist caught her above the ear. She heard herself yelp in surprise. She landed on her shoulder and hip. A rushing sound—the ocean, as clear as if she were on the beach in Waikiki—filled her head. She grabbed at her right arm, the one she'd fallen on. It felt like she was squeezing rubber. She heard herself yell again, but it wasn't because of the arm. The man had grabbed her hair and the back of her shirt and was dragging her into the street.

The day had started so well. Winnie had woken up feeling sexy—all those hormones jumping through her bloodstream had turned her into one big raw nerve. She liked it. She'd gotten Johnny going when he was still sound asleep, and she'd climbed aboard and reached the bursting point almost immediately. If this was what you could expect from pregnancy, she'd sign up for a dozen kids. She'd lazed in bed for half an hour after Johnny left for work, then groaned to her feet and stepped into the shower. She had just thrown her wet towel on the bed in the front guest room and was admiring herself in the full-length mirror when she saw Margie Buchanan running down the street. Margie yelled something, seemingly to the heavens. Did she say "aliens"? Was it "mammalians"? Winnie peered out the window, first to the right—the direction Margie was running—and then to the left.

Realizing she was still naked, Winnie stepped back from the window, feeling her face flush, and returned to the mirror. But now she couldn't concentrate. She looked out the window again, this time keeping her torso behind the curtain. Margie was a ditz, but surely she hadn't taken up jogging. Something was up. Maybe a raccoon had scared her. Or her son had forgotten his science project about mammals and she couldn't find the car keys. Winnie looked at her feet; her theories didn't satisfy her. Something definitely was up. She crossed to the bedroom, pulled on a wrinkled blouse and Capri pants, slipped into a pair of Top-

Siders, and walked outside to look around. She marched down to the Buchanan place. No one answered the door when she rang. She started back toward the house but then kept going. Before she realized it, she was downtown.

Winnie had never imagined she'd end up in a little town like Mammoth View. She'd figured she would be in Washington, D.C., during her twenties. She had been a poli-sci major at the University of Oregon, a member of the student senate. Her parents were befuddled when she brought Johnny home for Christmas during her senior year. She was dating a police officer? Winnie marched in demonstrations against the war, drove to San Francisco to campaign door to door for Shirley Chisholm. She was supposed to hate the fuzz—the pigs—whatever the kids were calling policemen these days. And, true enough, Winnie had tried to resist him. Johnny Lloyd never read novels. Guns and other weaponry fascinated him. But he was so much more than the cop cliché. He was kind and thoughtful. And, of course, he was gorgeous. A tall, powerful man with broad shoulders. She'd had her fill of pretentious, insecure little twerps in John Lennon glasses.

Winnie kicked out with both feet, but she managed only to pull a muscle in her side. She lay back, trying to will away this new ache. The blood on her face had dried by now; she felt the crust crackle when she moved her mouth. She touched her right cheekbone where the man had hit her; the sensation ripped through her, the touch of a scalding iron. Her head jerked involuntarily, the back of her skull banging against something hard. She blinked, and tears flushed out her eyes. She must look horrid, she thought, and then chastised herself. She loved the way men responded to her, she always had, and since learning she was pregnant she'd worried about how her looks would change. Now the shame she felt for having such feelings had proved justified. Now her vanity had found its dark side.

She tried to turn onto her side to wipe away what was happening. She could think about terrible things happening to her, but she couldn't believe they actually would. She was twenty-seven years old, she thought. The prime of her life. The world shook, lifting her up and banging her down. She was in a car. In the trunk. She couldn't deny it. She pushed her hands into her temples and squeezed her arms tight against herself as the car's movement forced her into a roll. She didn't want to think about what was going to happen when the vehicle reached its destination and the trunk opened. He—whoever *he* was—would kill her. There, she had thought it and believed it. Because it really was the only possibility. Another pretty young victim of the Zodiac Killer, or whoever this lunatic was. Her nose pulsed, and she worried it was going to start bleeding again. Her breathing sputtered. She gulped and sucked at the fug around her head. *Heavenly Father,* she prayed. *O Heavenly Father, I call on you.*

Johnny would find her, she told herself. This man in the plaid shirt was some ex-con Johnny had put away in Eugene, some psychopath. Had to be. And Johnny would know by now that the man was in town and looking for the cop who had sent him to prison. He'd know by now that the ex-con had grabbed his wife. Johnny was probably chasing him—that was why the car was going so fast; that was why she was being tossed around in the trunk like a pinball.

Winnie tried to sit up, and banged her head. She rolled onto her sore shoulder. The car had stopped. She listened: to a door slamming, to boots on gravel, to a key in a lock. She'd watched too many movies. Johnny wasn't going to swoop in and save the day. She was going to be killed. She was going to die. She and her baby. She held her breath to stifle a scream as the trunk swung open. A hand grabbed her, turned her.

"I tell you, Melvin, I can pick 'em. She's a stone fox."

"Shut up"—an older, sharper voice.

"Come on, look at her . . ." The hand grabbed her wrists and yanked her arms away from her face. Winnie squinted into the sunlight. She could just make out two bearded faces. She knew who these men were.

"She's pretty. You've got to say."

"I told you to shut up. Get her out of there."

The dumb one leaned in, pressed his hands into her spine, and hefted her onto his shoulder.

"No, no, no, no," Winnie whined.

"Shut up," Melvin said. His motto.

Fear ripped through Winnie's body. Her extremities went cold, her knees locked. She had to do something. She had to act. She swung her right arm, hitting the man on the back of the head with the upswing. *Clonk.* He adjusted her on his shoulder. She swung again; this time she whacked her elbow feebly against his neck. The man squeezed her torso like a fresh sponge, forcing the air from her lungs. Desperate, she stuck a hand into her mouth. She felt him squeeze her again. She pushed her index and middle fingers to the base of her tongue, as far back as she could. Then further. Tears filled her eyes, the ocean returned to her ears. She couldn't get it. The tickle stayed just out of reach, shimmering in her mind's eye like a gold ring.

"Aww, shit!" the dumb one yelled. He dropped Winnie with a shrug, and in the same motion swiped at the vomit on his back. The ground knocked the wind out of her. Winnie struggled to her knees, heaving, gasping for air. Melvin kicked her, his new red running shoe catching just under the ribcage. She went fetal. She grabbed her stomach with both hands, tried to hold herself. The *baby*, she thought. Melvin seized the front of her blouse and lifted—a mistake. On her feet, her blouse halfway over her head, Winnie thrust her knee up as hard as she could. She felt the man's nuts elongate against her kneecap like a dividing cell. Melvin buckled with only the tiniest *ooof* worming out of his mouth. The other man had no idea what was happening; he was inside the car, rooting around for something to clean himself off.

Winnie staggered in the opposite direction. A dirt path swirled and bounced amidst her flapping shoes. Trees soared into the sky on both sides. "Get after her, goddamn it," she heard Melvin yell. She gagged on the remnants of her upchuck and twisted her head to take in a building that had suddenly cast her in shadow. It looked like a ski lodge. A grandiose porch wrapped around the entire second floor. Large windows stood behind it, shooting reflective lasers into the sky like beacons. But something was wrong with the building. The porch sagged in spots. The chimney above it leaned. Shingles along the ground floor had been peppered by what looked like gunshots. She spotted a door and tried to sprint.

CHAPTER FOURTEEN

Stepping down from the Bronco, Hicks noticed the postal box on its side. Scorch marks reached down the container like jungle vines.

"What the hell?" Lloyd said when Hicks pointed it out.

"Yeah," Lundstrum piped up. "That's when everything went to hell."

Hicks and Lloyd turned to him, and Lundstrum returned the look, clearly stunned that the town's cops really didn't know what was going on. He started from the beginning: Toby Berenson and Eleanor Raskin coming into Benny's within a minute of each other, both in a state, talking about half a dozen dead at the lake, Otis's suicide, some Bakersfield reporter from KERO reporting live on the scene. Then the explosions started. The dumpster behind the travel office went first, later the post box here. There might have been another one in between. Somebody reported a fire out on Lake Road. "Downtown emptied out fast," Lundstrum said. "People were crying—and not just the women, I can tell you. That's about when the Johnson boys showed up."

"Is that right?" Hicks said.

"Yeah, sure, ol' Melvin was in high spirits. Whoopin' and hollerin' like he does."

Hicks led them into the police-department office, Lundstrum still offering up tidbits: Terry cursing out her father for refusing to get out of his chair and into the car; Scott Lansing, the barber, organizing a convoy to Bakersfield. Hicks picked up the phone: still dead. He slammed it back into its cradle. "You got a CB radio?" he asked Lundstrum.

Lundstrum raised his hands. "Not me. Toby, probably."

The chief eyed Lloyd. The lieutenant gave a quick, definitive headshake. Nope, no CB.

"Well, we better take a look around," Hicks said.

Hicks, Lloyd, and Lundstrum headed toward Main Street. They walked down the middle of the street, three abreast. The quietness, normally an attraction of Mammoth View, had begun to weigh on them like sickness. Almost every door stood open. Lights burned unnaturally in empty rooms. The men popped their heads into storefronts here and there. The five-and-dime had been ransacked. Same with the liquor store. Hicks's stomach plummeted. He had screwed up. Really screwed up. How could he leave Marco on his own? Dammit, where *was* Marco? The kid probably ran like everybody else.

Reaching Main Street, they paused, Lloyd and Lundstrum looking east, toward the mountain, Hicks gazing west: at the hotel, the barbershop, the dry cleaner. He spotted the bank beyond, at the fuzzy edge of his vision. The broken glass glinted and swirled in the sunlight. Lloyd noticed it, too. The lieutenant ran toward the dazzle. Hicks, with Lundstrum in tow, took his time, knowing that whatever had happened in there had happened quite a while ago. Hicks had long wondered when someone would realize the bank was easy pickings. It employed a guard during business hours—tubby, slow-witted Vernon Dumar—but no security cameras. The twenty-year-old alarm system was only turned on when the bank was closed. He'd talked to Jim Ferguson, the president, about upgrading security, but Fergie liked to think of the place as just a sleepy little savings and loan, even though he obviously knew that a fair amount of cash passed through it every ski season. Jim Ferguson was a fool, Hicks thought. Almost as big a fool as Hicks himself.

"Chief," Lloyd said from inside the building.

Hicks kneeled down and eased his way through the broken door.

"We've got two dead," Lloyd said. "One's Mister Towson. James Towson. Gunshot to the head. Not sure about the other one. Oh. Christ. It's Alice Krendel. Shit." He looked up at Hicks. "It's Alice Krendel," he said again.

Hicks nodded. He took his hat off, pressed it to his chest. As Lloyd bent down for a better look at the teller's body, disappearing from view behind the counter, Hicks felt his eyes fill with tears. He blinked hard. No phone or police radio or CB. No giant voice system, no emergency-preparedness plan. In his nearly two years as chief—the first police chief ever of the newly incorporated town—he'd done nothing to be ready for this moment. Nobody had done anything. He couldn't recall any discussion with the mayor or the town councilors about something like this. It was the county's job. Now here he was, right in the middle of the impossible. He had no idea what he should do. Except run. That was his urge. He could admit it to himself; he wanted to run just like everybody else. Though he wouldn't be running for his life. He would be running from his responsibility. From his incompetence.

Go West, young man—that was the famous saying. Everybody knew it. They taught the kids in school that the pioneers were courageous men, taming the wild country. But plenty of them went West because they had no choice. Because they were failures in civilized society. Because they were losers. That had been the real lure of the West. The romance of it. But where were the failed *old* men supposed to go? And where did you go when you were already West? Hicks wasn't Jack Lord. His America stopped at the ocean. He touched the gold badge on his shirt, tapping it lightly, letting the pads of his fingers bump over the impressions. "Chief of Police," it said. Chief of Police. He figured he'd be given his walking papers by the end of the week.

Lloyd would be made interim chief. What was he, twenty-eight years old? Hicks rubbed his head, rubbed away the self-pity. No time for that right now. He spotted the boots lying on the floor and immediately recognized them. Next to the right boot, a bloody footprint simmered on the marble floor.

"Don't touch anything," he said to Lloyd, who was slowly circling Alice Krendel's body like a photographer searching out the best angle.

The Johnson brothers. The goddamn Johnson brothers. Hicks never would have guessed they had it in them. He supposed that was the problem. He underestimated people and the things they were capable of—not a good trait in a cop. Melvin and Gordon Johnson had been a problem for years. They lived out at the old Sky Flower commune that had gone belly up a few years back, before Hicks was hired. He'd heard about the hippies—everybody in town had a story about them. They built a large, modern building, with meeting rooms, individual works spaces, and dorms. They laid out a soccer field and a vegetable garden, erected a playground for all the children they were going to have. They had grand plans for an international headquarters, like the Maharishi had in India. Some former A&R man at Capitol Records funded the whole effort after turning on and dropping out.

Homer Johnson bought the place at auction in '73 or '74, but just a few months later cancer got him. His boys didn't have the wherewithal to do anything with the property. They tried to start their own commune, but they couldn't find anyone who would believe that two mouth-breathing good old boys had the secret to enlightenment. They'd leased it as a corporate retreat a few times, until the rot started to set in. Now they simply burned through their daddy's money and caused trouble around town—hassling the tourists, shooting at raccoons and cats, that kind of thing. It had gotten worse lately.

Over a handful of months, three vehicles driving on Renton Road near the Johnson compound had been hit by buckshot, though Hicks couldn't prove it was Melvin and Gordon. A teenaged girl on vacation with her family last year accused Gordon of assaulting her on the slopes—he'd grabbed her after she'd fallen and lost a ski—but the girl's father decided not to pursue charges. When the time came to pay taxes on their land, the Johnsons became ardent anarchists, spouting off in court about their right to govern themselves.

Now it looked like they were murderers. Hicks sent Lundstrum running to the hardware store one block over. When Lundstrum returned with canvas sheets, Hicks and Lloyd covered the bodies. The chief pushed Alice Krendel's right arm under the canvas, and something behind the flesh crackled. The beginnings of rigor mortis, he supposed. That done, the three men returned to the street and started walking.

Hicks took the lead, his head down. His hands felt like catcher's mitts. He wondered if he was in shock. He figured he should be.

James Towson and Alice Krendel. Dead on his watch.

He didn't know either of them well. He'd seen them at Benny's now and again. Never together. Towson was not the kind of man who'd socialize with his subordinates. Certainly not the kind to fool around with them. And Alice . . . she had to be nearly thirty, but he'd bet a month's salary she was a virgin. He shut his eyes against the thought, but there was no stopping it. Now she would be innocent forever: no husband, no kids or grandkids. Alone in eternity forever.

Christ, Towson had two teenagers, he remembered. He couldn't think of their names. He was going to have to break the news to Olivia Towson. And to Alice's mother. What a day.

"Crime of opportunity," Lloyd said from behind him. "Had to be."

Hicks, his head still down, watched his boots flashing against the pavement, one after the other. "You figure?"

"Yes. Definitely. Too messy to be planned."

"Melvin declared that he was in charge," Lundstrum said.

"What's that now?"

"Yelled it at the top of his lungs. He and his brother were standing in the middle of the street."

"Marco might have gone after them," Lloyd said.

Hicks nodded. "Maybe."

The three men reached the police station. They hadn't seen a soul over the two blocks. Lloyd climbed into the Bronco.

"You best stay here," Hicks told Lundstrum, retrieving the storeowner's shotgun from the front seat and handing it over.

"You sure, Chief? I don't know."

Hicks slapped him on the shoulder. "Don't worry, Frank. Whatever's happening, it's already moved on. You can lock yourself in the office, if you want. There's a piece of almond cake in the fridge."

Lundstrum avoided eye contact. Terry's almond cake was a temptation, but not if it meant being alone again.

"It'd be a good idea to have someone here to answer the phone, if it starts working again," Hicks said. "We sure would like to get ahold of the state police as soon as possible."

The appeal to civic duty did the job. Lundstrum put his hand out, and Hicks clapped the keys into his palm.

Lloyd started up the Bronco. He'd never been to the Johnson compound, but he'd heard about it. "All right," he said, "let's go find these guys."

CHAPTER FIFTEEN

Billy closed his eyes and tried not to think about Becky. The rumbling of the car's engine and the shaking of the seat lulled him. He'd tried to move on, he reminded himself. He'd had serious girlfriends. One, at least. He met her in Tahoe, where she was a dealer at the Cal Neva, Sinatra's casino. Billy spotted her about two minutes after entering the casino floor, when she stepped out from behind her table and sashayed toward him. A leering imaginary trombone accompanied her; every man in the place felt it, deep in his groin. *Oh, baby, I want you*, it groaned. *Oh, baby, just like that.* She strode past him, and Billy turned to watch, just like everyone else. She continued on to the end of the long room before disappearing through a side door. And she did this—held the room in suspended animation—in black slacks and a ruffled, buttoned-up white shirt that offered not a smidgen of cleavage. This was a girl Billy had to get to know.

He followed her, out the door, around the corner, down the corridor. She was being seated at the coffee shop, in the front window. He suspected the manager always insisted on seating her there, that he kept the table open for her. Billy convinced her to move to a back booth where they couldn't be seen. He bought her a meal and let her bum a post-bacon-and-eggs cigarette. It immediately proved to be a mutual—and a mutually beneficial—crush. She saved him from a big loss at the blackjack table later that night; she made a card disappear and replaced it with another one, without a moment's hesitation. He would have married her that night if he hadn't blacked out from the Cutty Sark.

Jillian Bingham was her name. Jilly. Billy and Jilly, she liked to say. She thought that was hilarious. Fucking hell. He let it go. How could he not? She had a wop nose—her mother was Italian—but it didn't matter. Everything else was perfect. Almost six feet tall. Broad shoulders. Legs up to here. Ta-tas floating in space like planets. Every man at her table hit on her, over and over. No, the schnoz didn't matter. Men's eyes rarely got up that far.

She knew it, of course. She wanted to go to France so she could strut on the topless beaches. *Oh, bébé, I want you. Oh, bébé, just like that!* Billy wasn't interested. A trip to Europe cost an arm and a leg. And he didn't want a bunch of frogs looking at his girl. Her naked ta-tas were for him and him alone. But that conversation happened later, months later, near the end of things.

She came to Bakersfield with him after a weekend of gambling and sex. Because of her, he came out ahead in both, a first. They walked into the house at two on a Monday morning, exhausted from a lack of sleep and too much bad coffee. He sent his stepmother home without introducing her to Jillian. What would have been the point of an introduction? Jillian didn't look like marriage material even in the best light. And this wasn't the best light. It was dim, tawdry. Jillian had taken something, some kind of pill to stay awake on the long drive. She was blinking furiously, humming to herself. Mom could formally meet her another time, when Jillian was rested and wearing a straightforward dress. Billy peeked in on Tori. His daughter was sound asleep, curled up on her side, her fists clenched under her chin. He expected Jillian to be behind him, peering over his shoulder at little Tori, but she wasn't. She'd headed straight for the master bedroom, thrown her clothes off, and climbed under the covers.

Billy joined her in bed. He let her snuggle in close, let her reach into his drawers. Jillian loved the idea of shacking up with Billy. She'd never lived in an actual house. She'd grown up in used Dormobiles and shabby little apartments with carpeting that stank. She told him all about it during the drive, her whole childhood. Her drunk, degenerate-gambler father. Her drunk, showgirl mother. Her sister who died at six years old after falling out a window. Her bit part as a go-go dancer in *Viva Las Vegas* when she was seventeen. Her apprenticeship on the casino floor at Caesar's. Her marriage to a pit boss that lasted eighteen months, the implosion of which forced her to flee to Lake Tahoe.

Now, finally exhausted and out of the car, she didn't want to talk anymore. She wanted to do it, in her new home, with her new man. Billy didn't argue. Here's to swimmin' with bowlegged women, he thought, diving in. Jillian immediately lost herself in the sex—she couldn't help it, she was that kind of girl. She squealed and thumped her palms on the bed. Arched her back and bucked, again and again, until she felt him spasm. That done, she shoved him over and swung her legs off the bed. "Lordy, I'm parched," she said, putting on an accent of some kind. She got up and flung open the door.

There, standing in the doorway, was Tori, riveted in place, her flared-match eyes surely the prelude to a scream. She gripped her pajamas at the thighs with both hands. Jillian, naked as a jaybird, barely paused. She patted Tori on the head and strode toward the kitchen. Billy watched this scene, strangely fascinated. He had no idea what to do. Would an eight-year-old girl realize what had been going on? Nine. Christ, she was nine. He knew that. When Tori's eyes shifted and landed on Billy's, he snapped at her to go to bed. It was all he could think to say. She pivoted as if on skates and hurried back to her room.

When Jillian found out what Billy did for a living, she made noises about reforming him, about getting him into some kind of legit business. But her heart wasn't in it. For starters, she'd known from the moment she met him what kind of man he was. He had the smile of a conman. She'd seen it before, had always liked it. So the bookmaking, the various forms of robbery—these things did not shock or surprise her. It was a core part of his charisma; it helped make their life together exciting. Sure enough, she soon started helping out with the Spanish Prisoner scam, just for kicks. A beautiful woman always made it more likely that a man would fall for what was obviously a trick.

It was wonderful for a while. Billy thought hard about popping the question. A new marriage would make his parents happy. And Tori liked Jillian—she was in awe of her. Tori followed her around the house, helped her with the laundry and the grocery shopping. In return, Jillian showed her yo-yo tricks, walking the dog and shooting the moon and whatever.

Jillian wanted to get married, she made that clear. She wanted to be a wife to Billy and a mother to Tori. Have a kid of her own with her man. She believed she could be an excellent mother. She figured all she had to do was the opposite of everything her own mother did.

The problem was that as the newness of the sex wore off, Billy grew bored. His dissatisfaction bewildered him. Jillian Bingham should make him happy, he told himself. She should make him ecstatic. A nice girl. A beautiful girl. Helpful and kind and full of life. Of course, Jillian wanted him to be different, which was a problem. She wanted him to open up. She wanted to *know* him, to relate and share. She was always seeking meaning in their conversations, in their meals and their lovemaking. Billy didn't understand what she was trying to achieve.

His thoughts turned to the girl in the bank, the one Sam had punched in the face. Billy was worried about her. She didn't move again, not even a twitch, after Sam hit her. Her head had banged hard against the floor. Could be bad. Internal bleeding. He hadn't had the time to take a good look at her. Plain face, he remembered that. A librarian's face. He couldn't recall seeing a wedding ring on her finger. He figured she had to be married, though. She was young, but she was the type to marry the first boy who cupped her breast. He started to convince himself that he did see a ring. A little thing, cheap but cute, bought on credit at the St. Vincent Jewelry Center in L.A. before she and her man had lunch at the deli next door. Los Angeles would be a big outing for them, like going to New York or Paris for regular people. They probably had a couple of kids by now. They always started young out in the sticks.

Listen to yourself, he thought. Billy blinked hard, shifted his gaze to his right. The mountain rocketed past him, an endless wall of rocks and trees climbing into the sky. He had the girl's life all worked out when, in truth, he didn't know a thing about her. She was fine, he decided. A bump on the head. A concussion, at worst. A broken nose. She'd remember that a black man hit her, but she'd be foggy on the details. It would all work out. Her husband—a lump of a guy but sweet, a lumberjack or a skimobile operator— would nurse her back to health. She'd live a long and happy life, with a great story to tell her grandchildren.

He returned his eyes to the road, to the long hood of the car eating up the white lines in the asphalt. He knew what the problem was. She wasn't Becky. Jillian couldn't make him laugh like Becks had. She wasn't curious about the world like Becks. She didn't have Becky's talent.

He remembered Becky going to the library to read about Carole Lombard. That's who Becky wanted to be, the next Carole Lombard. She showed him black-and-white pictures from a book, and true enough, Lombard was something. Platinum-blond hair that rolled along the side of her head like a barrel wave. Pale, almost translucent eyes that forced you to look deep into them until the whole page went blank. And the body: she wore gowns that clung and eddied in all the right places. How was that allowed back in the 1930s, when everyone was a prude? But she wasn't just beautiful and glamorous, Becky said. She was funny. *Really* funny.

Becky saw *My Man Godfrey* at a second-run theater with a girlfriend, and that was it. She was hooked. "I'd like to sew his buttons on sometime," she would say whenever Billy was getting dressed. It was from the movie. A double entendre, she said. Whatever it was, she made it sound dirty, not funny. Which was fine with him. Shortly before she got pregnant, she cut her hair like Carole Lombard. It looked kind of funny in real life, in color, but she liked it. She told him Lombard came from a wealthy family but she never acted like she was better than people. Just like in *My Man Godfrey*. Billy never did see the movie. He remembered Becky scanning the movie ads in the paper for revivals and flipping through the TV Guide when they were at the newsstand. No luck.

He came out of his daydream, glanced furtively to his left. Jackson had his left arm crooked on the top of the door, the elbow pressing against the window. The right arm hung limply over the top of the steering wheel. He looked like he was about to fall asleep. Billy glanced in the rear-view mirror. Sam sat hunched forward, his eyes downcast, chewing his cud. Billy leaned back in his seat again, closed his eyes. He didn't like to think about what had happened between him and Jillian, but he did, all the time. He became depressed—that was what happened to their relationship. He could admit it to himself. He became so depressed that he took to bed. He slept for fifteen hours one night. It was in December; he couldn't remember what year. Cold. After the fifteen hours, he'd gotten up, peed, made some toast for himself, and, without even thinking about it, gone back to bed. It was the morning when he woke up again. He had no idea what day it was. His joints ached from disuse, his mouth felt like a garbage disposal.

"You sick?" Jillian asked when he tottered into the kitchen. She was sitting at the kitchen table in a bathrobe. The nub of a cigarette hung from her mouth like a snaggletooth. She looked sick herself. Sick of everything.

"No. I'm not sick."

"What's wrong with you, then?"

"Where's Tori?"

Jillian stubbed out the nub, extracted a new cigarette from her pocket, and lit it. She puffed, took the stick out of her mouth, and waved the smoke away from her face. "I told her she could go to what's-her-name's house."

"Who?"

"I don't know. What's-her-name."

"Why'd you tell her that?"

"Why not? She's over there all the time. You were dead to the world. I thought I was going to have to call an ambulance." Jillian got up, went to him. She pressed the back of her hand to his forehead. She turned him and rubbed his back. "My poor baby. Can I make you something to eat? Some toast?"

"Toast? I just had toast."

"You've been asleep for hours. Do you want some breakfast?"

"I had toast. I remember I had toast."

"Right, you had toast. I remember, too. The *highlight* of the fucking week. It was very memorable toast."

Billy smiled. Look at that—Jillian made him smile. That was funny. Not Carole Lombard funny, but a start. It was progress. He decided to go back to bed again, except this time with Jillian. She was giggling as they headed for the back of the house, untying the bathrobe. And, sure enough, it was like old times. She banged her palms on the bed. She yelped and bucked. When it was done, Billy fell straight to sleep and was out for another five hours.

He got up in the middle of the afternoon and looked out the window at the empty street. He walked down to Tori's room and peeked in. Empty. Still at what's-her-name's house. Or maybe she was at the record store. She wanted that Partridge Family LP. Billy couldn't bear the thought of it, that song—the one at the beginning of the show—playing over and over in the house.

He returned to the bedroom, lay down, but now he was done sleeping. Now he had to think. He had to figure out how to end things with Jillian with as little mess and upset as possible. Tori, after all, liked Jillian. She was the closest thing Tori had ever had to a mother.

"Why didn't you tell me about this route?" Jackson said. "I'm the driver, man. I should have known."

Billy opened his eyes, startled. "What?"

"I said, why didn't you tell me about this road, man? I should have known about it."

Billy sat up, blinked away the past. "Yeah, you should have known," he said. "You're a professional. Why didn't you know?"

Jackson shook his head, chastened. "Shit, who knew they even had maps for places like this? Why would I go up a mountain? Do I look like a ski bum?"

"Me neither," Billy said. "But I looked at a map. Planning. That's what being a professional is all about."

"Don't tell me about being a professional, man. Two seconds in that bank and I knew it was an easy score. That's being a professional. That's why I signed on for this thing."

"Right. The money you owe me had nothing to do with it."

"Why don't you just shut up with that, okay? You never had a cold streak? I just paid off my debt. You and me is clear. You owe *me* now."

"Jack, what were you doing, trying to pay your bills with the horses?" Sam had come to life in the back. He stretched his legs out on the seat and laughed, a high, short burst.

Jackson looked at him through the rearview mirror. "I have a job, all right?"

Billy turned in his seat, raised an eyebrow at Sam. "He cleans Porta-Potties."

Sam's eyes widened into saucers. Realizing Billy wasn't joking, he clapped a hand over his mouth. "Shit, Jack," he said. "There are a lot of places to get work."

Jackson glared in the mirror. "Hey, I got disadvantages, all right? I told you, man, I was in prison."

Billy watched the trees chunk past on the side of the road. He'd liked Jackson right off. The man bet with daring. He had the courage of his convictions. He took a big loss on the Colts when he should have known better. That team hasn't been the same since Unitas retired. Everybody knew that. Afterward, Jackson admitted his head hadn't been in the right place. He'd needed money fast because his girl, his *ex-girl*, had shown up and told him she was pregnant. When she said she was on the pill, she must've meant aspirin, Jackson said. Billy chuckled, remembering the conversation. He'd met the girl once, before she and Jackson broke up. White girl. Pretty. Jackson had a way with the ladies.

"We're going to split up the money in Stockton?" Sam said.

Billy sat up, annoyed. "I told you, I got to clean it. I know a guy. It'll take a couple of weeks."

"Right," Sam said. "I remember now. We got to trust you."

"Yeah, you got to trust me. You think I'm going to double-cross you, Sam the Man?" He turned and punched at Sam's knee. "I'd have to be crazy."

Sam laughed, slapped at Billy's fist. "Yeah. You're crazy, all right."

"Boys . . ." Jackson said, his eyes on the rear-view mirror.

"Right, Dad," Billy mocked, "no horsing around in the car."

"No, not that." He nodded at the mirror. "Look who's back."

Billy and Sam turned around in their seats. The lumber truck. Coming on hard. They watched the driver reach up and pull something. A horn blasted, rolling over the Buick like thunder. Jackson stomped down, and the car responded like a whipped horse, jerking and surging forward.

Billy placed a hand on the dashboard to steady himself. "Ease up. He's just trying to scare you."

Jackson kept his eyes on the road ahead. "I don't think you understand the redneck psychology."

Billy looked back again. Jackson could be right. The truck driver was bent over the truck's steering wheel like a rutting dog, a look of grim determination spackled on his fat face.

The race was on. The Skyhawk zapped along the little road, Jackson leaning forward to hold the car to its course. Billy couldn't see the speedometer, but it felt like they were going eighty. The car became airborne for a moment—the road suddenly went quiet, and Billy had the sensation of floating, his stomach yawing, a foul taste rising in his throat. The Buick bounced on its shocks. Billy's hands flew up, his fingers scrabbling at the headliner. Jackson pumped the brake, but only for a moment, only to regain control. Booming into a wide turn, the car pitched and shook. Billy held onto his seat. He heard Sam tumble in the back. The look on Jackson's face—the set of the jaw, the hard little eyes with the exploding irises—scared Billy. Was Jackson in control of the car—or was the car in control of him? Billy thought of the racers dumbly going around in a circle at the Indianapolis 500. The redneck's Super Bowl. It was easy money for him every year. There were no dynasties in car racing, no Yankees or Steelers. It was impossible to pick the winner of the race. The fans—Billy believed they secretly wanted the crashes. Actually, it wasn't such a secret. Spectators always tried to get as close to the track as possible before the race, thrusting programs and slips of paper at the drivers as they marched through Gasoline Alley in their space suits. The fans wanted to be able to say they got their man's last autograph ever. Billy turned and looked out the back window. The goddamn truck was keeping up. How was that possible?

The noise of the thing was incredible. It seemed to growl and roar at them, taunting them to go ever faster.

"We need to cut this out," Billy said. "We don't want to get pulled over."

"Don't worry. Flying off the side of the mountain and bursting into a fireball is a much stronger possibility."

"This shit isn't funny. You really are going to get us killed."

"*I'm* going to get us killed? The redneck asshole has nothing to do with it?"

"If you hadn't passed the sonuvabitch—"

"Don't you start, man. Don't go blaming this psycho Klansman on me."

"All right, fine. But we've got to stop this."

"You got any suggestions?"

Billy swung around and squinted until he had the truck driver in focus. The man was munching on something. And he was smiling. The fucker was smiling. Billy grabbed onto the small compartment between the seats, which rattled in his hand. The rattling pulled at him like a falling anchor. The man is back there smiling, he thought. He has no margin for error—the smallest error could kill him—and he's smiling and eating Funyuns. Because rednecks are dumb and they always feel safe in their trucks. They love their trucks. The bigger the better. Pick-ups, dump trucks, semi-trailers, ballast tractors.

Lumber carriers.

Billy had never seen a truck so big. This was not a machine for pussies, and the redneck driving it wanted everyone to understand that. The truck shook. The truck coughed. It spewed enough exhaust to choke the Man in the Moon. With every bump and pothole, the whole apparatus centipeded from the cab to the trailer's rear end, the logs mumbling, the axles pumping. How long would it take the truck to stop after Redneck stomped on the brake? Billy pictured it: the trailer swinging around, the tires throwing off rubber like bolts of lightning, the engine grinding into itself. Had the redneck ever stomped on the brake? Billy didn't think so. The man's face was unmoving, his plug-like eyes gleamed in the windshield. He looked like a full-speed-ahead man, a damn-the-torpedoes man.

Jackson's right arm jerked, and the car did the same, throwing Billy against the dashboard. Sam screamed as if giving birth. Billy wiped his hands on his pants. He felt like his stomach was lodged halfway up his esophagus.

"What the hell are you doing?" Sam yelled at Jackson.

"I didn't do it on purpose."

"You thought you could fake him out? It's a one-lane road!"

"I don't need this right now, okay?"

"You're jerking off up there!"

"Jackson," Billy interrupted. "What do you think would happen if we just slowed down? If we didn't play his game?"

"He'll run right over us," Sam screeched.

Jackson nodded. "We'll end up ass over teakettle."

If they went over the cliff, would they ever be found? The truck driver obviously wouldn't report it. If the car missed the trees along the side of the road it would simply disappear, Billy thought. There were a lot of mountain crevices and lips that could eat a Skyhawk. And the snow would come in a few months, and then no one would ever find them. All that money in the trunk: gone from the civilized world. That was deflation, man. A nice little bonus for the economy.

Billy unbuttoned his shirt and peeled it off. Next he pulled his undershirt over his head. "Slow down," he said, balling the top of the undershirt in his fist.

Jackson glanced at him. "You want to go out of this world the same way you came in?" His voice broke, spiraling off into a girlish yelp at the end.

"Jackson, slow down—just a little bit."

The car shuddered as it decelerated. Jackson held it steady. Billy began rolling the window down. The wind shouldered its way into the car and boxed his head. Behind them, the truck's engine roared: it was right on top of them. Billy shoved his right fist out the window and shook the undershirt, which snapped into a full stretch. He shook it as hard as he could, back and forth.

The truck grazed the Buick's back bumper. The Skyhawk jounced, and the truck made contact again. Sam pressed his forehead into the seat in front of him, prepared for the smashup. Jackson's arms vibrated; a quiet moan slipped out of his mouth. Billy continued to shake the undershirt. The g-forces battered his arm, and he strained to keep the wind from snatching the shirt away. Waving the white flag, he flashed on Jillian again, the night of the breakup. The screaming. The stomping around. She didn't care that Tori was right down the hall. She wanted to be out of control. She wanted to hurt him. She wanted him to beg her to stop. The car squirmed, caught in the truck's beam. Jackson pressed himself into the steering wheel to maintain control. His biceps bulged; veins popped down his forearms. He pressed his foot down on the accelerator, jerking the car free of the truck's gravitational pull. Redneck didn't follow suit.

The truck fell back half a car length. Billy swiveled, his eyes darting until they landed on the truck's windshield. The driver was still smiling, but it was different now. The man was pleased. The winner. The redneck nodded, up and down, mentally patting himself on the back. He raised his hand and flapped it like a fan; he wanted them to get out of the way.

Billy retracted the white flag and rolled up the window.

Jackson tossed an eye at him. "What should I do?"

"Move over."

Jackson pressed the car as close to the mountain as he could. The truck moved into the oncoming lane and rumbled alongside. It stayed there for a minute, two minutes, the huge log carrier and the small Buick filling every inch of the road. The truck's banging and jouncing sounded like an artillery barrage. Massive wheels filled the driver-side windows: Sam watched the backward-spinning illusion of the rims, his fingers digging into the seat. He felt his nails bend backward, the pain jolting up his arm, but he kept at it. At last the truck pulled ahead, inch by inch and then foot by foot, and, once the carrier cleared the car, it swung back into the right lane. The operation complete, the truck bellowed—Redneck was blowing the horn in triumph. Jackson, sweat beaded on his face, rode the brake, allowing the truck to lengthen its lead. The lumber truck disappeared around the side of the mountain, and half a minute later when the Buick rolled out of the turn, the men saw nothing but empty road ahead of them.

CHAPTER SIXTEEN

Hicks and Lloyd checked their revolvers. They eased toward the black Cadillac Eldorado, Old Man Johnson's car. The trunk gaped. The driver's side door also stood open. A sour smell hit them, the smell of a dead animal left out in the sun. No, not quite. Human vomit. Hicks found a splotch of it in the dirt like an undercooked egg. More puke had been wiped on the side of the car. Lloyd peered inside the Eldorado, shoved a hand onto the floor of the backseat. Nothing and no one.

Hicks started up the path to the building, Lloyd a few steps behind. Hicks had been to the property a handful of times. Every time he came out it looked worse for wear. The architecture mimicked Louis Kahn: the building was heavyset and graceless; it showed off its seams like battle scars. The mock-monumental size surely impressed the kind of hippie kids who were drawn to cults.

"Pretty cool," Lloyd whispered.

"Something like that."

"Should I go around the back?"

"No," Hicks said, holding up a palm. "We can't cover all the exits. Best to stay together." The front door was straight ahead, but he remembered that a hanging balcony overlooked the large, open entryway. They'd be sitting ducks if the Johnsons had evil intent.

He pointed, indicating that they should go around the side of the building.

They gave the front walk a wide berth, staying near the tree line. The building was designed to suck in natural light, making it impossible to pick up any clues about which, if any, rooms might be occupied. Turning the corner, the soccer field came into view. It had been recently mowed, which surprised Hicks. He couldn't picture either of the Johnson boys pushing a mower. Metal bleachers stood on the far side. A multicolored blanket flopped over a corner of the top-row bench.

Standing in the shade cast by the building, Hicks stopped and turned, taking in the four corners of the field, the woods beyond. Of course it reminded him of the park where he used to meet Elaine Krupp. He saw himself stretched out on his back, his head in Elaine's lap. She's smoothing his coarse gray hair as he talks about the details of his day, always so much talk about nothing: what calls came in, the patrol routes taken, a catalogue of speeding tickets issued and abandoned cars noted. He never saw Sarah coming—somehow he didn't hear a single footfall—until she was right on top of them. "Hello," Elaine said to her, squinting into the afternoon sun. "Can we help you?" The look on his wife's face as Elaine said this—*"Can we help you?"*—dug into Hicks's gut, sent out tracers.

Lloyd called him back to the moment. "Chief. *Chief.*" Hicks crouched and wheeled around, blinking through the ghostly afterimage. Hicks felt himself breathing hard, the huff of fear. He'd actually gone away, he realized. Drifted off into his head, right here with a gun in his hand. He should resign, he suddenly thought. He should call the mayor at the end of the day and tell him he was through.

"What's the plan?" Lloyd said.

Hicks settled himself, scanned the property. Porthole-style windows studded the second and third floors. The top floor offered large bay windows for panoramic views of the Sierra Nevadas and Inyo National Forest. "That door there," he said, pointing to a small, second-floor entrance at the top of a multilevel wooden path that wound decoratively up the side of the building. "That'll do."

They hurried across a corner of the field, paused at the first step, and then began to move sidelong up the stairway. They were positioned shoulder to shoulder, looking away from each other, trying to keep both corners of the building and the door in their sight. They were halfway up when a voice cut through their thoughts: "Stay right there, Sheriff." Hicks and Lloyd, taken by surprise, skittered out of the sun, their boots banging on the wooden planks. They pressed themselves against the building, hoping they were lost in the shade.

"This is private property, Sheriff," the voice said. "I kindly ask you to remove yourself from the premises."

"Melvin?" Hicks called, looking up. He was pretty sure it was Melvin and that the voice was coming from the third floor. "Melvin, it's Chief Hicks. We need you to come with us."

Only a bird responded, a long, sharp *caw* from somewhere in the trees. Lloyd caught Hicks's eye, nodded toward the door. The gun in the lieutenant's hand quivered like a plucked guitar string. Hicks shook his head. He figured Melvin had ducked away from the window and was heading into the bowels of the building. Finding him would be a slow, dangerous undertaking.

"You got an arrest warrant, Sheriff?" the voice finally answered. "What'd I do? Is it illegal for a man to mind his own business in his own home?"

"We want to talk to you about what's going on, Melvin. It won't take long. Where's your brother?"

Another round of nothing washed down on them. This time even the bird stayed quiet. At last a window shut with a clap. Hicks strained, but he didn't hear anything at all from inside the building.

Hicks looked at Lloyd. "I think we have probable cause for entry," he said.

Lloyd indicated with his head that Hicks should move first.

Hunched over, the chief stepped forward, eased up the last level, and duck-walked to the door. He pressed himself against the side of the building again. Lloyd jogged up behind him, jumped in front, and tried the door handle. Locked. Holding his revolver with both hands, the lieutenant reared back and kicked. The door shook. Lloyd kicked again, and the handle jumped into the air. The door swung wildly into the building. Hicks heaved his bulk through the doorway, arms out, finger on the trigger.

Linoleum flooring guided him to a stone counter. A refrigerator hummed against a wall. He was in the kitchen. Or *a* kitchen. The building probably had three or four of them. The chief stayed low, willing his eyes to adjust to the new environment. Lloyd stepped beside him. The lieutenant swung his gun to the left, then to the right. A beam of sunlight from a porthole pocked a far wall. The rest of the room marinated in speckled gloom.

"Melvin! Come on out, now," Hicks called. "We don't want anybody to get hurt. No reason to make this a bigger thing than it has to be."

The men stood still, listening. No footfalls. No pin-drop. Nothing. The building had swallowed Melvin Johnson.

Lloyd moved through the kitchen's entryway into the long, white-walled room beyond. Hicks poked his head through the opening a moment later. The room didn't have any furniture or carpeting. Lloyd was moving carefully, but every step declared his location. Easing into the next room, a hallway, he threw a look back at Hicks. He stuck a finger in the air: stairs.

Hicks joined Lloyd in the hall, followed his eyes to the end. This was odd. The building had an open design—big, high-ceilinged rooms, no doors, one room flowing into the next—but the staircase was enclosed. A small, elegantly lettered sign was affixed to the door. "Stairs," it said.

"No need for breadcrumbs, I guess," Hicks whispered.

Lloyd started to reply but a noise interrupted him—the sound of something falling and hitting an unforgiving surface. It sounded like it came from the floor below them, not above.

"Johnny!"

The voice pierced the floor, resounded in the souls of their shoes.

Hicks, stunned, dropped into a deep crouch, both arms out at his sides. It was Winnie Lloyd's voice. What the hell? Hicks turned to his lieutenant, but Lloyd was already racing toward the stairs. Hicks wanted to call out, to stop him, but he knew nothing was going to stop him. He also knew that to call out to him, to order him to stop, would tip off their quarry, show that they were weak and undisciplined. Not in control.

The stairwell door closed behind Lloyd. Boots clomped down the stairs, two or three at a time. Hicks made it to the door a few moments later and flung it open. He stepped forward, listening to Lloyd's footsteps dissipate into nothing. As the door closed behind him, he realized there was no light in the stairwell. He watched his hand and gun disappear into blackness.

"Winnie!" Lloyd yelled from below.

Hicks put his left foot down, secured it on the stair, and brought the right one down to join it. He heard something, way off in the ether. The chief wondered what it cost to heat and cool this building every year. The utility bills had to be steep. General maintenance costs, too. No wonder the Johnsons always seemed so stressed. The old man's estate couldn't be throwing off much income. The boys had to figure something out, and they clearly had no clue what that might be. They had no skills. No work ethic. Homer long ago sold his feed business. Of course Melvin and Gordon had decided to knock off the bank. Of course.

Feeling for terra firma with his boot, Hicks tried to locate the sound of Lloyd's footsteps; was his lieutenant heading east or west? He found the next step, transferred his weight, dropped the other foot down. He shifted to his left to put his head over the railing, to try to judge how many steps he had to go—and lost his balance. His knee hit the railing, sending a spasm up his leg. He fell backward, a silent-movie pratfall, and his gun flew up, slamming him in the face and then hurtling beyond his head as if released into deep space. He hit the wall, bounced. This all seemed to happen in slow motion. He felt like he had hours to catch himself: to reach out for the railing and grab it, to jam his shoulder against the wall, to thrust his leg out. But he couldn't do any of those things.

He crashed onto the landing, wrenching his shoulder. His left foot screamed. It felt like the foot had twisted all the way backward. He pictured an owl's head swiveling around, and he grimaced. He turned onto his back and let out a quiet howl.

He didn't know if he could get up. He had a sprained foot, at the least. He might have broken something. When he was in the hospital, the nurses told him every day he had to walk. They shook their heads and clucked at his protests, pulled him to his feet and steadied him with his arms over their shoulders. He hated those women. They always left the curtains open and paid no mind to his flapping gown, his bare buttocks exposed to anyone passing by the window. At least that wasn't as bad as being harangued about his bowel movements. Whenever he heard a nurse padding down the hall, he wanted to escape, to hide in the toilet. But if he did that, she'd just knock on the door, maybe even open it up. The john had no lock on the door, in case the nurses had to come barging in to save him. One thing he knew for certain: now that he was familiar with hospital life, he wanted to die young. Which would have been ten years ago.

He forced himself to his feet, felt around for the walls to get his bearings. His foot ached but it wasn't as bad as he'd first thought. He didn't think it was broken. Shaking it, pressing it down to test the pain level, he thumped into something, sending whatever it was sliding away and then bumping down the stairs. A plastic bottle. He became aware again of the sound of shoes— or something like shoes—in the hallway below him. He held his breath for a moment. He still couldn't see anything. The gun had disappeared on impact. He lifted himself up a step, toward where he thought he heard the gun land. He kicked out with his good foot. He bent down, patted a stair with his hand. He grasped the railing and pulled himself up further, patted the next step. Nothing . . . nothing.

An explosion shook the building—a shotgun—and he dropped onto his side, slid back to the landing, and pushed himself into a corner. The noise bounced around like a pinball. Shoes padded away, a door clanged open. "Gordon! Where are you?" he heard someone say. Melvin. Hicks waited, making sure Melvin had indeed gone off to another part of the building. He thought he heard another door open far away. He heard something, anyway. He dropped onto his hands and knees, pushed himself upright. He forced himself down the stairs, threw open the door. He leaned against the doorframe and spun into the hallway.

Silence met him. He could see now. Not well, not clearly, but a static mist was better than blackness. Staying close to the wall, he moved as quietly as he could, trying to orient himself. The only light—muted, the source distant and diffused—leaked into the hallway in concentrated spills. It was natural light, more or less. The sun, passing through the wide windows on the outside of the building, crossing the exterior rooms, and finally pushing through beveled glass that broke up the wall at regular intervals. Hicks made it down one hallway, turned, and kept moving. More of the same: tile underfoot, doors, beveled glass, fractured light. This floor wasn't open like the one above. Instead of high ceilings and large rooms, it resembled an old Art Deco office building. It was cramped, claustrophobic. "Lloyd?" he whispered, wondering if he heard something.

No, he'd heard nothing. He wasn't even sure he was going the right way. He couldn't trust his senses. The tight hallway bounced sound around indiscriminately. Melvin Johnson—and Lloyd—could have headed in the opposite direction than Hicks had thought. Hicks crouched down, hoping for a flash of inspiration. He realized he had no idea which way Lloyd had gone or how to find the Johnson brothers. He had lost his revolver and hadn't brought a backup. He was defenseless. And Lloyd could be dead, the recipient of that shotgun blast. He had to consider the possibility. He gazed down to the end of the hall—or at least as far as he could see before the fuzzy darkness took over. The hall and the doors had an institutional feel to them, making him think of the nurses again. He figured this must have been the commune's executive offices. Did a commune have executives? He squinted at a glowing, beveled-glass window as if he could see through it, out toward where he thought the soccer field was.

He thought of Elaine. Her graceless, stout-legged walk, the lulling jiggle of the fat around her waist. She had visited him in the hospital just the once, he reminded himself. She was there barely ten minutes before she started making excuses: the long drive back, an important meeting in the morning, her grown son's various problems. He hadn't seen or heard from her since. She was a middle-aged cop groupie, nothing more. Hicks had probably known it all along, but he'd ignored the signs for a chance to do something dangerous for once, something foolish. Sarah, to his surprise, drove to Mammoth View while he was still in the ER. Lloyd had called her. She put the house in order, cooked for him after his release from the hospital. She stayed a month, until he was back to his old self, more or less. Then she packed up her suitcase again—the blue canvas one she brought on their honeymoon thirty years ago—and drove back to Fresno. Their daughter, Joey, didn't come up from L.A., not even when he was in the intensive-care unit. She called a few times, but only to talk to Sarah. She was her mother's daughter. She might stay mad at him for a very long time.

Hicks rose, his knees popping. He knew what he had to do. He had to guess which way Lloyd had gone, where Winnie's voice had come from. He chose east, into the mountain. It just felt right. Bent double, he sneaked past a door and moved further down the hall. He listened, turned around, and watched the misty air loosen up behind him. He continued forward, inching along the corridor, craning his neck to give himself the best possible chance of hearing Lloyd rounding a corner or Melvin Johnson cursing to himself. He picked up his pace, worried that he was going in a circle. He might come around to the stairs soon, assuming there was only the one stairwell. He needed to look for the gun again. He couldn't leave it behind.

He stopped, took a step backward. He kneeled, steadied himself with a hand on the floor. The sound of fast, ragged breathing gurgled somewhere. He put his ear to the nearest door. Yes, it was coming from in there, he was sure of it. Something crashed to the floor inside the room, followed by a series of violent grunts. Hicks opened his eyes wide, straining to see through the beveled glass next to the door. He stared deep into his own indecision. He couldn't see a goddamn thing. He had no weapon. He was useless. But he had to do something. He felt the scream a moment before he heard it, and when the sound arrived—thick and panicked, a woman's voice—it released something in him, broke the dam in his synapses. He swung the door open and lurched forward, into the room. Darkness jumped up, like he was back in the stairwell. He threw a punch, a right cross, but he hit only air, his feet sliding.

He crashed into someone—a man. He grabbed hold: a neck, the back of an elbow, but the body parts slipped away like eels. The man went down, out of reach, but his stench swarmed over Hicks. Trying not to retch on the B.O., the chief threw another punch, his fist cracking on the linoleum floor. He punched again, connected with a thigh, a bare thigh. The man's pants were down, bunched at his ankles. Enraged, Hicks swung wildly. He landed blows on the man's chest and neck, and he heard him grunt and roll away.

"Got a gun," the man said. It sounded like Gordon Johnson.

"So do I. I'm police."

Hicks heard the man grunt again, and he prepared for a blow. Instead, the darkness wavered, followed by a stab of weak light. A few moments later, a distant door banged. The assailant was gone. Hicks had let him get away.

"Hello?" Hicks said.

"Chief?"

Hicks winced. Winnie. It really was her. He moved forward in the dark. He realized she was weeping.

"You okay?" he asked, not wanting to know.

Silence rolled out before him like the open seas.

"Yes," she finally said, her breath a series of small, rattling heaves. "Yes. You showed up just in time."

Hicks stood, brushed himself off. He watched Winnie's silhouette rise as well—it looked like she was pulling her pants up. "Well—" he said. He turned away, tried to think what he should say. A sound stopped him from continuing. The noise came from down the hall. Or above them. He really had no idea where. It could be boots. The sound seemed to be growing closer. Maybe Lloyd. Maybe the other Johnson. Hicks mindlessly patted his pockets. He didn't even have a pen he could use as a weapon. He turned and waved at the darkness, hoping to find Winnie in it. She had moved away, into the depths of the room. "Let's go," he whispered. "We need to get out of here."

"Wait."

"We can't," he whispered, urgently this time. "We have to go. We have to go now."

"Hold on, goddamn it! He ripped my blouse. I'm almost naked."

Hicks felt his face burn. He listened to Winnie scuffling around, pulling something metallic apart, piece by piece. Comprehension hit him; they were in a dressing room. She was opening lockers. After a minute, she grabbed hold of his arm. They stuck their heads out the door and, seeing no one, ran down the hall. Turning a corner, they pushed through a pair of doors.

The summer air washed over them. Hicks shivered, scared and shocked. He pulled Winnie along until they were out in the open, away from the building's shadow. It felt safe—safer—in the open.

Winnie slumped against him, sucking in air. She was wearing a grey uniform top—for a waitress or a maid—over smudged white Capri pants. The nametag on her chest read, "Carmela."

"The car's right up there," Hicks said, indicating the road above them. "Your husband's probably waiting for us." Hicks couldn't even guess where Lloyd was, but somehow it seemed like the right thing to say. He started to move toward the road, but Winnie stopped him.

"Chief." She dipped her head toward the ground, reading the gravel like tea leaves. "I'm sorry about my language back there."

Hicks relaxed, patted her arm. "That's fine, Winnie. Just fine." He started to move again, but she held him in place.

"We don't have to tell Johnny about . . . you know. What was happening in there." Her eyes bore into him.

Hicks realized all at once that he was going to lose control, start crying right in front of her. "No, of course not," he croaked, struggling to keep his voice from breaking. "After all, nothing happened."

He turned away so she wouldn't see his face; he strode toward the Bronco. He wanted to get the rifle from the back of the vehicle—he needed a gun in his hands. He heard her padding along behind him and realized she was barefoot. He blinked hard as his eyes watered: what the hell was wrong with him? He was a police officer—he had to start acting professional.

He unlocked the Bronco and angrily wrenched open the door. He had gotten Winnie out safe. That was good, but now he had to go back in and get the Johnson boys. Lloyd was still in there, alone and probably outgunned. He'd lock Winnie in the back of the truck, tell her to stay down, out of sight. He brought out the department's precision rifle, checked that it was loaded. Leaning the gun against his shoulder, he slammed the door and noticed what was in front of the Bronco: nothing. "Shit," he said. The Eldorado. It was gone.

CHAPTER SEVENTEEN

Jesus, that girl is choice, King thought, gazing into the backseat of the station wagon. He stared at the blonde's breasts, at the folds of the Jefferson Airplane T-shirt that held them in place. He'd polish those apples any day. He placed a foot on the car's running board and leaned in. He couldn't make out any bra lines at all. His mind jumped to Janice. He hoped she was halfway to San Francisco by now.

"He's not sitting on my lap!" the blonde barked, turning away from him. She crossed her legs—bare, shiny, endless—and folded her arms across her chest.

Taken aback, King looked past the fox to her seatmate in the middle. The skinny redhead peered up at him. No tits at all. Legs like knitting needles. The girl offered him a sympathetic smile.

How old are these girls? King suddenly wondered. These sure weren't Swedish airline stewardesses vacationing in the Great American West. They were kids. Probably high school. His hard-on wobbled and began to retract.

The redhead scooted over a few inches, banging hips with the frizzy-haired girl on the other side of her. "You can probably fit," she said. "Might not be very comfortable, though." She grabbed the blonde's arm and pulled. "Come on, Mary, move over."

"Don't touch me," Mary Bowen snapped, jerking her arm free. "He can't fit in here. There's no room."

"Come on, now, girls, we're all in this together," the man in the baseball cap said from behind King. "I'm sure we can squeeze him in."

"We can't, Coach," Mary Bowen said, her eyes beseeching him. "You can see we don't have room as it is. I've had Summer's elbow in my side the whole way."

"Oh, you wish!"

The coach sighed. "We can get one more up front next to me, then. Robin, come on up."

"No, I want to stay back here," the frizzy-haired girl said. "Summer can move up."

"You're smaller than Dana," the coach said. "I need to be able to move my arms. I'm driving the car, remember? Come on, let's get moving."

"We have to catch up to those men," Mary said. "We have to really hurry."

King stepped off the running board and straightened up. "You know what? I've changed my mind," he said.

"What do you mean?" Coach Prinzano asked.

"I've decided I don't want to go to Stockton. That was my girlfriend's idea."

"Well, we're not going to take you back."

"I'll be fine. It's only a couple of miles."

The coach pursed his lips, like he was holding in a fart. "It's farther than that, friend. And it's not safe in Mammoth View. You know that. Don't mind Mary. We can all fit."

King slapped the man on the shoulder. "Thanks for the concern, Coach," he said. "Really. But I'll be fine. I was an army ranger in a previous life." He turned and headed back the way he and Janice had come.

Coach Prinzano stood there dumbly, watching him walk away, until Mary Bowen piped up. "He said he's fine, Coach. Let's go."

King smiled to himself, pleased to have the station wagon

behind him, out of his sight. He'd rather shoot himself than sit next to that little bitch for the next four hours. In a couple of years she was going to turn on the Johnny Carson Show and see him on the couch next to Ed. She'd remember this moment—she'd realize she blew it. That she'd had the chance to chat up a Broadway star and passed it up. King thought about the time a few years ago when Carson made a joke about a shortage of toilet paper, causing a run on the stuff. People were so stupid, so prone to fearing the worst. A world without toilet paper! He smiled to himself, satisfied. He stepped off the road and breathed in the mountain air. He was going to miss this air. He refused to look back at the car as it pulled away. He was going to make it on his own.

King felt good for the first half-hour or so. The trees shooting up into the atmosphere, the sounds of birds, the perfect human aloneness of the enterprise. It blew his mind. He should do this more often, he thought. Had he *ever* done this? He listened to pine needles crackle under his shoes. He closed his eyes against the breeze. He touched tree trunks as he passed them, rolling the palms of his hands over the rough bark. His paranoia was lifting. He decided that was all it had been. He had nothing to worry about. There was no reason for him to run from Mammoth View like everyone else. No one knew anything. It wasn't his fault everyone had freaked out. There'd been an earthquake! They couldn't blame that on him. He skipped through the soft padding of the forest floor—throwing his arms out and kicking his legs—before he realized what he was doing. He pulled himself back into a normal walking stride. The jocks had called him a drama fag in high school. His own brother, the basketball star, had called him a drama fag. King had been an athlete, too, but being in theater had trumped sports. The problem was, no one respected artistic creativity. At least not until you became a celebrity. That was the problem with the whole country. People laughed at artists, taunted them at school, beat them up for dressing different and acting different. Unless they were up there on the big screen. Somehow that changed everything. Did anyone call Burt Reynolds a drama fag when he was in high school? Probably. But now he had the biggest movie in the world—that insipid *Smokey and the Bandit*—and every boy in the country wanted to be just like him. Kids imitated his high-pitched cackle. That was a drama-fag laugh if there ever was one.

King let his mind drift to the start of the day. It felt like ages ago. Epochs. He saw himself flipping on the lights at the station, one by one—*tick, tick, tick*. Stepping into the booth and closing the door behind him. Sitting in the chair and cracking his neck. Testing out his announcer's voice as a warm-up, going as deep and resonant as he could. He had tried out a girly scream and grinned at the result. He did a good girly scream. It must have been great to be in radio in the '30s and '40s, when it was glamorous and daring. When it involved actors, *real* professionals, not disc jockeys. He had taught himself all the old-school sound effects: twisting cellophane, shaking metal sheets, squeezing a box of cornstarch. He could make it sound like a thunderstorm or a man staggering through the desert. He could perfectly simulate the sound of a knife stabbing deep into flesh. Janice hadn't said a word about his show today. It annoyed him that she clearly didn't bother to listen, even though he'd specifically asked her to tune in. That hurt more than her breaking up with him and leaving him on the side of the road. Not so long ago Janice had wanted to marry him. She was *grateful* for him, and for good reason. He'd made her who she was, taught her about sex and how to be an adult. How to be cool. Her next boyfriend, whoever the hell that turned out to be, should send him a thank-you card. King snapped his head around, as if someone might be following him. His foot came down on nothing—he'd misjudged the incline—and he stumbled. As the foot clunked awkwardly, a spasm of pain rolled through him, traveling up through the spinal column.

King stopped walking. He dropped his head, rubbed at his back with his knuckles. His euphoria had gone, just like that. Weariness replaced it, not so much physical as emotional. He had to think about what he was going to do next. What he was going to do until he was flush. How he was going to eat and pay bills without a paycheck coming in. He shook his head, shook out his arms. Not now, he decided. He took a deep breath of that pure mountain air and let it loudly whistle out of his lungs. This was not the time to figure out such things.

He made his legs move again, took long strides to work the pain out of his spine. He tried to pick up where he'd left off with the nature-loving. The trees, the sky, the breeze. All that. He wondered what nature lovers think about when they're out in nature.

His mind jumped back to his show today, his last one ever. He considered it a triumph, even if no one else did. He certainly wasn't surprised no one else did. No one had any taste anymore. No one had any class. He'd tried to prove otherwise time and time again. He'd tried to make a real career in radio by being more than a stupid record-spinner. He wrote a letter a couple of years ago to Norman Corwin, the legendary radio dramatist, asking for a meeting. He'd wanted to pick the great man's brain, suggest a collaboration. Corwin wrote back—three typed sentences on an otherwise bare white page—informing him that he was teaching a college class in the fall and inviting him to audit it. Once the rush of receiving a letter from Norman Corwin had worn off, he tore it up and tossed it down the garbage disposal. A college class? He was a colleague, not a wide-eyed undergrad. He'd been nominated for a San Diego Radio Broadcasters Award. He had it on good authority that he placed a close second in the voting.

King leaned against a tree—he needed to rest. He didn't have enough thoughts to sustain him on a long walk in the woods. That was the problem, he decided. He was a doer, not a thinker. He needed to play a game while walking, like looking for state license plates during a drive on the Interstate. Something to keep his mind occupied. He stretched his back and slowed his pace. What he needed was to get high. That was obvious. He could walk for hours if he was high. He could do anything when he was high.

He was seventeen years old the first time he tried the demon weed. He was wearing his James Dean jacket—the red breaker with the high collar—and feeling rebellious without a cause. His friend John Davis had bought the grass from a mechanic he worked with at the gas station. John had been Slim in *Of Mice and Men*, Grant High's biggest theatrical success in its history. King obviously had been George. He and John had been fast friends since the eighth grade. John was kind of his Tonto, his faithful second. King had mentioned that he wanted to try marijuana a few weeks earlier, and so John had gone out and made it happen. After school, they sat under an elm tree at the far end of Mister Magnusen's orchard, rolled the cigarettes as best they could, and lit them. They hadn't been smart enough to bring girls with them. They hadn't known that when you're high any girls will do. He took to marijuana right away—he loved the way it made everything go soft—but it wasn't until his sophomore year in college that he became a regular user. That was when his roommate introduced him to a guy who sold the stuff out of his trunk.

It made sense that weed scared the government. Free thinkers always scared people who were invested in the status quo. That was a good thing. He wanted to scare the old men who ran the country, the old fools who decided what was acceptable and what wasn't, the politicians who started the Vietnam War and the justices who stopped Milton Luros from illustrating the *Kama Sutra*. He wanted to be dangerous. He lit up whenever he needed a burst of dangerous creativity. When he needed to finish the bridge of a song, or nail a reaction look that wasn't in the script's directions, or get through a monologue that went on too long. He did his best work while high, which had to be why he felt so exhausted after just half an hour of hiking. He'd been working at a top level for weeks. He saw it all come together this morning, but it had happened so suddenly—and ended so suddenly—that he hadn't had time to properly come down from the high. That was dangerous too, hanging out there on the edge, being mentally and creatively blue-balled. He trudged on, toward the town that soon would be a permanent part of his past, just one more bad memory on the way to greatness.

Tori knew exactly what to do when she was in danger. Head straight to the study, do not pass Go, do not collect two hundred dollars. She'd snatch the key that was taped behind the empty fish tank, unlock the desk, take out the pistol. The thing was heavy—she thought that every time she hefted it. Sometimes, when no one was home, she held it in both hands and dropped her arms, like she was a grandfather's clock. Just to feel the full weight of it. Dad always told her to respect the gun, that it was a serious thing.

She wouldn't mess around with it when someone was actually after her, of course. When that happened she would grab it, check the chamber (nothing's more useless than an unloaded gun, her father said), and lower herself into a crouch. This was not mere theory. Her father needed her help, needed to know she could protect herself if he couldn't. He wasn't a young man anymore. He loved to say that, and it was true. His hair had gray flecks in it. His eyes—*those eyes!* her friend Brianna had grossly chirped that time, after he smiled at her—had developed permanent half-circles under them.

Her father showed her how to use the gun when she was twelve. Took her to the range, held her arms the first time so the pistol wouldn't fly out of her hand when she pulled the trigger. They went back and did it again the following weekend. Three days later came her initiation. They were sitting in the den watching *Laugh-In*. She was slurping up the last of her bowl of SpaghettiO's while he smirked at the TV, a cigarette hanging from his mouth. The man didn't even knock, like a civilized person. He just called out, "Hey Billy, it's Austin," causing Dad to tip his head slightly, as if he wasn't sure whether the words had come from inside his head or real life. He nodded at her. She put her bowl down and ran—she was fast even then—staying low so the unwanted visitor couldn't see her slip through the entryway and into the back of the house.

Her father walked to the window between the kitchen archway and the front door. He peered around the curtain. "What the hell do you want?"

"Can I use your john?" the voice responded. "Mine's broken."

Dad snorted his annoyance. "Are you fucking kidding? You came all the way over here to use the can? Use the McDonald's. Go to Garrity's." He eased into a crouch when Austin didn't immediately reply.

Tori inched up to the window on the other side of the door and looked outside. She spotted a large man in a leather coat standing on the mat and holding his crotch. He had a jungle adventurer's hat on his head, pushed back off his forehead. She leaned closer. She could feel the cold through the single pane. She resisted the urge to put her finger on the thin mist of condensation where her breath had hit.

"Come on, Billy," the man said. "I've got to drop a deuce. I don't want to do it at goddamn McDonald's. I'll air it out, I promise."

Billy flicked his eyes at Tori, who held the gun against her shoulder. She set her legs in the ready position. She felt her pulse pounding in her neck. The gun slipped in her hands and she tightened her grip. Billy waved at her with his whole arm—*Go away! Go away!*—and, stung, Tori took a step back, into the doorway, just out of sight. She let her arms drop, felt the gun swing. She could relax, she told herself. Everything was all right.

She heard her father open the door.

"Thanks, Billy, you're a life saver," the man said.

Tori quietly backpedaled into the den to return the gun to its hiding place. She was heading over to the desk when the bang made the floor jump and she fell. Her knee throbbed—the pain radiated up her leg and zeroed in on the small of her back—but she forced herself to her feet and ran into the foyer. The front door hung open; somehow it had popped off the top hinge. Then she saw her father on his back, flailing. Three men were on top of him. One of them punched him in the head. The big man, Austin, stood off to the side, watching, hugging himself. His brows rose as if magnetized, and he froze at the sight of her. The other strangers soon stopped what they were doing. They all looked at her.

"Hello, honey," the puncher said. "Why don't you go in your room and leave the adults to talk?"

Tori stretched her arms out, her finger rubbing the pistol's trigger.

The man smiled. He had a large gap between his front teeth that matched the dimple in his chin. His black hair was slicked straight back, but a handful of strands had fallen into his face. It looked like a toddler had finger-painted on his forehead.

The gun bobbed at the end of Tori's sightline. She wouldn't be able to pull the trigger; she was sure of that. But the men didn't know it—or at least they didn't know it with certainty. The man with the gap stood up slowly, his hands flapped upward in a jokey "I surrender" gesture. The other two did the same, glaring at her the whole time.

"All right, Billy. You got a good girl there," the puncher said without looking at him. "She must love her daddy—God only knows why."

Gap-tooth waved his minions out the door, including Austin. He smiled at Tori again, whacked his foot against Billy's leg, and walked out, closing the broken door behind him. Only then did Tori's father turn over and face her. Blood had collected in the groove over his upper lip. His right eye drooped.

"Dad, you're bleeding!" she cried.

"I'm okay."

"Who were those men?"

"You should have stayed in the back," he said, sitting up and wiping the blood from his lip. "You know better."

Tori couldn't believe he was mad at her. He was really P.O.'d. "Why were they beating you up?" she demanded.

"An argument," he said. He stood up, stepped over to the window, and looked out.

"You were arguing with them?"

"Yeah. It was just an argument. About . . ." he sighed. "About politics."

"What?"

"Politics. Never mind. It doesn't matter. It was a disagreement at a bar." He was beside her now. He took the gun from her hands and dropped it in his pocket. He held Tori by the shoulders. "Well done, T. You looked after your old man."

Tori squinted at his face. It was beat up but inviting. A comforting face. One eye still twinkled. "You're not mad at me?" she said.

"I am. A little." He rested a hand on her head, cracked his back with a groan. "Now let this be a lesson to you, Victoria. You treat people the way you want to be treated. And you never, ever talk politics with strangers."

Tori looked behind her. Seeing an empty road, she stopped running. Nothing like that had happened since. It could have been the reason they moved to Oildale the next year. Worse neighborhood, but bigger house—an L-shaped ranch-style with three bedrooms. But she still went to the range with her father a handful of times every year. She still checked for the key taped behind the empty fish tank every week or so. She still woke up with a start whenever the wind blew a tree branch against the side of the house.

Her legs ached. The camp was farther up the mountain than she realized. She craned her neck, her eyes following the road up and around until the asphalt disappeared into the swampy-green miasma of the forest. She started to run again, but side to side now, to save her hamstrings. It wasn't much faster than walking, but it felt better. Made her feel more in control. Of course, she would need to pick up the pace or it would take her hours to make it back to Spritle's. She understood what she had to do; she had to embrace the pain. She pumped her knees and felt the propulsion throw her forward. To really get moving, she had to visualize it. She had to see herself bounding, not zigzagging, up the mountain.

Victoria Lane, the Olympic champion famed for training on the steepest hills in the world! Victoria Lane, Wonder Woman's protégé!

She closed her eyes and threw a knee forward and out, then the other one, forward and out. Her weight bounced down on the balls of her feet, the Achilles tendons stretching and catching. She could feel the difference, the surge of power. She quickened the seesaw swing of her legs. She concentrated on her hips rotating in their sockets. Air heaved out her nose. She imagined Eileen Blum trying to churn up this road, her stomach bouncing, the waistband of her shorts collapsing under the assault. Tori wondered where that image came from. She didn't even know Eileen; she had never spoken a word to her. God, could being an athlete be turning her into a lesbian? The fear of it caught in her throat, and she hacked at it with painful coughs.

She wiped away the thought, brought up a more pleasant one. She thought about the first official race she ever ran. That was better. She saw herself coming over the finish line. She'd never felt anything like that in her life. Everybody looking at her, applauding her. She pulled the finish-line tape off her chest and looked up to find Coach Berman running toward her. He embraced her, swung her around. Pulling back, he held her at arm's length and squeezed her triceps. He was smiling like a maniac. "I knew you could do it," he said. "I knew it." Tori remembered being amazed by those words.

Just twenty minutes before he said it, at the beginning of the race, she had been certain she would end up dead last. Maybe just dead. All of the girls had sprinted off the line. Sprinted! They did not pace themselves, like Tori and her teammates did during practice races, saving themselves for a kick down the final stretch. These runners bolted along the paved walkway that circled the pond, before signs directed them up a ridge, dumping them onto a dirt path in the woods.

Tori had sprinted too, because it would have been embarrassing to be left behind in the dust. But she knew she couldn't last long at this speed. Her feet burned inside her shoes; she could hear the air screaming as it banged down her throat. She felt lightheaded. She was having trouble keeping her eyes open. She became convinced she could hold her form longer if she closed her eyes, let her mind take her away. Not that it really mattered. Tori looked up ahead; she couldn't even see the leaders. They'd already made the turn into the woods. That's how far behind she was. The soles of a dozen shoes bounced in front of her like rebukes. Pebbles flew out of their nooks and crannies, off into the air. She counted fifteen or so runners ahead of her. Plus at least a handful more who'd already made the turn. That put her among the very last group of runners, the losers who didn't belong there in the first place.

The race had just begun, and she was already blasted, just completely wiped out. She strained to look ahead again, past the girls in front of her, to the turn that led into the trees. *I can make it that far*, she thought. She could slow down or stop up there, once she was under the cover of trees, where no one would see her give up except the handful of sad sacks running behind her. When she finally made it to the finish line, she could say she fell and twisted an ankle. Everyone would believe that. She closed her eyes so she could will away the discomfort in her chest and stomach and knees. She might miss the turn and accidentally complete the circle back to the starting line like a fool, but she had to take the chance.

Coach Berman had started the girls' cross-country team at her school. He had a framed photograph behind his desk of the marathon champion Jacqueline Hansen running along an asphalt road. A dirt field stretched out next to the road and a grey barn stood behind it, like the road separated two dimensions of time. Hansen's elbows were pressed against her sides—perfect technique—her left leg reaching out for the road, the muscles bulging. "That was the year she won Boston," the coach said the first time he noticed Tori studying it. "Just a few years before that, just a few years *ago*, another woman—a friend of hers—tried to run the marathon, and the race director ran after her and yanked her off the course. Women weren't allowed then. You were born at the right time, Victoria," he said. "The whole world is open to you." Tori nodded. She didn't know who the woman in the picture was. She figured it must be Coach Berman's wife.

She learned later that the coach wasn't married, that he'd never been married. By then, she realized that Coach Berman wasn't like the other teachers. On the first day of practice, he had read to them from a mimeographed sheet of paper. "We are all familiar with the stereotype of women as pretty things who go to college to find a husband, go on to graduate school because they want a more interesting husband, and finally marry, have children, and never work again. The desire of many schools not to waste a 'man's place' on a woman stems from such stereotyped notions. But the facts absolutely contradict these myths about the 'weaker sex' and it is time to change our operating assumptions." The coach looked up then and smiled at them, at each one of them, these pimply, freckly adolescent girls in T-shirts and shorts, standing in a semi-circle on stork-like legs. That was Senator Birch Bayh, he said. Speaking on the floor of the United States Senate. Coach Berman took off his Oakland A's baseball cap and wiped his forehead. He followed that by wiping his nose on his sleeve. "All right," he said. "Let's get to work."

Tori looked up, searching for Mammoth Mountain's peak, knowing she wouldn't be able to see it. She pondered that speech. She pictured the look on Coach Berman's weathered, lonely face as he made eye contact with each one of the girls on the team. The speech had saved her during that first race. She didn't want to disappoint Coach Berman. That was what drove her on. It was a regional invitational—a big deal. He'd chosen her and only one other girl—PJ, a senior, the best girl on the team—to run.

Coming up to the first turn, Tori realized that she hadn't seen PJ up ahead, that she might be one of the few girls behind her. One of the losers. Right then she banished the plan to stop. She successfully negotiated the turn. She was in the woods. She vividly remembered the dramatic change. The sun could no longer blaze at her. It filtered through the trees only in thin, diffuse angles, harmless and pointless. The dirt path was soft, or at least softer than the pavement. The rattling in her head with every stride had ceased. She concentrated on pumping her arms, on pulling her knees up. The girl right in front of her went down. A tree root tripped her. Tori leaped over the girl. Her heart leaped higher. That was one fewer girl she had to outkick at the end.

She began to feel different. She couldn't explain it. Like she was watching herself run. Like she was an electronic toy she could control with a remote. She made her knees pump higher and longer and harder. She made her arms pump faster. She could feel the back of her shirt poof out, the air current trapped in there between the fabric and the skin on her back. She imagined her skin glistening. Flashing in the spots of sun that cut through the trees. Girls backpedaled to her, their faces obscured by grotesque masks. Their pain only drove her on. She felt nothing. Nothing at all.

Even now, all these months later, Tori couldn't explain how she'd done it. All the other girls came back to her, one by one. She remembered doing mind whammies on them, focusing on the numbers on their backs, locking onto them like a magnet onto metal. Finally, the finish line was in sight, the tape quivering in the breeze. Tori smiled at the memory, one of her all-time favorites. She came up on the strangely placed pond, the one she'd admired on the way down the mountain. Okay, she'd actually run a lot farther than she'd thought. She'd gotten all mixed up. She could be back at the camp by nightfall. She looked at the sky. No, not by nightfall. But not too long after that. She wondered why she was going back to Spritle's Racers. She hadn't thought about why until now. She was fleeing, that was all. Her feet took her back the way she had come. Well, why not? The coaches would return for her when they realized they didn't have everybody. They would have to. It was the law or something.

And if they didn't? She'd be there all by herself, in the middle of nowhere.

Tori sang to herself in her head. *Silly Love Songs*, her favorite song. Some people want to fill the world with silly love songs—and what's wrong with that? Tori knew it wasn't cool to like Paul McCartney. The boys at school, if they even knew about the Beatles, dug John Lennon. He was a tough guy; he raged against the corrupt world, the war machine. He pointed out hypocrisy. Even George Harrison had a mystique that made him alluring. He looked crazy, with the beard and the hair and the intense little eyes, but in a good way. She saw an interview he did on television once, and he kept saying "Hare Krishna," as if it were a secret code. But Paul—Paul was the Beatle their parents liked, their mothers. Well, Tori liked him, too. He seemed like he'd be nice to her if she ever met him. He seemed normal. And his songs made her believe it was possible to be happy, that everybody could have somebody to love, if you had an open heart.

Tori turned: she was hearing the echoes of her shoes banging along the street, even after she'd stopped. Funny. The wide-open world, outside of cities, did crazy things with sounds. She listened, fascinated, as the *tuck-tuck, tuck-tuck* tinkled across the evening air. A figure appeared around the bend below her. Startled, Tori screamed. She scrambled up the road, tripping, scraping her hands.

"Wait!" a voice called. "Wait! Stop—please!"

It was a male voice, a deep voice, but child-like. Tori didn't believe it could belong to either of the men she'd seen attack the basketball boy. She slowed and turned around to look at him. He was still a relatively small figure in the distance. She backpedaled a few steps, as a test, to be sure she could start running again in a flash.

The man held up an arm. "Yes, thank you. Hello."

"Stay right there!"

The man stopped. She couldn't make out his face but she could tell from his posture that the directive confused him.

"I'm sorry?" he said.

"I said *stay there*. Who are you? Why are you following me?"

Her voice broke; she discovered that she was screaming at the man.

The man put his hands on his waist. His shoulders heaved. He put his head back and drank from the air above him. Then he looked at her again.

"I'm King. King Desario."

"Right. You're a king."

"Sorry." He smiled, still catching his breath. "Nickname. My name's Oscar. Oscar Desario. I was coming out onto the road when you jogged past. You looked like you knew where you were going. So I followed. I'm glad you stopped. Jesus. Why are you running up the hill?"

"Two men were chasing me."

"Really?" He looked behind him. "Who?"

Tori felt her face flush. "Maybe they weren't. I'm not sure. They *might* have been chasing me."

"Why were they maybe chasing you?"

"I saw them beating up a kid."

The man's mouth ticked downward. He tilted his head, judging her. "What'd they look like?"

"I don't know. There was a tall one and shorter one. I think the shorter one had a beard."

"The Johnson brothers."

"You know them?"

"I know of them. Melvin and Gordon Johnson. They're kind of the bad seeds around here." He paused, put his arms out, palms up. "May I come closer?"

Tori shifted her weight, left foot to right. She accepted that she wasn't afraid of this man, Oscar Desario. He looked like Danny Shapiro, her old boyfriend. A grown up version of Danny. Kind of. He had the same big, soft lips, the same square head. The same small, sloped shoulders, like a squirrel on its hind legs. When Tori didn't respond to his question, he began to slowly walk forward. Tori pegged him as being her father's age, but he had long hair, blown dry into a Robin Gibb poof and then sweated into a prickly mullet. When he reached her he put his hand out, and Tori, feeling weird, shook it. He smiled: a nice smile. "So, I'm King, like I said. What's your name?"

The clammy warmth of his hand made Tori want to cry. It felt so good. She lurched forward and embraced him. King, below her on the slope of the road, staggered, belatedly grabbed her around the back, and steadied himself.

"Whoa! Whoa!" he said, stifling a laugh. "You okay?"

Tori held him tight around the neck. Tears leaked from her eyes, and she wiped them on his shoulder. She was embarrassed to be hugging him, but she didn't want to stop. Finally, she released him and stepped back.

"I'm Tori," she said, feeling the heat in her face.

King tilted his head to survey her, which made Tori uncomfortable and pleased at the same time. He seemed to be memorizing her, imprinting what he saw on his brainpan. An urge to kiss him suddenly washed over her. He was old and sweaty, but it couldn't be worse than her kiss with Danny, her first and only. Her teeth had hurt the rest of the day after it, and he'd ended up with a cut lip. They'd gone their separate ways—Danny to the baseball field for practice, Tori to the bus—without another word. She'd tried to meet Danny's eye and smile, but he turned away with his head down.

"Don't worry about the Johnsons," King said. "They're harmless. Well, not harmless, but not as bad as they seem. And I'm here now. I'll stay with you. If you want."

"Okay. Thanks."

"So. Where are you going?"

"I was going back to the camp—I'm at summer camp—but no one's there anymore, so I'm not sure I really want to go back. I need to call my dad."

"Sure. Your dad's probably worried to death."

"There's no one in the town. It's a total ghost town."

King reflexively looked over his shoulder, toward Mammoth View. "I know. That's why I'm out here. My girlfriend wanted to drive to Stockton, and I went with her, then changed my mind. But I bet a lot of people are starting to come back. Like me. It's safe."

"They left because of the earthquake?"

"The earthquake. All sorts of reasons. It was much ado about nothing."

"What do you mean?"

"That's Shakespeare. Much ado about nothing."

"I mean, why's it nothing?"

"Well, it's like if you yell fire in a movie theater, everyone runs out even if they don't see any smoke." King turned and looked off down the road toward the town. "I live on the east side—a couple of miles from here," he said. "You can call your father. Have something to eat."

Tori looked down. She watched herself flex her right foot.

"Or I can take you to the police," King said. "They'll call your father for you, I'm sure."

Tori continued to study her shoes. She felt paralyzed.

King got the drift. "Okay, well, I'm heading back. The police are on Second Avenue, right downtown. Across from Benny's Diner. You can't miss it. It was nice meeting you, Tori." He turned.

Tori lifted her head and watched him walk away. She watched him shrink with every step, and when he was the size of a Lilliputian, she started to follow.

CHAPTER EIGHTEEN

They spotted a used car lot on Hunter Street—Enterprise Car Sales. Jackson parked the Skyhawk about four blocks away, next to a squat industrial building whose windows were all either broken or caked with dirt. Billy threw the door open and stepped into the street, with Sam clambering after him. The car wobbled as Sam jumped to the pavement. On the other side, Jackson stepped out and straightened up with a groan. He pulled off his driving gloves, shook out his hands. He left the window wound down, the key in the ignition. He figured the Buick would be gone before sunrise.

Billy cradled the bag of money in his left arm and slammed the trunk. He faced Sam. "You got everything out of the car? Absolutely everything?"

"Even my chakra."

"Okay." Billy pointed toward the dealership. "You're up first."

Sam glanced at Jackson, who nodded, and Sam began walking down the sidewalk. After four strides he burst into song: "That's the sound of the men, working on the chain *gay-a-yang*. That's the sound of the men, working on the chain, *gang*."

Billy and Jackson leaned on the car, watching Sam walk away from them.

"You sure he's okay?"

Billy looked at Jackson. "Sam? Absolutely."

"I'm thinking he seems like the kind of dude who needs money. All the time. He'll come calling on you."

"Well, we'll see. You don't have to worry about that. He won't even know where you are."

"What are you going to do if he comes and demands his share? Waving a gun around."

"You've got Sam all wrong."

"I don't think that I do."

"Well." Billy squinted and picked Sam out of the falling sun. He was now a pinprick moving against the oncoming traffic.

Forty-five minutes later, Sam pulled up in a red Datsun, and Billy and Jackson climbed in.

"What took you so long?" Jackson demanded. "How long's it take to hand over a wad of cash?"

Sam chuckled. "If you don't dicker a little bit, it looks funny. Those are the guys they remember. And there's paperwork, you know. I almost gave him the wrong I.D. This thing's a bad little mother, though." He punched down on the accelerator, throwing Jackson off-balance in the back seat.

The car rumbled past boarded-up storefronts with dilapidated signs advertising last-ditch sales. The streets were deserted, save for the occasional sad sack trudging seemingly nowhere. The boxy brick buildings along the road gave off the air of some long-dead civilization, as if Sam had accidentally taken a wrong turn into a massive archeological dig. Billy, sitting in the front passenger seat, craned his neck skyward, looking for evidence of downtown in the distance. He'd been to Stockton before, remembered a bustling commercial district, the colorful S&L Society Bank building curling elegantly around the corner of Main Street. He wondered if this lousy economy had swept it all away.

They found another used car lot, and Billy and Jackson decided to both go in. As long as they acted like they didn't know each other, who would ever be suspicious? Billy chose a Chevelle with a blue-and-white racing stripe. Jackson scored another

Buick, an Electra this time. They both paid with cash. The three men then drove separately to a Denny's, where they left their cars running, climbed out, and huddled together in the back of the parking lot.

Billy gave his prepared speech. "Just a reminder. I don't want to hear from you. I don't care if your mama needs emergency surgery or you have inside dope on a hot stock. I'm taking the risk here. You put me at risk by calling me or coming to find me. We're all agreed?"

"A couple of weeks," Sam said.

A gold Camaro pulled into a space opposite them, jerked to a stop. A young woman with hair cropped to look like an old-fashioned leather football helmet unfolded herself. A three-inch-long metal cylinder fell from her lap and bounced on the pavement. She vigorously kicked it under the adjacent car. Goal! The three men watched as she adjusted her skirt: slender legs, decent rack—possibly no bra. She spun around but didn't notice them. She had a flat, button nose. Too-small eyes. A smattering of brown freckles. She jerked her head and sniffed hard. Billy couldn't take his eyes off her. Not because she was a looker—she wasn't—but because he recognized her. Or thought he did. Had he bagged a girl in Stockton? A large drop of sweat fell from the woman's nose. It hit the ground and sprayed like a tiny lawn sprinkler. She didn't notice that, either. She sniffed again, the little helmet of hair shaking like gelatin, and strode into the restaurant. Billy's eyes stayed on the ground. It wasn't sweat. It was a drop of blood.

"Those were your words, man."

Billy looked up. "What?"

"You said you'd have our money in two weeks."

"Yeah, right. But don't count the days. It could be three weeks. It could be a month. All right? This is an art, not a science."

"We got it. Don't worry." Jackson put his hand out, and Billy shook it.

Sam extended his hand too, but when Billy reached for it, Sam pulled it away and playfully patted Billy's face. "Just remember that we *can* find you," he said, flashing a Joe Cool smile.

Billy returned the grin. He understood that the macho dance was necessary in situations like this. "I think we understand each other." He thumped Sam's arm—"Go the speed limit," he said—and ducked into his new wheels. He backed out of the parking slot and rolled toward the exit. As he passed the front window of the restaurant he took a long look at the waiting area. He didn't see the woman. They must have seated her already. He swung the Chevelle into traffic and headed south. He watched his rear-view mirror until he saw the Electra bound onto the street and turn in the opposite direction, and then the Datsun. He looked at his watch. Should he hang out at a bar or get a motel room? He figured the caravan from Spritle's was about an hour behind them, so his answering service should have a message from Tori at any time. He decided on a room. After talking to Tori, he'd have to wait three hours while he pretended to drive from Bakersfield to Stockton. He might as well be comfortable; he'd rather watch TV or take a nap than chug beers on a barstool.

Inevitably, he compromised. He decided he would have a couple of pops at a place called Ware's he'd spotted from the road, phone his service, call Tori back, and then take a room at the Motel 6 next door to wait out the fake drive. He walked into the bar and stood, squinting, waiting for his eyes to adjust to the gloom. It was a dump, which was what he wanted. He sat at the bar, ordered a beer. He swiveled on the stool so he could survey the place. Only a handful of customers, mostly pensioners. The waitress, a Mexican girl who couldn't possibly be old enough to drink, was sitting in a booth with a newspaper, working on the word jumble.

Billy's bladder rebelled after he finished off the third beer. He dropped from the stool and walked to the back. A sign directed him to the second floor. The old wooden steps barked with every step, and he tried to lessen the sound by putting his heel down first and rolling forward. Now the stairs moaned. The bathroom was at the top, tucked into the wall. He turned the doorknob—

locked. Some old drunk was already in there. The smell hit him then, and he stepped back. He put a hand to his nose to try to squeeze off the receptors. The guy was going to be in there a while—or forever. Billy went around the corner, where he found a narrow, dark hallway. Decades-old photographs of men raising steins, their arms around one another. Billy couldn't tell if the pictures had been taken in this bar. Near the end of the hall, a door on the right stood partially open. Billy peeked into an office, no doubt belonging to the owner. A short desk, the desktop tidy, pushed against the window. The only light issued from a lamp out of sight behind the door. Billy stepped inside, glanced behind the door. There didn't seem to be anything here worthy of his attention. Maybe he'd find a gun or some cash in one of the desk drawers, but he wasn't about to start rifling the place. There was, however, something that did catch his interest: a small room at the side—a private bathroom. He closed the door behind him, flipped up the toilet lid, and let loose. He shuddered, and dropped his head in satisfaction.

Stepping back into the hallway, he saw the door at the far end whisper shut. His view of the room behind the closing door lasted less than a second, a blur of shape and color, but he knew exactly what was going on in there.

He felt the moisture in his mouth. Dear God, he was salivating. He stepped to the door, listened. Nothing. Not a sound. But he knew.

He descended the stairs slowly, considering his options. He should just finish his beer and go. That was the best of his choices, and of course it was off the table. You didn't walk away from a sure thing. Back on his stool, he waved to get the bartender's attention.

"How do I get in on the game upstairs?"

The bartender, a big, middle-aged man with a fu manchu mustache, gave him a sidelong glance and the expected response. "The what?"

"Come on, the *game*."

"Sorry. Don't know what you're talking about."

Billy stood again and strode out the door. He unlocked the trunk of the car and grabbed the bag filled with the money. He pulled a handful of cash out, counted off five thousand dollars, put what remained back in the bag, and shut the trunk. He found a rubber band in the glove compartment and bound up the five grand. Back in the bar, he returned to his seat and waved the bartender over. He smiled, his guy's guy smile. He leaned in, confidential-like. "I know you can tell I'm not a cop. I'm just looking for a diversion." He flashed the roll of bills. "Maybe you can check upstairs. You might be surprised at what you find."

The barkeep sucked on his tongue. Billy could tell the man didn't want this aggravation. He almost felt bad for him. "All right, you're not a cop," the bartender said. "So who are you?"

Billy broke a Benjamin free and stuffed it in the man shirt pocket. "I'm a man on a lucky streak."

The bartender fingered the hundred. He removed it from his shirt and made it disappear in his fist. He walked around the bar without a word and climbed the stairs. A minute later Billy noticed the bartender and another man, a fat guy in a faded white button-down shirt and a skinny black tie, gazing down at him. The fat guy's hair had to be a toupee. Off the shelf. Billy lifted his beer, silently toasted them, took a swig.

The bartender rematerialized behind the bar and gave Billy the nod. Billy gulped the last of his beer and eased up the stairs. As he reached the door at the end of the hallway and raised his hand to knock, it jerked open. A large, round man with a babyish face filled the doorway. Not the same fat man who had checked him out with the bartender. A thundercloud of smoke hovered around him, leaking into the hall.

"Show me what you've got," the baby said.

Billy handed him the roll of bills, and the man riffled through it and handed it back. He nodded him inside, stepped aside.

It was a surprisingly big room, with at least half a dozen tables going and wait staff in penguin outfits flitting about. Billy suddenly wondered if this was a syndicate operation. Did they have the mob in Stockton? He wouldn't have thought so. He scanned the place. It didn't seem to fit the dimensions of the rest of the building. Mindlessly, Billy guessed it had been added on. He imagined the room hanging from the back of the building, held up by two rickety ten-foot-tall wooden beams. The poker table he'd first noticed from the hall loomed in his path. Five men in various stages of distress and exhaustion surrounded it, slumped forward over their cards. They looked like they'd been there since last night, and they probably had. Billy's eyes jumped to the next table. Blackjack. He felt himself start to grin. You expected poker in the back room of a bar, but they were playing *blackjack* here, too. Billy bypassed the poker table. Who could resist blackjack? It wasn't you against the vagaries of the cards. Not really. It was you against the dealer. Like two boxers going fifteen rounds. It was about whether you had the nerve to discover the weakness when you couldn't see it, whether you had the courage to go the distance.

Billy prided himself on his courage and nerve. He ordered a Scotch from a passing waiter, found a table with an open spot, and sat. He ran a hand over the green felt. The dealer was tall and thin. Female. She smiled down at him, a smile full of promise. She wore a button-down white shirt and black slacks, basically the same outfit Jillian wore the first time he laid eyes on her. But with this dealer, he couldn't tell what kind of body she had under her clothes. She could be delectably svelte. She could be pudding. He pulled out two hundred-dollar bills and handed them over. She pushed a small stack of chips at him. Cards started to fall in front of him. The game was on.

Focus—concentration—overcame him at once. There was only the ocean in his ears, numbers and colors before his eyes. He held a card to his forehead and closed his eyes, like Carson doing Carnac the Magnificent. "Hit me," he said.

She hit him. He grimaced. A seven and a five.

"Hit me," he said again.

She dropped another card on him. A king. Bust.

He glanced up at the dealer, whose face remained utterly blank. Well played, he thought. He rolled his neck. He felt good. The power was with him, he could tell. He should be dead, after all. That trucker earlier today had them right where he wanted them. They were within moments of hurtling off the road, down into the valley below, gone forever. But Fate—and Inspiration—had been with him. And so here he was.

"What's your name?" he asked the dealer.

"Jane."

Jane. Good name for a dealer. Plain. Unadorned. Professional. She fit her name: she dealt without flair, but with obvious skill. The fingers grasped and clutched the cards with precision; the cards didn't seem to bend at all, as if they were made of wood. He held at eighteen, lost to twenty.

A pimply teenager showed up with his drink. Billy pressed a chip on him, downed the Scotch in one swig. He would have preferred to have Jane deal by hand. He didn't trust the mechanical, eight-deck shoe, believed it could be rigged. He thought about moving over to the poker table. Jane smiled at Billy, and he returned it, shaking off his paranoia. She dropped a card in front of him, and he scooped it. He suspected she was flirting with him.

He immediately felt his luck change. Two hands later, he had sixteen, no-man's land. Jane had a king showing, a brightly colored illustration: a pointy gold crown pressed down on a square, Dick Tracy-like head. He was paying close attention to the distribution of cards, focusing so hard he was getting a headache. Looking at that king, at the bold colors in his robes, he saw the future as plainly as the cards in front of him; he was going to take a low number next but not as low as the dealer. There wouldn't be another picture card in this game.

Confidence surged through him. Before the game he'd asked for more chips, and for the first time he saw Jane's expression change when he told her how much he wanted. She asked him if he was sure, which made him smile. He was always sure. He was always positive.

She put another card in front of him. A jack. Holding a dagger.

The burning started as the dealer reshuffled the deck. Billy's brain felt like it was on fire, like it was going to burn up and fall out his ears in ashes. But the cards kept coming, and the chips kept moving. He downed another Scotch. He felt the breath of men behind him, smoke hitting him in the back of the head. They were urging him on, these men. He was winning! His prognostication had simply gotten ahead of itself, that was all. Reality had to catch up to the rapid-fire workings of his brain. He would leave these saps with nothing!

Drink and exhaustion hit him all at once. He reeled from the table, stumbling. He crashed to the floor, felt himself bounce. Parquet flooring, like the Boston Garden. Nice. He burped up something, drooled it onto the floor in a long string. Two men, one on each side, grabbed him and lifted him up. They began to march him toward the door.

"What the hell is this?" Billy said, squirming, trying to drag his feet. "You're throwing me out? Afraid I'm going to break the bank?" He chuckled at the thought of it: a second bank robbery in one day.

One of the men plowed a hand into Billy's back pocket, pulled out his wallet. The man removed all of the bills and counted them. Eighteen dollars.

"This is your life-insurance premium," the man said. "It's good for the next sixty seconds. If you're still here after that, we're going kick your head in."

The man slapped the empty wallet into Billy's chest. Billy tried to shake the gauze away from his eyes. He looked around the room: everyone was looking at him, waiting to see what he would do.

He ran a hand through his hair, cracked his neck. He turned and walked out, thumping into the doorframe on the way. The door clicked shut behind him. He felt his pockets. They'd taken all five thousand off him. Ripped him off like he was nothing and nobody. Of course they did: they could tell he was about to go on a roll, that this nobody hick tourist passing through town was about to make them all look like fools. He thought about getting his gun out of the car and coming back. Had he disposed of the gun yet? He couldn't remember.

He hurried down the stairs and into the night. He opened the Chevelle's trunk, pulled a handful of cash out of the bag—way more than five grand this time—and stuffed it down his pants. That was no good. He looked like Johnny Wadd. And he could barely walk. He removed the money, put it back in the bag and closed the trunk. He looked around to see if anyone was watching him. He considered finding a cop, telling him he'd been robbed, but he immediately thought better of it. He was five-grand lighter, a victim of the fucking Stockton mob, but he had to look on the bright side. He could've had a lot more on him, the entire amount from the bank, however much that was. Maybe he'd take the whole five G's out of Sam's end. Sam would never know. Billy walked over to the Motel 6 and into the lobby. Low ceiling, brown walls. The top of the counter was scuffed and chipped from a million keys being pushed across it. He banged on the bell, and when the clerk showed his pasty face, Billy asked for a room away from the noise.

"Noise?"

"From the drunks coming out of the bar. From the cars on the street."

"Oh, right."

The man gave Billy the best room in the place, way in the back, on the other side from the bar. Billy tossed the key onto the dresser and stepped into the bathroom. Sitting on the toilet, he smoked a cigarette and thought of Wilson. He should track that S.O.B. down, he decided. Get his and Becky's fair share of the Seattle job—plus twelve years of interest. In his grief he'd let it go, thinking of it as blood money, like accepting it would be payment for Becky's death. But money was money—he knew that.

Whether he had the Seattle cash or not, Becky was dead. Long dead. So dead, if he were honest with himself, he had trouble remembering her. What she was really like. He could picture her—and he did it all the time—but was it the snapshots on the wall he was seeing in his mind? He couldn't hear her laugh anymore. He probably wouldn't recognize her voice if she dialed him up from the Great Beyond. He flushed the toilet, stubbed out the cigarette, and washed his hands, gazing at himself in the mirror. He'd started to notice his age not too long ago: the dark gullies under his eyes, the explosion of tiny lines. What would Becky have looked like at forty? Would he still be attracted to her? Would they still be doing it every night? Billy turned away from the mirror. He should get married again, he thought. Let the past stay in the past where it belonged. It'd be nice to have someone in the house who knew how to properly cook a meal and iron a shirt. He chewed on the inside of his cheek, shook his head, and walked out of the bathroom. He dropped down on the bed without even deciding to do so.

As he lay flat on his back, his muscles seemed to unclench as one. His brain stuttered, like a bad ignition switch. He imagined all the people who'd been on this bed over the years, all the sweaty couples having sex, the lonely traveling salesmen watching the TV alone, the drunks too whacked out or embarrassed to go home to their wives. Their faces, indistinct and without character, swirled around him. Impending sleep pressed down on Billy's head. He wasn't sure he could arrest it even if he wanted to. This was what his father had always been like after coming home from work. Bone weary, he'd say. Big Bill he could picture as clear as day. The old man couldn't wait to retire. Couldn't wait to sit around for a living.

Billy figured his father would be dead within two years of getting his gold watch. What was he going to do, watch the soaps? The man didn't have any hobbies. He'd never play golf, the rich man's sport. And anything else—softball, tennis, basketball— would give him a heart attack. He didn't want to travel to the other side of town let alone Paris or London. He hated his job, but it was his life. Without it, and without the union and the bitching and the physical exhaustion, he'd go crazy. Mom left twenty years ago—God only knew where she was. *The woman had coasters on her heels*, Big Bill told him once. *She's probably skated all the way to Hell by now.* Nice, Dad. Gwen, Billy's stepmother, could roll with Big Bill's moods better than Mom, but that only went so far. She would walk out as well, once she had to deal with her husband for whole days and weeks at a time.

His father might just end up moving to Bakersfield, Billy thought. A lot of parents did that in retirement, started making their kids miserable all over again. Big Bill knew his son was a career criminal, so Billy wouldn't really have to hide what he did with his days. His father had silently accepted it. Billy was his only son. It wasn't as if he'd become something unforgivable, like a fag or a Republican. Still, they never talked about it. *How's business?* Bill Senior would ask, and Billy would say, *I'm getting by*, and that would be the extent of it. Billy wasn't sure why. He wanted to talk about it with his father. Every business was a con—Big Bill understood that. Why else did unions need to exist? There was no such thing as both sides in a deal winning. Billy believed he was more honest with himself than so-called legit businessmen, than the CEO of U.S. Steel. He wanted his father to know he wasn't ashamed of what he did.

On the brink of sleep, Billy struggled to set Becky in motion. Becky at twenty, not forty. He wanted to see her walking, that was all, just walking down the sidewalk on Hollywood Boulevard, stepping over and around the stars of her favorite actors and directors, looking like she might bust loose like the love interest in a Gene Kelly movie. That loose, cheerful, Girl Friday stride, her shoes clicking on the pavement. That was it. He could still remember.

He zoomed in for further proof: her hair in a teasing knot at her neck, bouncing against the pink flesh; the abnormally long, beautiful neck itself with the string of moles along the clavicle; the fragile slope of her shoulder, intersected by a thin white bra strap. She began to run. She loved to run, just like her daughter. Not fast like Tori, but joyously. That was what she had. Joy. Billy didn't have that. Tori didn't either. Becky ran for the same reason a dog ran—to feel herself being alive—and now, his eyes closed, Billy watched her do a loping jog to the end of the block and head back toward him. "Let us run with patience the race that is set before us, looking unto Jesus," she said to him once, laughing.

She had laughed high and loud, often at the strangest things, but he couldn't hear it anymore, couldn't quite make out the sound. What did her laugh sound like? She raised a hand to reach for him. She stumbled then and had to pull her arm back to catch herself, but it was too late. Her knees grazed the ground, her hands slapped against the pavement. All of a sudden she was a heap on the sidewalk, unmoving, her dress settling softly around the curves of her buttocks. The gaping wound in her back burbled like a water fountain. Watching it all over again, Billy screamed. He screamed bloody murder.

CHAPTER NINETEEN

Melvin snapped the radio on and flipped through the channels in search of Vin Scully's euphonious voice. Baseball was still Melvin's game, and Scully's Dodgers were still his team. Carl Erskine had been Melvin's favorite player when he was growing up. Ersk pitched as if he were double-parked, Scully said about him, and wasn't that the truth? Melvin had fantasized about stepping into the batter's box and seeing Erskine on the mound cannonballing into his windup. Time and again he'd seen himself crunching one of Erskine's slingshot fastballs out of the park. Melvin was a power hitter. A four-bag man.

He was sixteen years old when Maris and Mantle took out after the Babe's home-run record; it was the same year Melvin almost broke Mammoth High's all-time dingers tally. Many old-timers hadn't wanted to see Ruth's record fall. Melvin couldn't understand that attitude. If you loved baseball, why would you want that fat clown to be the face of the game? Maris was a much better baseball icon than Babe Ruth. Better looking, better manners. Mantle, with that cheese-eater's grin, looked like an American, too, but he tried to be Hollywood. Roger Maris was a working-class guy. He was a man who earned his place and didn't brag about it. Maris, Mantle, Killibrew—they were a dying breed.

The blacks had taken over the league. That was the main reason Melvin never got his shot. Willie Mays and Willie McCovey and Willie Stargell—those boys all gave him the willies. Gordon had laughed at that line when Melvin came up with it. "Yeah, why're they all named Willie?" Gordon cackled. "Their mamas can't think of any other names?"

Melvin slowed into a turn. Gordon, zoning out in the passenger seat, hit his head against the side window. Gordon grabbed at the dashboard and righted himself. He had been Melvin's biggest fan during his brother's baseball career. For years he went to every practice to watch. Homer didn't give him a choice—there was no one else to look after him—but Gordon was happy to be there. Melvin couldn't say who wanted it more for him, Gordon or Homer. Homer drove Melvin to Bakersfield and San Luis Obispo for tournaments. He made sure Melvin had a bat that perfectly fit his hands and a jock strap that snugly secured his balls. "That boy's going to be the next Ted Williams," he liked to announce during games. The others parents would smile grimly. No one liked it when Homer started crowing, and they liked it even less when he might be right.

Melvin looked out the windshield at the twisting road in front of him, trying to follow the asphalt after it disappeared into the forest. He had a plan. Simple but smart. He and Gordon would hide out for a couple of days in the hunting shack, until everyone figured they were gone, then they'd sneak down the mountain and head south. Straight on to the border. He didn't know why he hadn't thought of it years ago, when no one was chasing them. After all, the Mexicans were serious about baseball. Melvin figured he could become a scout for the Dodgers, tour around the Mexican League looking for the next Bert Campaneris. He flipped the Eldorado's headlights on; the sun was falling behind Mount Dana at the edge of the western horizon. He'd have to learn to speak Mexican, of course. Gordon wouldn't be able to do it, but Melvin would translate for him. Gordon would be fine with only talking to him.

Melvin wondered what he'd miss about Mammoth View. He liked the house, even though it was too big and smelled like piss and linoleum. He liked sitting on the roof and watching the tiny skiers blip into view on the corner of the mountain and disappear just as quickly, like spiders falling off their webs. He went into town more often during the winter because of the ski bunnies in their tight pants. He enjoyed sitting on the public bench across from Benny's and watching the girls climb the steps to the diner. He whistled when the best-looking ones came out, and sometimes they'd come over and bum a cigarette. Thinking about it now, he banged a stick out of the pack, jammed it in his mouth, and dropped the pack back into the cup holder. He punched the lighter button. There'd be ski bunnies in Mexico. Senorita bunnies. There were bunnies everywhere.

He thought about the last time he traveled south, after dropping out of school. There were bunnies in San Diego, that was for sure. Melvin had walked into Westgate Park for tryouts feeling certain he'd never go back to Mammoth View. He was eighteen years old and had figured out his entire future. He'd spend a season or two with the Padres for seasoning, then move up to the big club in Cincinnati. After another couple of years proving himself as a Major Leaguer, he'd demand a trade to the Dodgers. That was as close as he'd come to returning to Mammoth; back in California, but three hundred miles from Homer.

He remembered the three schoolgirls who stood behind the backstop fence on that first day. They hooted and laughed at him when he came up to bat. The girls grabbed the fence and pressed themselves against it like prisoners on visiting day. Their bodies were so ripe their flesh must've hurt. Digging in at the plate, Melvin had to force himself not to turn around to see what they were doing.

The Padres had an old guy throwing from the mound—he had to be fifty if he were a day, with white hair and a pot belly—and Melvin missed three straight pitches before he got ahold of one. Fouled it into the seats behind first base. He was sure the old man was throwing spitters, just to screw with him. They always hazed the new guys. Everybody knew that.

Later, when the coaches thanked him for coming in and wished him luck, Melvin didn't say a word. Two days before he'd been sure of his success. But after being out on that field, with all those empty seats staring down at him, he convinced himself he'd known all along how it would go. He accepted the rejection as complete and final. He wasn't good enough for the Pacific Coast League or any other professional league. He wasn't good enough to make money playing ball. He got up and walked out of the room. The others who'd been cashiered were milling about, kicking at the floor, hoping for a reprieve, but Melvin picked up his bat, walked straight out of the stadium, and headed for the Greyhound station.

He walked down Friars Road, his head down, bat on shoulder. He carried his duffel bag in the other hand. Off to his right, the blue of the ocean melded with the blue of the sky. He thought that if he veered from the road he might disappear into that blueness and come out in another dimension. He began to remember how far it was to the Greyhound station: about a twenty-minute drive, which meant a couple of hours on foot. He swore to himself. Sometimes he just stopped thinking and found himself in these situations. He pivoted and started walking backward, eyeing the vehicles as they overtook him. He stuck his thumb out. He probably looked kind of funny to people driving along the road. He'd changed into a T-shirt and jeans, but he was still wearing his cleats and, of course, carrying the bat. Yet it only took a minute before a pickup pulled over.

The driver waved for him to get in the truck bed—Melvin couldn't even see the man's face—and Melvin climbed in and banged the side to let the guy know he was ready to go. He closed his eyes and let the rumbling of the truck lull him. For some reason, the decision to get into the pickup felt momentous. He wondered if this unknown driver saw something special in him, if the man was going to drive him to some secret hideaway where big plans were being hatched, like in a James Bond movie.

When he opened his eyes, Melvin saw warehouses and rundown storefronts. An old orange dog stretched out on the shoulder of the road, dead or sleeping. Melvin recognized the neighborhood; the Greyhound station was right around here. He felt paralyzed with indecision, but he forced himself to act. He jumped out at a red light and strode away from the truck. He didn't bother to wave at the driver. Turning the corner, the traffic noise dropped away. He walked along the curve of old streetcar tracks that died in the middle of the street. He crossed an abandoned lot with thigh-high weeds that pushed themselves at him like street vendors. A warehouse rose up beside him and he feared he'd miscalculated, but he continued on and soon came right up to the station. His sense of direction never failed him.

The next bus wasn't for four hours, so he decided to get some sleep. He was exhausted from the stress and the disappointment and the walking. He claimed an open bench in the middle of the bus terminal and stretched out. Not long after he had settled in, a smudged, scrawny girl tapped him on the shoulder. She was wearing an Army field jacket over a soiled summer dress. "You want a go?" she asked. Melvin sat up and leered at her, wondering if it was a joke. She smiled back, her mouth a shaky brushstroke on a blank canvas. She asked for five dollars.

Melvin only had two bucks after buying the bus ticket, but she nodded, led him out of the station, and around the corner. The southern side of the building pressed up against an empty lot; beyond that was an onramp to the highway. The girl faced him, her back to the station's outside wall. He'd brought his duffel bag and bat with him. He dropped the bag and propped the bat on his shoulder as she undid the clasp on his belt. The girl was pretty, he decided. He liked them petite like this one. He pushed at the stringy strands of blond hair that had congealed on her forehead. Her eyes were small and strangely fixed, like two Phillips-head screws. She leaned back against the building and hiked up her skirt.

Melvin pulled his hand away from her face. Anger seized him. It was clear she didn't really like him, that she didn't want to do this. She just wanted the money. He punched her in the face. The back of her head banged and momentarily stuck in place. She dropped into a sitting position, a smear of blood trailing her down the wall. He stepped away, surprised at what he'd done. The girl turned over with a whimper, her hand brushing the top of his right foot. Startled, he kicked her in the stomach. He felt the shoe go in, meet resistance against the spine, and spring back. He was still holding the bat, and he had to stop himself from using it. He didn't want to kill her.

He fixed his belt and returned to the waiting area. When his bus arrived, he stretched, picked up his duffel bag and bat. He followed his fellow passengers, but instead of joining the queue, he stepped around the side of the building. The girl was gone, but the splat of blood was there, proof that he hadn't dreamed the encounter. He gripped the bat, turned, and climbed onto the bus, glad to be putting the big city behind him.

When he arrived home that evening—the home he'd planned on never returning to—he announced right off that the Padres didn't want him and that was that. Homer didn't say anything. He was too busy sitting on the porch with his lemonade and gazing off at nothing. Finally he looked at Melvin without looking at him and told him they'd eat in half an hour. Sure enough, Homer got around to the subject during the meal. "If I told you once, I told you a thousand times, boy. You've got to be a hustler to make it in this world. Talent will only take you so far. Coaches, employers, what-have-you, they're all looking for a man with hustle."

"That wasn't it," Melvin told him. "I hustled plenty, let me tell you. You don't know what you're talking about." He hadn't called Homer *Sir*, probably for the first time since he was five years old. He was through with that.

Homer pushed his plate away and glared across the table. Melvin knew exactly what was coming. "Blow, blow, thou winter wind," Homer hissed, his voice as sharp and bloody as razor wire.

"Thou art not so unkind as a son's ingratitude." Melvin refused to look at his father. It was downright creepy when he spoke in tongues like that. Melvin stared out the window. It wasn't winter and it wasn't windy out, but there was no point in saying so.

Melvin couldn't find the Dodgers or any other game on the radio. Not much reception way out here. He switched the radio off and wiped away the memory of the San Diego trip. He rode the brake as the car rolled into another steep curve. He let go of the pedal on the straightaway, and it felt like they'd been set loose in space, halfway between the moon and Mars.

"You don't want to listen to music?" Gordon asked.

Melvin shook his head. He grew up on Elvis and Eddie Cochran, but music had never been central to his life. It was something for the background, for when you were putting it to a girl. But Gordon loved music. It carried him away, into himself. What was the saying? Music soothes the savage beast? Especially the new crap Gordon liked. David Bowie and Gary Wright. Dr. Hook and Electric Light Orchestra. All those gays. Their music soothed and soothed until you were drooling. Good thing Homer was dead. He wouldn't have put up with that stuff for a minute.

Melvin clicked the radio back on. "You go ahead," he told his brother. "You can choose any station you like."

Hicks was halfway down the path when he saw the man. The Bronco's tailgate was open, and the man was standing there at the back, all but the side of his head and an ankle obscured by the truck. A shoulder, too, moving up and down. Part of an arm. A flapping pant leg. Blood rushed to Hicks's head. He pulled the rifle off his shoulder and hunched low. He eased into the trees. He put a finger on the trigger, tested the gun's weight with his other hand. Step by step the man's profile came into view. Hicks relaxed. It was Lloyd. He was hugging Winnie, who sat on the end of the truck, her arms around her husband's waist, face pressed into his shirt. Hicks thought of Sarah. He thought of begging her to come back to him.

Lloyd spotted him and turned, wrenching his wife's neck with his hip. Winnie looked up, eyes lit with trepidation. Seeing the chief, the irises settled, and she smiled.

"We must have just missed each other coming and going," Lloyd said.

Hicks placed the rifle in the back of the truck. "Must've."

"I was going out of my mind. I turned that place inside out. It was quite a shock—a relief—when I opened up the car door to get the rifle and found Winnie hiding under the blanket in the back."

Hicks caught Winnie's eye. He hadn't actually expected her to stay out of sight as he'd instructed. "Good girl, Winnie," he said.

"Thank you for going back for him, Chief." Winnie looked ready to cry, but her smile seemed genuine.

"They're gone, obviously," Lloyd said. "But the good news is I got the radio to work. I guess being up higher helps. Marco's talked to the sheriff, who didn't know what the heck was going on. Sheriff's contacting the state police and Bakersfield PD, then coming up to help out."

"All-points on the Johnsons?"

"Yes," Lloyd said. "The sheriff's doing that. Armed and dangerous."

Hicks opened the passenger-side door, put his foot up on the runner. So he had about an hour left of being in charge. He'd sure like to catch Melvin and Gordon before the cavalry showed up. He felt confident his heart could take a little more excitement. "What's Marco doing now?"

Lloyd smirked. "He's at Benny's. He didn't know where to go or what to do."

Hicks chose not to comment with Winnie present. He flipped open the glove box and pulled out a map. He asked Winnie to get up, and he spread the map out on the floor of the trunk. "You know where old Homer's hunting cabin is? By Meyers Lake?"

"Never been there," Lloyd said. "You think that's where they've gone?"

"As good a guess as any. That's where Gordon went after the incident with the teen girl, the skier. I'm willing to bet they're going into the mountains. They're not dumb. Not Melvin, anyway. He'll know they'll stick out like a sore thumb on the roads or any of the towns around here."

"Makes sense."

"So I'm thinking I'll take you and Winnie into town and then head out there. There's more than a few hours of light left. You'll coordinate with the sheriff."

Lloyd looked at him, confused. "You want to go up there alone?"

Hicks put a finger on the map to hold his place. He tried to crinkle his forehead in a father-knows-best kind of way. "Winifred has been through an ordeal. You should take her to get checked out. Be with her."

Winnie seemed startled that her name had come up. "I'm fine," she said. She tried to open her eyes all the way to prove it. The right one, limp and browned like a fast-food burger, refused to cooperate. It fluttered at half-mast. She soldiered on anyway: "Drop me at home. I just need a bath."

Hicks started to speak, stopped himself. He grimaced at Winnie.

"Really," she said. "I need some rest is all. I'm okay."

"We need a statement from you."

"She can do that later, Chief," Lloyd said. "I can't let you go up there alone. Those boys are going to be armed. Marco can call the doctor for her."

"Marco has done enough."

Lloyd shifted his weight and glared, as if he were considering holding his breath and stamping his feet. "It's not safe for you to go after them on your own," he said.

Safe? It wasn't safe for the two of them to go, either. Hicks folded up the map. It infuriated him that his lieutenant's desire for action trumped his concern for his pregnant wife. It saddened him that Winnie was trying to play tough for her man. He walked around to the driver's side and wrenched the door open. "Suit yourself," he said.

They left Winnie at the office with Marco. Hicks said as few words to the young officer as possible to show his disapproval of his performance; just told him what to do and that was it. On the way out of downtown they spotted four cars in quick succession, all coming from the direction of the highway—the exodus, it seemed, was starting to reverse itself. By the hardware store on Main, they saw Terrence Galloway stepping out of his pickup. Terrence waved at them to stop. Lloyd flicked the siren light as he drove past so Terrence understood they weren't ignoring him.

Hicks noticed the bank in the rear-view mirror. "Shit. See if you can get Marco on that thing," he said, pointing at the radio. "He needs to secure the bank. We can't have looky-loos poking around in there before the sheriff arrives."

"Right. The bodies are still in there." Lloyd reached for the radio.

Hicks couldn't believe he'd left the bank like that. That was one more screw-up he could add to the ledger. He should have told Frank to hammer a board over the door. James Towson and Alice Krendel's blank faces rolled through his brain, and he tried to push the images away. Thirty years as a cop, and he'd seen only a handful or so of dead bodies, and most of those had been homeless men who'd frozen to death. TV shows made it seem like cops were looking over murder victims every day, but it wasn't as normal as people thought. Maybe in New York City but not in Visalia and Fresno, Hicks's ports of call during his career. He had never before seen a man's face half blown off. He'd never before seen a caved-in eye socket, and a flap of fried forehead skin tossed backward, shifting the hairline like an askew wig. He'd never before seen a young woman in a demure blouse-and-skirt combo flat on her back on the floor, her big, plaintive eyes filled with blood. Hicks wondered if he was going to be sick.

"It isn't working," Lloyd said, dropping the microphone back into its cradle.

"It's a block and a half away!" Hicks barked. "Pull over. Pull over right there."

Hicks jumped out of the car and walked into the liquor shop, which was empty and a goddamn mess. He picked up the phone behind the counter: no dial tone. He looked down and saw that someone had yanked the cord out of the wall. Jesus Christ, can you believe this? He slammed the phone down and stormed out of the store. He waved at Lloyd in the truck and jogged down the street to Terrence Galloway, who stood by his pickup, watching. Without letting Terrence say a word, he quickly explained what had happened and that he needed Terrence to hustle over to the police department and tell Officer Barea to secure the bank's door.

"My God, Chief, how can this be?" Terrence said.

"I know, Terrence, I know," he said. "And we're going to catch the men who did it. We're on our way right now." Lloyd had backed up the Bronco and opened the passenger-side door. Hicks climbed in and Lloyd stepped on the gas. The chief kept his eye on the rear-view mirror until he saw Terrence Galloway running toward Second Avenue.

CHAPTER TWENTY

Melvin got out of the car and began to walk. This was it, he told himself. It had to be.

The drive out here had left him confused and frustrated. Everything had changed since the resort had been built in the Sixties. Roads had been added; others had been altered or abandoned. Vacation homes had taken chunks out of the forest. He'd missed the turnoff because of the bait shop. The shop was gone and the lot had been cleared. It probably would be replaced by a fancy luggage store. The junction was different as well. Dirt had been good enough for years—for Melvin's whole life—but now it was blacktop. Tourists wanted to know that their nature land was safe, that it was part of the regular world. Melvin stopped in his tracks, looked to the north and then back at the mesa in front of him. The access road should be right here, but there was nothing.

"This it?"

The voice startled Melvin. Taking a breath, he waved dismissively at Gordon. He'd told his brother to stay in the car. He couldn't concentrate if Gordon was yabbing at him. He marched on, farther from the car and Gordon. The lake should be over there, but when he reached the ridge, there was only a roll of shrubs below. He remembered the flannelbush and spreading gooseberry, but the stand of white fir where they'd always left the car had disappeared. Aspen surrounded them.

He couldn't blame this on development. No, this just wasn't the place. But they were close. He could feel it. He returned to the car and pulled himself behind the wheel. "We're almost there," he said.

"Okay." Gordon knew not to question Melvin about such things.

Melvin started the car and maneuvered it back onto the blacktop. He tried to remember when he'd last been to the hunting cabin. It'd been a long time. Back when he was still talking to Homer. Back when Homer was alive. He looked over at his brother, who was staring blandly out the windshield. He never thought to ask Gordon for help, and for good reason. Gordon's shirt—white, unadorned—probably hadn't been laundered in a month. His jeans, rolled up to the top of the ankle, looked even worse.

Melvin flicked his eyes to the dashboard. He put his left hand on the inside of the door, felt it quiver under the spell of the engine's power. This Eldorado was a monster. It could roll all night and all day, through the California desert, through Arizona's scrubland, right on into the teeming hordes across the border in Mexico. He thought of the Speedy Gonzales cartoons that always got Gordon cackling: *Andale! Arriba! Arriba! Epa! Epa!* He looked out the windshield and up at the black sky. Ol' Homer was up there somewhere, smoking his hand-rolled and snickering. *Another fine mess.* That's what the old man liked to say whenever Melvin had screwed something up, and now Melvin said it to himself.

"What's that there?" Gordon said.

Melvin tapped the brake. He followed Gordon's finger to a small dirt road that jutted out of the forest and linked up with the blacktop. He was amazed his brother had spotted it. He would have blown right past it without an inkling. Bringing the

Eldorado to a lifeless roll, he peered at the hole in the landscape. He had to admit it looked familiar. He turned into the road. The car jounced, and he had to hold tight to the steering wheel to stay in his seat. Gordon grabbed onto the dashboard. The headlights poked and flickered at nothing: dirt and gravel, flashes of greenery as the road meandered. Cottonwoods hung low overhead. Their branches banged the roof and scraped at the windows, like strikers warning off a carload of scabs. Melvin remembered the cottonwoods from his childhood. They made him think the woods were haunted, that when people died they left the town and settled in the forest. Homer had laughed at his son's fear. "I got to toughen you up, boy," he'd said.

Melvin thought about how easily he could have killed Homer out here. He could have shot him in the back so easily. No one would have thought he did it on purpose. He was just a kid. A kid who needed toughening up.

Melvin pulled the Eldorado into the tall grass, shut the engine down, and climbed out. This time Gordon also stepped out of the car. Melvin squinted in a vain search for the opening with the white fir trees. Seeing nothing, he tried to picture the cabin. It was small and rudimentary, he remembered that much, but it did a pretty good job of keeping the elements out. He and Gordon didn't have any supplies with them. They'd left in too much of a hurry. No food. No clothes. Nothing. That's why Melvin had thought of the shack. Not only did no one know about it, but Homer always kept it stocked. The canned food would be ancient but edible. There were sleeping bags. A couple of blankets. The lake water tasted fine. It would do for a couple of days until the sheriff assumed they were long gone and they could hightail it out of the area.

Melvin froze in his tracks. A dog was yowling. No, not a dog, not way out here. A coyote. Gordon, walking with his head down like morons did everywhere, bumped into him from behind. The yowling stopped, replaced by a whooshing through the trees above them. Melvin crept forward. He could smell rancid water and so he slowed, worried that he would fall into a gulley. Where the hell were those goddamn fir trees? He picked up his pace again, feeling desperation begin to gnaw away at his stomach.

"It's starting to get dark," Gordon said.

"No shit, Sherlock." Leave it to Gordon to state the fucking obvious. Melvin looked up. The sky had faded to a heavy, steely gray, like a gargantuan UFO was blotting out the real sky. Pretty soon they weren't going to be able to see anything. They could walk right past the lake, right past the cabin, and not even know it. They could end up out in the badlands.

Melvin pushed through a tangle of tall grass, stumbled, and his foot splashed. He pulled it back to dry land, felt water squelch inside his shoe. Jesus! He dropped into a squat, and Gordon eased up next to him. They'd found a stream. Melvin couldn't remember ever seeing it before, but it had to mean they were close. It had to be a tributary to the lake, and the cabin was right at the edge of the lake. Melvin stood, shook his foot, and starting walking again. They followed the line of the stream, swiping at the grass with their hands. Melvin felt like they were walking in a circle. The trees grew thicker; the low branches seemed to move with them, like a herd of dumb animals.

"I'm hungry," Gordon said.

"We'll eat when we get to the cabin."

"We're not going to find it. This isn't the way."

"Shut up, will you? We're close."

"Let's go back home."

Melvin wheeled on him, furious. "We can't, you moron."

"Why not?"

"Because you had to go and snatch that girl," he yelled. He felt the spittle fly from his mouth. It had to have hit Gordon right in the face. Melvin hoped so. "The sheriff's after us. They're going to blame everything on us."

"We can explain."

"Go ahead. Good luck with that." He turned away. "I'm going to find the cabin."

Gordon didn't have anything more to say, which was good because Melvin was ready to kill him if he did. Melvin thought about how good it had felt to kick the crap out of that boy today, and now he wanted to do it again. He imagined driving back into Mammoth View, finding the kid right where they left him, picking him up, and crunching him right in the gut. Melvin felt himself smile. What else could he do but daydream? He couldn't thump his brother, that wasn't right. And there was no one else around.

He walked on without comment for—what? Twenty minutes? An hour? Melvin had no idea. At this point the treeline felt like a wall. He and Gordon were prisoners out here, prisoners walking in the yard. The moon had popped into view, the watchtower's spotlight. Melvin realized he hadn't heard a bird or anything for ages. The wildlife had gone silent, watching them. He was supposed to be following a stream, but he'd lost track of it. He wasn't following anything but his intuition, which was shot. He wasn't no Indian. He couldn't put his ear to the ground and tell you which way was San Francisco. He was a modern man.

Melvin stopped. "This isn't it," he said. "We should go back."

"I know this isn't it."

"How do you know?"

"I just know."

"So you think we should go back?"

"Yes."

"Fine. Fuck it. We're going back."

Melvin turned and started back the way they had come. It shouldn't be hard to backtrack, he reasoned. They'd been plowing through tall grass most of the way; they'd just follow their own path out. They'd been wasting their time out here wandering around, but it didn't really matter. It just meant they'd be even more tired when they finally found the cabin and they'd sleep even better. He found a clutch of bent stalks, patted them, and plunged forward. He heard Gordon breathing heavily behind him. He thought he caught a whiff of the water, the smell of decay, of algae and dead fish. His eyes had adjusted to the gloom; he spotted more squashed grass and moved toward it. He had a good sense of direction; he felt confident he was heading in the right direction. He would find the car, he was sure of that much. But the cabin—that was probably a lost cause. Maybe they should just make a run for it in the car, he thought. There were some old logging roads back in the mountains—he was certain he could find them. He didn't know where they led, but as long as he was more or less headed south, it didn't matter. Once they were outside of the area, they could find the highway. Then they'd be fine.

He jumped at the sound of branches snapping. Was someone out there? He stopped and put his hand out to Gordon. He listened. All of a sudden, he heard nature again. Noises pinged from every direction: birds calling from treetops, the rustle of animals moving through dead leaves. For the first time, Melvin felt disoriented, like he truly was lost. *Was that a voice?* He crouched so he could focus his hearing. Words skittered along the night air, distant and undecipherable. A moment later, more followed, answering the first wave.

"Did you hear that?" Melvin whispered.

"What?"

"A voice."

"That was you."

Melvin stayed in the crouch until he was sure the silence had returned. The voices—whatever they were—had been swept away by the night. He had nightmares like this. He would be lost in the dark, beset by monsters, with no one to save him. It was always deathly dark in these dreams, and he was always flailing about blindly, the darkness turning in on itself like a black hole. He jumped to his feet, pushed forward. He was moving faster now just thinking about it, pushing through the underbrush, jogging through an opening in the woods. He recognized the clearing—they'd skirted it right before they came across the stream. By this point, the car had been his destination all along. The hunting cabin was forgotten. The warmth and solidity of the car would be their salvation. No one could get them as long as they were hurtling along at sixty miles an hour.

They found the road. The dirt road had a checkerboard of tracks crisscrossing it: deer tracks, tire tracks, footprints.

"What do you think of that?" Melvin said, pointing at the unmistakable imprint of a boot.

"I don't know."

Melvin kneeled down, ran his hand over it. It was hard and crusty. He couldn't tell if it was fresh or not. He still wasn't an Indian.

They continued down the road, ducking under low branches and pushing through wayward grass stalks that stuck out into the road. Finally, they came up on the back of the Eldorado. For a moment, Melvin thought he was going to cry. He hadn't let himself believe they were lost, but they had been and he knew it. They'd made it out because he was smart and had a good sense of direction. Of course, there was luck involved, too. He had to admit it.

He wanted to admit it. They needed luck right now. The night was just beginning. They still had to get out of town unseen and find someplace to hole up for a while. He climbed into the driver's seat. Leaning back against the leather, enjoying modern comfort again, he felt the sweat and dirt on him. He wiped at his forehead with a hand, adjusted himself so that his underwear mopped at the line of sweat above the waistband. Once Gordon dropped down into the passenger seat, Melvin started the car. He turned the vehicle around and eased slowly down the road—on and on, it went—until at last he found the blacktop. He paused to take a breath, then slammed down on the accelerator.

Melvin followed the road as it skirted the mountain and dropped toward the town. He came up on County Line Road, stunned to find it way out here, and turned the car onto it, due south. When he saw Ernest's gas station up ahead, it surprised him. He was closer to Mammoth View than he thought. Closer than he wanted to be. The lighted sign on top of the pole—"Gas

Cigarettes"—shimmied in and out, on the verge of going dark for good. He tried to remember if the gas can in the trunk was full. They were going to drive all night and he didn't want to stop. Why give someone a chance to get a good look at them? He pulled in and rolled up to the pump. He could trust Ernest to keep quiet, he thought. Ernest had spent time in prison for assault. The old guy didn't think much of the sheriff. Turning the car off, Melvin looked down the road. With the light fading, he couldn't see far.

A splash of water made him jump in his seat. A rubber blade swooped down, cutting away the liquid. Melvin blinked, peered harder out the windshield. Ernest's gaunt, leathery face heaved into view. The man looked like a skeleton. For the past year, Ernest's son-in-law had been filling in for him on the weekends. It was supposed to be for only a few weeks while Ernest recovered from some kind of ailment. But Ernest had come back from the hospital a different man, a toothpick wearing a hat, and so his son-in-law kept working weekends. There'd been days when Melvin had pulled in—Mondays, Tuesdays—and found the place closed. You couldn't expect an ex-con to have much of a work ethic, Melvin thought.

"Evenin', Melvin," Ernest said, appearing at the open driver's side window. He leaned down further, squinted past Melvin. "Evenin', Gordon."

"Evening," Melvin said, trying to sound normal. "Ten bucks' worth, all right?" He held out a bill.

Ernest took the money and stuffed it into a pocket. He popped the lid off the gas tank, stuck the nozzle into the hole, and slung the pump's crank down. He leaned a hand against the pump, watched the numbers turn on the dial.

Melvin looked out at the empty road some more, trying to make himself see something. He listened to Gordon picking at a scab on his palm. He turned, looked back at Ernest. "What do you hear, Ernest? Anything?"

The old man shrugged. He paused, counting off the dial, and slammed the lever back into place. "People scared," he said, screwing the cap back onto the tank.

"About what?"

Ernest shrugged again. "The boogie man."

"Guess it's been a busy day, right?"

"Shit." Ernest leaned on the window. He wiped at his nose and inspected the back of his hand. Unsatisfied with what he found there, he hawked like a pro and let loose a stream of yellow mucus onto the ground. "Since they blocked off the byway up there, it's been deader than Abe Lincoln."

"What're you talking about?"

"The interchange. Right up there. It's the sheriff's doing."

Melvin felt his stomach give way. He gripped the steering wheel. He realized he hadn't seen any other cars since he'd pulled onto County Line. "What for?" he asked.

Ernest shrugged once again. "Like I said, people scared. Doesn't matter what about." The man strode away, disappeared inside the building.

Melvin wondered if he was giving Ernest too much credit. Why wouldn't the old man tell the sheriff he'd seen him and Gordon? Because he was an ex-con? A man of principle? It would be much better to know for sure he wouldn't talk. Ernest was a frail old bugger. He could snap the man's neck without breaking a sweat. He could blow on him and he'd fall over. Angry with himself, angry about what he had to do, Melvin threw open the car door and climbed out.

"Where you going?" Gordon asked.

"Shut up. Stay here. If the sheriff—or anyone—comes along, you hit the horn. Got it?"

Gordon nodded.

"You hear me?"

"Yeah, blow the horn."

Melvin walked into the building. He kept his head down, as if hoping Ernest wouldn't recognize him. Sure enough, the old man didn't seem to notice. He was behind the cash register, sitting on a stool and reading a magazine.

Melvin put his hand on the stack of the Bakersfield Californian. The morning edition, he noticed. The evening paper was probably sitting on an idling truck on the interchange, the driver wondering why traffic wasn't moving. Next to the Californian rack was one for the weekly Tehachapi News. "Water levels at record lows," the newspaper said across the front page. Melvin looked at his fingers, the tips now smudged with newsprint. He put his fingers in his mouth, sucked them clean. He stepped over to the counter.

Ernest still hadn't looked up. He was engrossed in that magazine. Must be a titty rag, Melvin thought. The old man's cheeks looked like they'd been carved by the wind for a thousand years. Ernest held the magazine in his right hand, and, with the left, tapped out a mindless tune on the counter. The fingers were like a spider's legs. Melvin figured he could take those spider fingers in his own hand, squeeze hard and bend them back. Ernest wouldn't be able to do nothing but scream. He'd go down on a knee, and he'd be at Melvin's mercy. Melvin could grab something with the other hand—this glass bowl filled with Dubble Bubble gumballs—and smash it into Ernest's head. How hard would he have to hit him so that he wouldn't remember seeing him and Gordon at all? He figured three or four whacks would do it.

Ernest looked up, let the magazine drop against his chest. Jesus, Melvin thought, the man was reading Fortune.

"What can I do you?" Ernest said.

"You can open the goddamn cash register," Melvin said. He had to make it look like a robbery. If it was a robbery, anybody could have done it.

The right side of Ernest's mouth ticked upward. One of the wisps of his thin white hair fluttered on the top of his head. "You robbing me, Melvin?"

Melvin was suddenly furious. He'd been getting his gas here for years, and all this time Ernest thought he was a common criminal.

Ernest's eyes flicked at him. His spider hand didn't move

toward the cash register; it just stayed right there on the counter.

"Jesus, Ernest, you son of a bitch. I just want some gum, all right? That okay with you?" He snatched a gumball off the top of the pile and slapped it down on the counter.

Ernest's hand still didn't move. His little gruel-like eyes had latched onto Melvin's and wouldn't let go. Melvin, flustered, pulled out his money clip and threw a dollar bill down on the counter. He grabbed up his gumball and turned away, away from those judging eyes. "Keep the change," he said.

"Much obliged," he heard Ernest say as the door slammed shut. Melvin started the car and pulled away from the pumps.

"What're you talking to Ernest about?" Gordon asked.

"Nothing. Don't worry about it." Melvin unwrapped the gumball and popped it into his mouth. He gunned the motor, turned the car onto the road and headed back the way they had come.

CHAPTER TWENTY-ONE

Tori spotted the car below them. She watched it swing out of a turn and straighten itself out on the ribbon of black tar. Relief rolled through her. She'd had enough of walking. She was sure she had sunburn on her nose and neck. She wanted a roof over her head; she wanted to loll back on a plush seat. King stepped beside her. He followed Tori's gaze until he noticed the marble-sized object heading up the mountain. A moment later the sound of the vehicle's engine—revving wildly, followed by the lull of the gear change—reached them. It sounded like a faraway woodpecker banging itself into a tree. Tori and King watched it together, watched it slowly grow into a real thing as it twisted up the mountain.

As the car made the turn to come level with them, Tori raised her right arm high over her head and waved. Pressure gathered behind her eyes; her sinuses popped. She was going to cry. This time they would be tears of joy. King grabbed her wrist and pulled her arm down to her side.

"What?" she said.

"That's them."

"Who?"

"The Johnsons. The guys you saw in town. That's their car."

Holding onto Tori's wrist, King jumped onto the shoulder of the road, wrenching Tori's arm. "Oww!" she yelped, but he kept pulling at her. King looked over the side of the mountain, searching for an opening that didn't involve a sheer drop. He began to run, letting go of Tori only when he was sure she was running, too.

The sound of the engine rose behind them like a teakettle coming to boil. King leapt for the trees as the engine roared in his ears. Tori stumbled, crashing to the thin strip of dirt between the asphalt and the edge of the mountain. The vehicle screamed to a stop, leaving a long, wavy set of skid marks in its wake. Tori felt the burn on her knees and along her wrists and forearms. She tried to turn over but someone grabbed her in a half-nelson. She was lifted up like a bundle of laundry and dumped onto the floor of the car's backseat. Her abductor crashed on top of her. He pushed a heavy, strong hand on her neck. Realizing what was happening, she screamed in panic, but the hand pushed harder on her neck, stifling her.

The Eldorado's tires squealed again. Tori felt the car swoop into another turn, as if it were on tracks. She tried to kick her legs, but, with her face pushed down to the floor, she couldn't manage it. The hand stayed on the back of her head. The pressure of it sent sparkles to her eyes. She thought she could make out shapes. Could her kidnapper send messages through his hand straight into her brain, like Mr. Spock?

"Where we going to take her?" the hand told her brain.

"You're not going to touch that girl." Another voice, not from her brain. Probably from the front seat.

"She's for you?"

"She's leverage!"

"What do you mean?"

"The pigs are after us, Gordo. How easy do you think it's going to be to get away? When you have a hostage, the authorities will give you whatever you want. Food. Money. Clothes. We can be like that Army deserter who hijacked the jet airplane. They gave him a hundred thousand dollars and flew him to Algeria."

"Where's Algeria?"

"Doesn't matter. We're going to Mexico."

"I don't want to go to Mexico."

"Well, you're going. When we're there, we can hire someone—a private dick—to clear our names."

"So why can't we do anything with her?"

"We just can't. Not while we're still in the country."

"You don't make any sense, Melvin."

"You're going to have to trust me, dammit."

Tori slammed into the back of the driver's seat. Her bottom teeth caught on the seat fabric and tore it as she flipped onto her back. She hacked and spit, thrashing. The hand had lifted off her head, and a body—a silhouette—appeared over her, suspended there, before flying away like a humming bird, back the way it came. She felt the sensation of turning, twisting. She was thrust upward—she could do a handstand with almost no effort, but she missed the chance because she immediately crashed down again onto her back. Sound finally arrived: metal scraping against metal, something or someone groaning. Her head banged into the door, and she realized she was about to die.

The stream moved with surprising force. At first Hicks thought he could jump from one rock to the next, but that dream lasted but two hops. His right boot slipped, dropping him thigh-deep into the drink. The cold water seized him; the entire lower half of his body immediately started to tingle as the water sluiced around him. He felt his boots fill with water. For a moment he thought he was going to fall to his knees, go all the way under. Lloyd grabbed him by the arm, but the lieutenant's foot slipped as well. Screw it, they decided. They'd driven for half an hour and walked for another twenty minutes or so. In for a penny, in for a pound. They held the rifles against their chests and waded across the stream, hoping the day's warmth would be enough to hold off anything more serious than the shivers. Once they were on the other side, they could see the lake through an opening in the trees. It wasn't much, placid and without ambition, barely a lake at all, which might have been why deer and birds congregated there to drink and ponder their fate. The breeze played upon the lake's surface, causing intricate ripples and shimmies. It was hypnotizing.

"You know where this cabin is?" Lloyd asked. "We really want to be back at the car by dark."

Hicks had come out here with Sheriff Davis the last time they were looking for the Johnsons, when Gordon had assaulted the girl skier. They'd knocked on the cabin door and called out loudly for at least a full minute before deciding to go in. When they pushed the door open, light flooded the shack like an evangelical's vision. Gordon was sitting on the floor in the far corner. "I didn't do nothing," he said when the sheriff's stern voice made him look up.

Hicks pointed to the northern end of the lake. "It's back in there," he said. A dense, seemingly endless wave of pines overtook the landscape beyond the water. No wonder this was prime hunting ground.

"What do you think? About twenty to get there?" Lloyd asked. "If we hustle?" He looked at his watch. It'd be dark in an hour. They'd planned on being there by now.

"Sounds about right."

They set off along the side of the lake, but even out in the open they found they weren't able to pick up their pace. Hicks's legs felt like they'd been filled with sand. He choked on the humidity. They'd managed to keep their torsos out of the stream, but now their shirts were just as soaked as their pants. Sweat spread across Hicks's chest like paste. It was going to take them longer than twenty minutes. A lot longer. Looking up, he blinked at the surroundings. The natural world seemed exhausted too, unhappy to have visitors. Plants drooped. The ground covering wheezed under their feet like flagellants. The color of the sky had taken on an ominous tint. This all could be a matter of perception, Hicks thought. He was tired. It had been a long, tiring, upsetting day. They were heading into the lair of armed suspects, where they didn't know the landscape and might not have the element of surprise.

Hicks had never been a fan of the Great Outdoors. He couldn't recall ever being impressed by a mountain vista or moved by a babbling brook. The Fresno area was brutal, nondescript scrubland, but in all his years there he'd never given it two thoughts, never wished for prettier scenery. He just didn't care about nature. He'd always wanted to be a big-city cop, walking the mean streets—the mean, *paved* streets. Fresno was supposed to be a steppingstone to L.A. or San Francisco or Oakland for him. He paused to catch his breath. He turned around and found where the stream bubbled into the lake.

On the far side of the water the land rose abruptly into a massive, curving mesa. The sides were jagged and angled, the top as flat as a stovepipe hat. The size of the mesa surprised him, and he stretched his neck backward to get a better look. The only sounds beyond their breathing were the birds, offering a repeating call and response in the trees overhead, and the occasional clicks and clacks of the forest—animals stepping on twigs and pine needles just like them, Hicks assumed. They needed to stay by the lake to avoid getting lost, but being in the open was taking too much out of them. They moved to the treeline. Now that he was in the shade, Hicks was able to breathe deeply and focus his vision again. He immediately spotted a wooden marker poking out of the water at the edge. Next to it sat a wide, three-seat canoe, the paddles hooked into their rings. "I remember the canoe," Hicks said. "I know exactly where we are."

The evening had begun to settle in by the time Hicks finally found the cabin; it popped in front of him like a goblin, giving him a start. He and Lloyd shined their flashlights against the building—it was a simple weatherboard structure. Realizing this was indeed it, they hastily clicked off the beams, put them away, and pulled

their rifles off their shoulders. Doubled forward, they eased up to
the south-facing side and listened. Nothing. Hicks duck-walked
around the corner and found the door. He motioned for Lloyd to
stay put, then crouched. "Hello?" he called out. "Anybody in there?"

The cabin leaned but had an air of permanence about it.
Hicks stood, pressed his back against the side of the cabin, and
reached out for the door handle. It creaked in his hand: there was
no lock. He turned the handle and pushed. It swung inward with
a slow moan. Hicks inched toward the doorframe and peered
inside. Empty. He stepped in, looked around. Lloyd joined him
a moment later. Two empty cans of Campbell's chicken-noodle
soup lay on the floor. Hicks picked one up and held it to his nose;
the pungent, pleasing smell made his eyes water. He looked at
Lloyd. "I guess they heard us coming," he said.

"You think so?"

"Yeah. They were just here."

The chief and his lieutenant blundered back the way they
came. The Johnsons could have headed further up into the
mountain, but that seemed unlikely. It was too easy to get
lost and freeze to death in the night. The brothers knew these
woods, they hunted and fished up here, but neither of them was
Grizzly Adams. Hicks and Lloyd reached the lake and dropped
down under the cover of a stand of trees. The heat of the day had
disappeared all at once, and Hicks found himself shuddering.
Lloyd crouched beside him.

"What do you think?" Lloyd said.

"There's only the one road out."

"They could be lying in wait for us somewhere."

"Could be. But they can only delay the inevitable out here.
The car's their only real chance for escape. They might guess that
the highway and County Line have blocks, so that narrows their
choices."

Lloyd nodded and rose. Hicks headed out behind him, but he
stopped after just half a dozen steps.

"Wait—hold up."

Lloyd looked at him. Hicks nodded toward the water, and Lloyd looked at the wooden marker and the calm, black water. It took a moment before the penny dropped for the lieutenant. The canoe was gone.

CHAPTER TWENTY-TWO

Winnie knotted her hair behind her head, stripped off her sodden clothes, and climbed into the bathtub. She slunk down so that only her head and knees were exposed to the air. The water was uncomfortably, wonderfully hot. She watched her toes being pulled upward, stretching for the surface. Tears collected in her eyes, and she extracted a hand from the depths to wipe them away. She grabbed a small plastic container and burped a dollop of thick green goo into her hand. She looked at the goo and felt silly, but she also felt good—she couldn't help it. She knew no one else in Mammoth View—probably no one else within three hundred miles—had this stuff. It was French, this facial mask. Catherine Deneuve supposedly swore by it. Winnie had to send away for the product, of course. No store in these parts would carry something like this. She rubbed it into her face, taking care under her damaged eye. She burped more of the product into her hand and lacquered it on top of the first layer. She lay back against the tile, resting her head on her hair knot.

Winnie considered Deneuve the most beautiful woman in the world, hands down. Everything about her—the steely gaze, the willowy figure, the cock of her walk—was perfect. Made personally by God himself. (Sophia Loren was number two in her book, though she and Deneuve shouldn't be compared—they were essentially different species.) What did it say about her that she thought the most beautiful women in the world were European? Was she a snob? She thought about who the most beautiful American was and settled on Cybil Shepherd. The depthless blue eyes, the sharp cheekbones, the lifeless blond hair. There was a stark, rural blandness to her beauty. Very ordinary. Very American. God, she *was* a snob. That's what college did to a girl.

Winnie stared at the tile walls. Johnny had made her promise to stay at the police station until he returned, but that was ridiculous. She was perfectly safe at home. Those hillbillies didn't know where she lived or even her name. They didn't know anything about her, except that she got away. She thought about what had happened to her today. She touched her swollen eye, her hand jumping away as if it had grazed fire. Snot, responding to the jab of pain, leaked out her nose. She began to weep softly. Winnie tilted her head back to get a good gulp of air and felt the mask resist and crack. She needed to talk to someone, someone who would understand, but there was no one. How had that happened? Winnie had been in Mammoth View for almost two years. She was on a first-name basis with almost everyone in town, but she didn't consider any of them a friend. Not really. Winnie lifted a foot, pressed it against the faucet and stretched her back. The water sloshed around her. She could call Dannie, she thought. She swiveled her head to find the clock on the shelf above the sink. No, it was too late in Chicago. Dannie got up early and went to bed early. In college, Winnie had poured out her life to Dannie. To Lisa and Tatiana, too. She'd had close friends all her life. She didn't know what had changed, why she was a loner in Mammoth. Maybe she really was a snob.

She sat up in the tub, cupped her hands and splashed water on her face. She wiped the mask away as if erasing herself. She knew exactly why she hadn't been in touch with Dannie lately. She had nothing to say for herself anymore. Dannie had a career and lived in an interesting place. Winnie had followed a man to Podunk. She didn't even want to tell Dannie she was pregnant. She was happy about it—she was *thrilled*—but she wasn't proud. Getting pregnant was a beautiful thing, a life-changing experience, but it wasn't exactly an accomplishment. Breathing hard, Winnie pulled her legs to her chest, rested her chin on her knees and closed her eyes. She had to decide whether she was going to see a doctor about her injuries. She figured Johnny would insist, but that didn't matter. She could tell him she went, and that would be that. She didn't really see the point of going. What could be done for her eye beyond putting a steak on it? The various bruises were just bruises—she'd had a million of them and would have a million more. And the other thing? The hick hadn't accomplished much. Close only counts in horseshoes and nuclear war.

She plucked the bar of soap from the dish and began to scrub herself with it. Like any good Catholic, she found solace in ritual, and cleansing was ritual. Cleansing was godly. *O God, I am heartily sorry for having offended thee and I detest all my sins.* Winnie crossed herself, accidentally flicking water into her eyes. She wasn't sure how much God mattered anymore, how much He affected the modern world, but she still felt comforted by the church. The physical place. The stained glass, the Stations of the Cross, the quiet. The experience of being in a church always removed all thoughts from her head, which was usually what she needed. She scrubbed her torso, her arms, and her pits. She held the soap under the water and scrubbed her legs vigorously, the insides of her thighs. Done, she let go of the bar and heard it clunk on the bottom of the tub. It came to rest against her right heel.

If she told her parents about what happened, would they come down to visit? Mom would, in a flash. Dad wouldn't be willing to close up the shop. He was keeping the place going on a wing and a prayer, and putting bread on the table had to take precedence. Actually, her mother might not come down. She'd ask Winnie to fly home. Her mother hated to travel. She'd never forgiven her only child for moving away. To California, of all places, with the hippies and crazies. If Winnie told her what had happened to her, it would confirm all of her mother's fears. Her mom would insist that Johnny look for work in Oregon and Washington. She'd start crying on the phone—big, retching sobs.

Winnie hugged herself. The heat had dissipated from the bath water, and she felt goosebumps crawling along her back and arms. She thought about how embarrassed Chief Hicks had been at finding her in such a state of disarray and not knowing what had actually happened. How kind he was, to not ask questions right then and there. She stood up and shook the water off her arms. Reached for her towel.

She knew what she wanted to do. She wanted to find the chief a girlfriend. A real one. He'd made mistakes in his life, and he'd paid with his marriage and his health, but he was a good man. He'd saved her, and he deserved to be loved. She'd find him a girl at the ski resort. They got new blood in there every season. People moved to Mammoth to work at the resort in hopes of escaping their lives and building new ones. Sometimes there were middle-aged women among the recruits. Winnie pushed her face into the towel and rubbed. Yes, that's would she would do, she decided. Then the chief's girl could be her friend.

Winnie put on a T-shirt and a pair of shorts—she didn't check which ones or look in the mirror. She pulled open her jewelry drawer and lifted out her St. Benedict replica medal. It was large and heavy, copper-colored. She'd attached it to a cheap gold chain she bought at Walgreens. She put the chain around her neck, placed the medal carefully at the base of her breastbone, tapping it into place. There was no one better at warding off evil than Benedict. She walked into the hall, opened the closet, and took the putter out of Johnny's bag. She hefted it, choked up on the staff. Next she grabbed a pitching wedge. The clubs were too long for her, but she wasn't going to go out to the garage in search of hers.

She slung the clubs over her right shoulder, walked through

the kitchen and, barefoot, out onto the porch. Johnny kept a coffee can filled with old balls on the railing next to the door, and she snatched it up on her way. The lawn was green but overgrown. Johnny hadn't gotten around to mowing for a while. It was a deep yard. If they had a boy, it would be perfect for Johnny to throw a ball with him. That was a father-son ritual, tossing a baseball back and forth, but Winnie preferred football. She didn't have a favorite team or anything, but she enjoyed watching it: the complex strategies, the substitutions, and the teamwork necessary for every single yard advanced or repelled. She understood why Southerners with their martial spirit loved the sport so much. Stonewall Jackson would have been a helluva quarterback, sitting in the pocket, waiting for his receiver to break free while the whole world was falling down around him, waiting, waiting. She liked the tight uniform pants they wore, too. Joe Namath, now that was a good-looking man, even if he did wear pantyhose.

The tall grass felt good on her ankles, ticklish but pleasant. She thought of the picnics her parents used to take her on. She put the can down and grabbed a ball from it. The ground was hard, but it seemed to give a little under her heel when she tried out a practice swing with the wedge. The ball all but disappeared when she dropped it. She turned her hip, brought the club back, and swung with an abrupt chopping motion. The ball popped into the air like a magic trick, made a neat parabola, and fell with a plop in the narrow utility right-of-way between their property and the Bakers' behind them.

Winnie smiled. That was pretty good. She'd taken golf for her physical education elective in college. It simply made sense. She'd always liked Arnold Palmer. Unlike Namath, who was just plain sexy, Arnie was appealing in an unthreatening, comfortable kind of way. A soothing presence in newspaper pictures and on TV. Like he could be your uncle. It was something she and her father could share, rooting for Arnie in the twilight of his career as he tried to score one last big win against Nicklaus, Casper, and Trevino. Her Dad never took her out to the public course, though.

Never asked if she'd like to play.

When she finally did play, she found that she kind of had a feel for the game. From all those times watching, she supposed. And the swinging motion relaxed her; it reminded her of the lulling bliss of riding a seesaw when she was a child. For her last two years in college, she would go out to the school's driving range during stressful periods: before a difficult final exam or after a bad date, that kind of thing. Seeing that little white ball soar into the sky—up and up and up, as if it might join Sputnik in orbit. It was nice. She would feel her shoulders relax and her neck unkink. All the benefits of beer with none of the calories. After five or six drives, her mind would start to white out, leaving her dazed and happy.

She gave up the game after she graduated and quickly forgot how much she'd enjoyed it. Arnie was essentially retired, so she didn't seek out the leaders list in the newspaper anymore. Then they moved to Mammoth View. There was a public course an hour and a half away, in Sanger. Back in Eugene, Johnny had only played now and again, with buddies or for cop charity fundraisers, and never seriously. But he didn't hunt or fish, which was what every man in Mammoth did during the summer, so now golf was his only available leisure activity. If Winnie hadn't started playing again, she'd never see him on the weekends. Besides, the closest Catholic Church, St. Bonaventure's, was in Sanger. She was able to get Johnny to go to church with her every Sunday before they hit the links; she was able to sell it as a two-birds-with-one-stone kind of thing.

The problem was, she wasn't a natural athlete like her husband. She quickly found out she wasn't nearly as good at golf as she'd thought she was. Johnny improved week after week on the Sanger public course. Winnie struggled. In fact, she had forgotten almost everything she learned in college—she was almost starting from scratch. At first, she was having trouble even getting the ball into the air on her drives.

Her second chip stayed in the grass. Instead of jumping

skyward and landing in the utility right-of-way, her objective, it merely shuddered and rolled forward a foot or so. Criminy, she thought. She found the ball with her foot, rolled it back to her, heel to toes. She turned her hip, chopped: this time the ball jumped, wavered in the air, and thumped against the three-foot-tall fence at the end of the yard. So close. She dropped another ball in front of her, turned her hip, and chopped. The ball barely moved again, spinning crazily this way and that before expiring. "Shit," she muttered, angry at the ball, at her club, at herself. What a stupid game this was. She stepped up to the ball, reared back, and swung. The ball shot into the air, clearing the fence by about five feet, zooming between the two ash trees in the right-of-way, toppling out of sight. The tinkling startled her into a crouch. Her throat closed, and she huffed to force air into her chest. She knew exactly what the sound was. She'd broken a window.

She didn't know what to do. She stood and rose up on tiptoes in hopes of making out what had happened, but it was too dark to see anything. She stood there for three or four minutes with the club in her hands, its head up in the sky like a periscope. When a blob appeared in the Bakers' back yard, she dropped the club to the ground.

The little blob grew and quickly took on the form of a human. It was Mrs. Baker. The long streaks of white in her hair made her look like a stockier Cruella De Vil from *One Hundred and One Dalmatians*. The Bakers kept to themselves—they were known for it. Practically shut-ins, at least according to the gossip. The couples waved at each other when they were both in their yards, but that was it. Johnny and Mr. Baker had chatted over the fence a few times, but she'd never said much more than "Hello" to either of them. Mrs. Baker was wearing a brown cloth coat over an airy nightgown. Her sausage-like legs were encased in rain boots. She held the golf ball in her hand. She stopped at the end of her yard and squinted across the right-of-way, grimacing violently. "I was expecting a boy with a baseball bat, not a woman with a golf club," she said.

Winnie's face burned. She hid the golf club behind her back. "I'm really sorry. I don't know what came over me. I'm so embarrassed."

"It's fortunate that I wasn't in the bathroom when this came through. I could have been seriously injured."

"I'll come over and clean up the mess. Just let me put on some shoes." She started to turn toward the house.

"No, no," the older woman said. "No need for that."

"Are you sure?"

Mrs. Baker nodded. "I don't like people in my home."

Winnie grabbed at her neck and rubbed, trying to cool herself down, trying to breathe properly. "We'll pay to replace your window."

"Yes, you will."

The two women blinked at one another through the darkness. "I don't know what else to say," Winnie said. "I'm terribly embarrassed. I was letting off some steam, and I just—I don't know—lost control."

Mrs. Baker crooked an arm, rested her hand on her waist. She took a step back, as if she were having trouble getting Winnie into focus. "Must've been a busy day for your husband," she said.

"I'm sorry?"

"The emergency. Whatever it was."

"Oh. Yes. Of course." Winnie felt herself starting to calm down. Her pulse disappeared inside her skin. "He's still at work. I don't know if he'll be home tonight."

"They're making fun of us in Bakersfield. The hard-faced blond girl who does the news on Channel Two. Smirked through the entire report."

"Uh huh." Winnie thought she'd misunderstood what Mrs. Baker said. Or that Mrs. Baker had misunderstood the news report. She didn't dare ask for clarification. "You and Mr. Baker stayed home all day? You didn't leave?"

"Mr. Baker's in 'Frisco. And me, where would I go? Whatever happens, I want to die in my own home, not in a ditch somewhere."

"A ditch?"

"You know what I mean."

"Yes, of course."

Mrs. Baker had a pack of Marlboro's and a lighter in her right hand. She lit a cigarette, sucked in a block of smoke, and blew it out the side of her mouth. She looked at Winnie sidelong, holding the cigarette like a teacup. "When are you due?"

Winnie's face flushed. "I—I didn't know you knew."

Mrs. Baker pulled on the cigarette. "Honey, look at yourself."

Winnie did. She discovered that her shirt had hitched up with her backswing, exposing the bottom of her stomach, her navel winking. Embarrassed, she pulled the shirt down. That could be a little beer belly, she thought. It was nothing. Nothing at all. No, somebody had told Mrs. Baker. It wasn't a secret. No way this woman could tell she was pregnant.

"Don't worry," Mrs. Baker said. "It seems overwhelming, but you'll be just fine."

Winnie gaped for a moment before comprehension grabbed hold of her. The pregnancy, she reminded herself. Mrs. Baker had no idea what Winnie had been through today. None at all. Winnie sighed and forced herself to smile. "You're right. It does seem overwhelming sometimes. I don't know why. I want children. Three or four, I think."

"Well, you'll get them," Mrs. Baker said, blowing smoke into the night air. "That husband of yours. He looks quite virile."

Winnie smiled, nodded. "He might even be the father of this one."

Shock paralyzed Mrs. Baker's face. Her mouth eventually opened, but no words came out.

Winnie realized with horror that her attempt at lightening the mood hadn't gone over. "Sorry," she said. "Bad joke."

Mrs. Baker forced out a smile. "That's very funny," she said.

Winnie watched Mrs. Baker walking away, her nightgown swishing, the outline of her stocky frame visible in the moonlight.

"I'm sorry," she called out to the retreating figure. "About the window, I mean," she added, not as loud.

Winnie kicked at the grass, decapitating a swath of turf. Friggin' neighbors, she thought. Adjusting to small-town life hadn't been easy for her. She still hadn't adjusted, in fact. When she'd lived in bigger burgs, being out in public always put her in a good mood. She'd loved drifting anonymously through department stores. People streaming around her, the pleasing smells wafting in from the cosmetics counters. She'd never lived in a *really* big city, like New York, so there'd always been the titillating possibility of running into someone you knew. But they were big enough towns that she knew it probably wasn't going to happen, which is what made the possibility exciting. In Mammoth View, it *always* happened. She now hated running into someone she knew, because there was no avoiding it. She knew everyone—or, at least, everyone knew her.

She turned around to face her own house, tapped a ball in front of her with her foot. She swung—pok!—and the ball lifted up. It banged against the gutter along the roof and dropped to earth. She pushed another ball into place with her club. Pok! She shanked it: the ball twirled in the wrong direction and clipped the side of the house, causing Winnie's heart to shudder as the ball skipped past the bedroom window and bounced harmlessly into the driveway. The close call made her focus. She didn't want to break two windows in one night. She patted a ball into place, eased the club back and swung again.

She caught that one just right. The ball sailed upward, shakily at first but then with real purpose, like the last chopper out of 'Nam. She followed through without even thinking about it, up on her toes, her hips torqued, the club finishing over her shoulder. The ball continued to rise—over the roof, way over. It shimmered in the sky, white on black, hanging there like a Christmas ornament. It never fell—it just disappeared from view.

Winnie held the pose for a long time. She imagined herself as a statue in the Galleria dell' Accademia, the female version of the David. No, that wasn't right. Too static, too lost in the past. She was feeling alive and very much present all of a sudden. She felt the night air on her cheeks, on her arms and legs and the strip of belly flesh that had once again been exposed by the swing of her arms. The thought of it—of being alive and present—made her crack. She brought the club down, let go, and dropped to her knees. The feeling was wonderful but also tenuous, so very tenuous. The fragility of it scared her. Already she felt it slipping away. She wondered if she'd ever get a solid hold on it again.

CHAPTER TWENTY-THREE

Hicks and Lloyd picked their way along the lake, shuffling through tall grass, waving at unseen flying bugs. Hicks pictured the TV images of Southeast Asia that had become so familiar, soldiers pushing through the jungle in short sleeves, humpbacked and sweaty, as easy to startle as cats. Lloyd had been in the army near the end of the war but he'd never been in Vietnam. Korea, Hicks remembered. Lloyd had spent his army days staring across the demilitarized zone. Hicks had almost been in Korea as well, back when the fighting there was hot. He'd been out of the service for only a year and a half when Kim Il Sung's troops crossed the thirty-eighth parallel. Hicks could have been called up, but he wasn't. The only combat he'd ever see would be on the television.

Vietnam had been very different than Korea, of course. Like almost everyone he knew, he'd supported the war in Vietnam and had said so every time it came up. Sarah told him once that he might think differently if they had a son, but Hicks insisted he wouldn't, that you couldn't let the communists run roughshod over the world, that any young American man should be proud to serve his country and protect freedom. He'd believed this with a religious certainty; he'd been unwavering throughout the war. He wasn't so sure anymore. Illness had made him soft. It sounded ridiculous, but having a heart attack made him realize what it must have been like for those draftees trudging through the jungle. They hadn't asked for Vietnam to happen to them, just as he hadn't asked for his heart to seize up. Sprawled on the bathroom floor, he'd been certain he was going to die, and he'd been surprised by how scared he was. When he woke up after surgery and saw Sarah standing against the back wall of the hospital room, looking exhausted and annoyed, he started crying. He couldn't stop for ten minutes. That alone, bawling in front of his estranged wife, was enough to make him a pacifist. How could he support any policy that put men through such an experience? No one needed democracy so badly that they should go through that.

Hicks thought about Nixon's secret plan to end the war. He couldn't remember what it was anymore. Had Nixon abandoned it? Did he implement it and it didn't work? The scandal over the break-in probably got in the way, messed things up. Hicks never paid much attention to the Watergate stuff. He watched that Robert Redford movie all the way through and didn't see what it had to do with Nixon. About halfway in, Jason Robards asks Redford and the little Jewish guy, "Where's the goddamn story?" Hicks didn't see where it was, either. The movie was all about the Committee to Re-Elect the President. CREEP this and CREEP that. So what? Campaign dirty tricks went back to the ancient Greeks. They were as American as apple pie. Hicks didn't understand the hoo-ha about it now. He liked Nixon—he'd grown up with guys like Dick Nixon—and hated to see the man getting attacked for being an ordinary American from an ordinary American town.

Hicks had been on the department's security detail the time Nixon came through Fresno in '62. When Hicks shook hands with the great man, Nixon looked past his shoulder and gave a little twitch of a smile. Hicks couldn't recall a word of the speech at the fairgrounds, but he did remember Nixon leaving. The candidate came down the steps at the back of the stage and walked straight for the car, right into the crowd on the right side of the pavilion. The crowd fell back to let him through, though arms shot out all along the collapsing line, like cattle prods. Everyone was desperate to touch him, to feel his flesh—as long as they were off-center, as long as it was a sidelong, glancing contact. "Hey, Dick!" someone shouted. Another called out: "We're with you, sir!" Nixon waved and smiled and threw his arms out to both sides, an umpire calling a close play at the plate. His face was flushed, he was excited to be in the middle of it all, but he kept his eyes cast slightly down and his shoulders slumped slightly forward, as if he didn't want to be recognized. He looked like a man who might die of embarrassment.

The nattering nabobs, Hicks thought, remembering Vice President Agnew's phrase about Nixon's critics. He'd had to look the words up. The college men in their sharp suits hated the president, hated that he'd come up from nothing to make something of himself. Hicks thought of Mrs. Nixon standing next to the president on their last day in the White House. The image had stuck with him, the look of brokenhearted horror on her face, her eyes blasted into unseeing shame. He'd always liked her, thought she was every bit as pretty as that conceited Jackie Kennedy that everybody so loved.

A rustling sound off to his right grabbed Hicks's attention. He couldn't tell what it was. Could be an animal moving through brush. Could be his imagination. He glanced at Lloyd, who was frozen in his tracks. Lloyd caught Hicks's eye and pointed, then bounded quickly into the woods. Hicks hesitated. He would have liked to discuss it first. He looked away from Lloyd's disappearing form and out across the lake. The rugged, green landscape on the other side, lit by moonlight, rolled eastward with a powerful order and beauty. White Mountain and Waucoba Mountain floated over the horizon like competing postcards of the Egyptian pyramids.

He turned back and noted that Lloyd was gone, sucked into nature. He scurried after him, his stomach aching. He hated going directly into the woods. He much preferred to stay along waterways—lakes and streams—and manmade paths. It was too easy to get turned around among the trees, to end up headed deep into the forest when you thought you were going back to the car. Up ahead, Hicks spotted Lloyd—he hoped it was Lloyd—ducking under a low-hanging branch. The chief's flashlight poked pathetically at tree trunks and grayish ground cover and darkness.

Hicks worried about how much noise they were making. They were so loud that the forest seemed emptied out; the animals had plenty of time to get out of the way, to watch them go by from makeshift hidey-holes. If the Johnsons were out here and nearby, they also could hear and probably see them, two city cops blundering along, tripping over roots in the ground, the beams from their flashlights bobbing. Hicks didn't actually know what kind of outdoorsmen Melvin and Gordon were. When the Johnsons had rented out the Sky Flower for corporate retreats, they'd advertised themselves as hunting guides, but the few hunting tours they'd led hadn't gone well. There'd been a threatened lawsuit from one CEO type who Gordon had almost winged. The county put a stop to the tours by getting Fish and Wildlife to enforce their license rules.

Lloyd—it *was* Lloyd, thank God—crouched at the base of a tree, and Hicks came up behind him. The chief patted him on the shoulder to let him know he was there.

"I don't hear it anymore," Lloyd whispered.

Hicks cocked his head. He'd forgotten they were following the noise. He didn't hear it, either. The sounds in the forest were strange. There was always noise in the woods, he'd noticed, but it always seemed far off, unthreatening and yet still unnerving. It was like they were listening to a factory's assembly line through a seashell, the *chick-chick* of widgets being pressed into plastic packaging on the other side of the world. That was what had caught their attention about this now-gone rustling sound: it was close, right around the corner—right on top of them. Hicks clicked off his flashlight, figuring he should only use it if necessary, in case the Johnsons really were nearby.

A tickle of fear crawled up Hicks's large intestine. The recognition of it—that he was afraid—made him angry. "What do you think?" he hissed at his subordinate.

"Let's wait a minute, see if it comes back."

Hicks dropped down and waited. He noticed that his teeth were chattering, which didn't surprise him. His pants and shirtsleeves were still damp, weighing him down. He hugged himself and rubbed his upper arms with his hands. His eyes caught a flash of movement, and he blinked. Lloyd stood up, his head jabbing forward like an English Pointer. Hicks stood as well. Did they see something? He couldn't be sure. Lloyd shuffled forward, ducked into the dark.

Hicks, feeling like the little brother no one wanted around, rushed to keep up. He broke into a jog, but Lloyd's lead lengthened. He dared not run any faster, lest he crash headlong into a tree, lest his damaged heart give out. He kept his arms in front of him to ward off the natural world, tracking Lloyd as much by the huffing of the lieutenant's breath as by sight. He rounded into a dry gully, his feet slipping on the powdery earth. He stopped, ducked his head. He'd lost Lloyd but spotted their quarry: figures in the gully moving in an orderly line. Definitely people, not animals. He noticed Lloyd a few yards away from him, squatting under the cover of a tree. He too was watching the forms up ahead. The Johnsons, it seemed, had accomplices.

Lloyd looked behind him, found Hicks, and held up four fingers. Four men. Hicks padded over to Lloyd. The two officers conferred quietly and then started down the ravine, staying low, staying within hearing distance of the Johnson Gang's footfalls. Hicks kept his eyes straight ahead. It was pointless to try and determine where they were going or what route they were taking to get there. With their flashlights stowed in their belts, Hicks's and Lloyd's only light was the moon, which peeked over the top of the mesa like a porthole in a sinking ship. They were relying chiefly on sound, and hoping the Johnsons would stick to the easy path.

The gully disappeared in places. Cottonwoods elbowed into the floodway, sending out low, pugilistic branches. Other greenery—bushes and shrubs of some sort that Hicks couldn't name—stretched across the opening in the forest, determined to close off any possible escape. At one spot, they had to get down almost to their knees to squeeze through the opening and then scuffle about in the dark to pick up the path's thread. Somehow they kept the Johnsons within hailing distance.

Hicks worried that the Johnsons could hear the footfalls behind them and were figuring out how to circle around for an ambush, but he knew this was probably paranoia. The men up ahead marched on slowly, their feet clicking and cracking on the forest's detritus, the occasional incomprehensible burble of a word uttered and batted back. Lloyd moved like a sumo wrestler in an effort to stay low and save his back. Hicks didn't worry so much about keeping his head down, figuring the forest did a good job of obscuring them.

He pulled up at a tree and waved at Lloyd to keep going. He had to pee and couldn't hold it any longer. Before he arrested the Johnsons, he had to take care of his own Johnson. Hicks snickered at his play on words until he realized Lloyd had hesitated and was watching him. Hicks, adjusting the rifle on his back so it wouldn't sling around on him, waved furiously, and so the lieutenant turned and kept going. Hicks unzipped, dug his heels into the ground, and unleashed a stream, resisting the urge to let out a long, loud exhalation. The piss left his body like a bucket overturning. It splashed his boots, created surprising little streams that forked around the base of the tree. As he finished, a shiver ran through him, as if his soul had just departed. He couldn't believe how much better he felt. He felt invincible.

He buckled up, stepped back into the gully and jogged into the nothingness. It took him about five minutes to catch up to Lloyd, who was still sumo-stepping slowly and deliberately forward. Hicks put a hand on his lieutenant's back just as his subordinate ran into some kind of thick, brambly plant. Lloyd hadn't realized the gully was curving. Straightening themselves out, they continued down the path as if in the middle of a tunnel. The moon had slipped behind the mesa, turning the night into a syrupy paste. They listened for footsteps and the rustle of plant life being shoved aside, but there was nothing. Hicks swallowed hard, hoping to break up the worry ball stuck in his throat.

The lawmen suddenly heard the sloshing of water. Shocked, they glanced at each other and then started running. They banged hips—there wasn't enough room for the men to run side by side, but Hicks wasn't willing to cede the lead to the younger man. His boots slipped on the crusty ground; with each step, he felt like his feet could go out from under him. He slapped a hand over his empty holster to hold it in place and pumped with the other arm, flattening out his feet as much as possible as he brought each one down. The forest opened onto the lake just as Hicks felt his breath give out, and he broke stride. *Damn it*, he thought, struggling to suck in air. Lloyd continued forward, and when the men they were chasing came firmly into view, he aimed his rifle. "Police! Stay where you are!" the lieutenant yelled. "Hands up! Hands up!"

Hicks also shouldered his rifle and stepped up beside Lloyd. Then the men came into focus, and he swore to himself. He pointed the gun skyward.

"Evening, Sheriff," said a short, bearded man wearing a plaid shirt and stained brown pants. He stood ankle-deep in the water, his back to the lake. Behind him, the three other men sat in the canoe, the canoe Hicks had first spotted by the hunting cabin.

Hicks recognized Plaid Shirt. The man came into town every month to collect a disability check from a post-office box. The chief didn't recognize any of the other men, though all four of them looked like they could be related.

"What are you doing out here?" Hicks said.

Plaid Shirt smiled and looked over his shoulder at the others with a bemused expression on his face. He turned back to the lawmen. "What are *we* doing? What are you doing?"

Hicks realized he'd asked a stupid question. The four men obviously lived out here. When he saw Plaid Shirt in town, he unconsciously recognized him as a mountain man. Not everybody liked the civilized world—and who could blame them?—so a scattering of men lived in the forest, hunting with bows, sleeping in hunting shacks or out in the open. Hicks couldn't imagine living in the mountains—off the fat of the land—but he saw the appeal. All your regrets would be washed away out here. All the failures, all the hurts you'd caused, it all would become meaningless.

"You seen the Johnson boys?" Lloyd asked, finally letting his rifle drop. "You know who they are?"

Plaid Shirt tilted his head to look at Lloyd. He scratched his matted beard. "Can't remember the last time I seen the Johnsons. Homer knows his way around these parts pretty good, but the sons don't take to it in the same way."

"They're wanted men," Lloyd said.

"Oh, yes, I can see that."

"If you spot them," Hicks said, stepping forward. "Don't engage with them. They're dangerous. We'd sure appreciate it if you came into town and told us you saw them."

Plaid Shirt nodded. "We surely will do that, Sheriff."

Hicks wanted to ask them where they were going, but he resisted. It didn't matter, and he sensed the men wouldn't want to say. Plaid Shirt pushed the canoe and climbed in. The night wiped them away in an instant.

CHAPTER TWENTY-FOUR

Janice told herself not to worry. She pressed her forehead against the steering wheel and closed her eyes. Don't worry, she repeated. That's exactly what brings on an attack—worrying. Her head still tingled from all the juice she'd sucked down during the drive, but she knew it wouldn't last. Now that her medication was gone, she was on her own. Her only defense against an attack was her will power, her own strength of character. She took in a deep gulp of air, let it out. The burger at Denny's had helped. It had settled her down, at least while she was eating it. She pressed down on the brake, felt the car quiver. The image of illegal aliens massing at Lake Crowley slipped into her mind, and, realizing it, she chastised herself. *Forget it*, she mouthed.

She couldn't help herself: the feeling of panic kept returning. The army must have the situation under control by now. Or the National Guard. Was there a difference? She didn't know. She tried to remember what else the radio had said, before the explosions happened and she'd started to have the asthma attack, before the mountain had cut off reception. She'd read an article recently about illegal aliens earning just a few dollars a week in Central Valley fields, how they were worried the farmers would have them deported if they complained. That could explain it, she thought. Desperate measures and all that. The earthquake might have something to do with it, too. A quake always got people worked up.

Janice told herself it didn't matter. Everything was different now. She felt like she truly was starting a new life. She pictured King's face in the rear-view mirror as she roared away in the car. The shocked, blank face of a moron coming to a realization. That was the only way to get something into that thick skull of his, by giving it a good whack.

She smiled at the memory. She'd never broken up with a boyfriend before. Never. She'd always been on the receiving end of the kiss-off. *I met someone else,* John Billings told her senior year, right before the Sadie Hawkins Dance. That someone else was Ann Larkin. The slut. Was there anything worse than the person you care about the most telling you he'd found someone better? That you weren't good enough? Not smart enough, not sexy enough, and not interesting enough. At least she didn't do that to King. She just drove away, as if possessed by the devil. That was better, she decided. He would never be able to forgive her for leaving him by the side of the road like that. No chance he'd still be in the apartment when she returned to Mammoth. He'd pack up and go sleep at the radio station if he had to. Male pride was a strange thing, but you could figure it out.

The first breakup she'd been through had been the hardest. She still thought about it, still dreamed about it. He didn't tell her he liked someone else. He just stopped talking to her, stopped standing near her, stopped looking at her. They were thirteen years old, eighth-grade sweethearts. She knew it shouldn't still bother her—they were children!—but you can't tell the heart something like that. It acts independent of the brain. It does what it does, feels what it feels. She hated her heart.

Janice turned the key, killing the engine, and climbed out. She needed a drink. She deserved a drink. If the world was going to hell, she didn't want to be sober for it. She straightened out her skirt and looked up: The Argonaut, the art deco sign said. It hung from the building's façade like a wedding garter, high up and inviting. By the look of it, this had to be the most expensive hotel in town. Tonight, she only wanted the most expensive. Who would save money on their last night on earth, right? She strode inside, located the bar, and headed straight for it.

The room was long and dark, but the bartender was easy to spot. "Hey," she said to him. "You heard the news today? We at war?"

The man cocked an eyebrow, smiled. He was about fifty, but he still had a full head of silvery hair and was clearly proud of it. "You a woman's libber, hon?"

Janice, surprised, laughed.

Encouraged, the bartender leaned forward, resting his elbows on the top of the counter. "There's no war here. Only the sweet song of love in this place."

"That's not what I'm talking about."

The barman shrugged, winked. "I got you. Your husband comes in, I'll tell him you haven't been hitting on me."

Janice looked around. There had to be an evening paper lying around. This was a bar.

The bartender straightened up, rubbed his hands together. "What can I get you?" he asked.

Janice sighed, ordered a whiskey, and walked to a corner booth that offered a good view of the rest of the room. She sat and tried to reorder her thinking. Forget about the paper, she told herself. Let's think about the here and now. She felt giddy and anxious, like anything could happen. Anything she wanted. After all, she was free. She was on her own, truly on her own, for the first time in years. The first time ever. She searched the faces around the room, trying to give off the vibe, certain she could do better than an old bartender.

A man in a business suit slid off a stool and headed her way. He was also a little on the old side, about the barman's age, but he was good-looking, trim. Smile lines cut deep into his cheeks, giving him a rugged, Western hero look. Janice ducked her head coquettishly and let a smile take over her mouth. She looked up from under her brows just in time to watch the man stride past her without a look or a pause. Her eyes turned to follow him. The toilet. The look on his face hadn't been sexual interest, it had been a full bladder. Janice pulled out her compact and checked her makeup. There was the problem. God, she was ugly, she thought. All these freckles. Her flat nose and squinty eyes. She looked Japanese, but without the exoticism. Shit, how had she ever gotten King?

She blew air out of her cheeks. Her ugliness shouldn't be a problem, she thought. It obviously *was* a problem in the larger scheme of things, but not tonight. Men in bars weren't picky. Especially men in bars in Stockton, California. She unhooked a button on her blouse, held the mirror at arm's length. Screw it. She unhooked another button. One more and she'd get arrested for flashing. She looked around. No one was watching her. One more button might be necessary.

A man in a yellow sport coat and black slacks appeared at the entrance. For a terrible moment Janice thought it was King. King had a yellow sport coat. But this guy didn't look anything like him. This man had a big, brown helmet of hair and a nose that was too small for his face. He looked like a pilot, which would be exciting. The man's eyes roamed the room, paused at Janice—she threw her shoulders back—continued their survey and finally settled on an empty stool at the far end of the bar. He made a beeline for it, sat, called over the bartender. Janice waited for the bartender to glance her way, thinking the pilot might send her a drink—he had definitely seen her—but there was no glance. The bartender retreated to his spigots, filled a stein. Janice put her compact away. Reaching for her glass, she began to ponder the possibility of sleeping alone tonight.

"You're down to the dregs."

Janice looked up at a man's crotch. The tight pants showcased the outline of what appeared to be Asia. She dipped her head back. An expensive corduroy jacket with leather elbow patches. It was almost as impressive as the man's tater. He wore a thin blue pullover under the jacket. She could sense the muscle, the power, behind it. Up to the face: a good face, round and full, with large, sleepy eyes. A thick forehead gave way to short, black, kinky hair. He was a Negro—a *black* man had decided it was okay to hit on her. Still, she would not describe him as the dregs. "Excuse me?" she said.

"Your drink. Nothing but ice left."

"Yeah. I'm a lush."

"That's not what I meant." He rested a hand on the table, next to the glass. The fingers were long and elegant. "I meant, can I buy you another one?"

Janice let herself smile at him. She had to admire his courage. To come up to her in a nice bar in a conservative town like Stockton. She wondered if hotel security would be along in a moment.

"Sure. I'll have another drink."

He returned with two glasses filled with golden-brown liquid, put one in front of her and slid into the opposite side of the booth. "Cheers," he said, holding his glass aloft. "So, what's your name?"

Janice licked her lips to savor the warm, musky fluid. "Janice," she said.

He grinned at her, satisfied with the answer.

"And you are . . .?"

"Jackson. Jackson Dupre."

"Jackson Dupre," Janice said, admiring the name even more now that she'd said it herself. "Where are you from? New York?"

He rumbled out a laugh. "New *York*? That's three thousand miles away."

"I don't know," Janice said. "Jackson Dupre sounds like a New York name. Sounds cosmopolitan."

"Oh, I'm cosmopolitan, baby. I was in Germany during my stint in the Army. Looked across the Wall at all those poor saps over there in East Berlin."

"Wow. What was that like?"

"Strange, I must say. They'd look back, the ones who lived in the upper floors of the buildings right there. They'd look at you with . . . I don't know . . . anger or longing or something. Can you imagine putting up a huge wall to keep your people from leaving?"

Janice drained her glass for the second time. "I can imagine it," she said. "We all got walls blocking our way. You can't always see them."

"Wow, yourself," he said. "Is it the whiskey or are you always this heavy?"

Janice couldn't tell if he was mocking her. She leaned against the booth's wooden backing. She felt the point of her spine jab at it and a little tingle of pain roll toward her stomach. She wondered how old Jackson Dupre was. If he'd ever been married. If he was married right now. She felt herself slipping down, her buttocks sliding, and she put her feet out to steady herself. The right one landed on one of Jackson's. She left it there. "I'm not heavy at all, Jackie," she said. "I'm as light as air. If I wasn't holding on to the table, I'd lift off and float away."

"I hear you. And it's Jackson."

"What was it like, being in the Army? Hard work?"

Jackson was looking right at her, right into her. His eyes twinkled. Janice blushed. Her hand felt around for the undone buttons on her shirt. She felt naked.

"It wasn't nothing," he said. "Easy as pie once you get through Basic."

"You didn't have to shoot anybody?"

Jackson chuckled. "Why would I do that?"

"You know, Vietnam."

Jackson gazed at her with his sleepy eyes. He seemed to know what he was doing to her. That smile sat on his face like a toy, waiting for her to reach for it. "I learned how to defuse bombs," he said. "I can make them, too. You know you can make a rather powerful bomb from common household materials?"

"Really? Like what?"

"If I told you, I'd have to kill you."

Janice put an elbow on the table and leaned on it, trying to match his sexy, sleepy gaze. "Don't do that. I'd like to finish my drink."

Jackson snorted in mirth. "Sometimes I think I should have stayed in the Army, you know? Not a bad life, an Army career."

"Why didn't you?"

"Well, I thought I had things to do. I thought I had ambition. I thought things were changing."

"You don't have ambition? You look like a successful man."

He liked that, she could tell. A successful man. She rolled her foot off of his and tapped it.

"What about you, Janice? What brings you to the Vogue Lounge on a Wednesday evening?" He took a drink, swished it in his mouth and swallowed. "You work in the hotel?"

Janice looked at her hands, at the chipped nail polish on her fingernails. The first wrong note in the conversation. He thought she was a lousy hotel clerk, sitting in the bar at the end of her shift. She tried not to let her disappointment show. It's okay, she told herself. A hotel clerk's not so bad. That's better than him thinking she was a bored Stockton housewife looking for excitement.

"I'm from Mammoth View," she said. "You know where that is?"

A look crossed his eyes, as if he were holding in gas, but he made eye contact again, smiled. "No."

"A little town up in the mountains. A ski resort. There's something going on up there—I don't know."

"What do you mean, 'something going on'?"

"An emergency. There was an earthquake this morning. I don't know. Roads were blocked off. They shut down the office where I work, and I just decided to get out of town for the day, let things settle down. It was nuts. You haven't heard anything?"

Jackson shook his head.

"Well, anyway. It's a nice little town. Quaint. Real pretty

during the holidays, with the lights and everything, and the snow. Like a picture postcard. It's out of the way, though. Living there, you sometimes feel like nowhere else exists."

"Sounds nice."

"Yeah, it is. It's different from what I'm used to. I'm from San Diego originally."

"That right?" His smile widened. "This here is fate. I grew up in Valencia Park."

Janice nodded. The black part of town. "I'm from La Mesa," she said. Nowhere near Valencia Park. Another world. She leaned forward. "You want to get out of here, Jackson? It's kind of hot in here."

Jackson stood, put a couple bills on the table, and held his hand out for her. Touched, Janice took the hand, let him pull her up. His skin felt different, she noted. Heavier. Was his black skin thicker? She couldn't even guess. But it was smooth. It felt nice. God, could she really do it with a Negro? She grimaced to herself. Afro-American—that's what they were called now. She chastised herself for her thoughts. She was as liberal as the next person. If she lived in Los Angeles, wouldn't she vote for Tom Bradley? Now that was a good-looking man. Yes, she could do it with a Neg—an Afro-American.

They reached the lobby, her hand still in his. She watched people's faces, trying to identify what they were thinking when they saw her holding this man's hand. Were they scandalized by this happy interracial couple? Were they pretending they didn't notice? A tingling sensation rippled through her extremities. A feeling of power burbled up in her, of righteousness. Or maybe it was hormones. Horniness.

Shit. She realized she hadn't gotten a room yet. What if they were booked up? Where would they go? How much would it kill the mood, the dealing with the clerk, explaining the lack of luggage, putting money down? She stopped herself. He probably had a room. Why else would he be in the bar? He didn't seem like the kind of man who trawled hotel bars. He looked like he had no problem getting women, at least black women.

"Would you like to take a walk?" he asked.

She cocked her head. He had surprised her for a second time, first by having the stones to approach her in the bar, and now, when it was obvious she would sleep with him, by offering to extend the courtship, as if he really wanted to woo her. As if he really liked her.

"Okay," she said, and with that, he guided her out the door and into the night. The entrance to the lobby shone like a movie premiere, but the road beyond quickly disappeared. Gooseflesh rolled along her arms. It felt good. The night was warm, but you could tell that coolness was coming. The air had an edge to it, a warning. Another hour and she'd need a jacket. Jackson walked her around the side of the building to fancy pebbled steps that dropped languidly. She squinted down to the bottom, where a path led to the waterfront. Janice blanched. She hadn't realized Stockton was on the water. The walkway—kind of like a boardwalk, but with concrete and brick instead of boards— stretched into a blackness made gauzy by periodic streetlamps. As they came down the steps she could see that this wasn't the ocean. The waterway looked manmade, shaped and molded to fit the town. But she sensed the ocean out there, close by, breathing quietly. Jackson squeezed her hand, pulled her along. She could make out a few other couples, all snuggling or strolling, all of them right up against the water. This obviously was the place for lovers in Stockton.

"You cold?" he asked.

"No, it's perfect."

Jackson let her hand drop, slipped his arm around her waist and pressed her to him. He reached across himself with a long arm and grasped her hand again, pressed it against her stomach. He would trap her like this when they were making love, Janice thought. In an hour. Half an hour. Her stomach rolled. She felt wonderful. She couldn't believe this man she'd just met—this black man—was making her insides do loop-de-loops.

She listened to the water slap softly against the quay. She peeked out at it from under Jackson's arm, wondering how far it was to the Pacific, how long they'd have to walk to reach the beach. She salivated at the thought of it. She'd spent every summer of her life on the beach, until she followed King inland. She missed the hot sand, the heat dazzle: the sense that the ocean went on forever, that escape really was possible—you just had to swim out there to the horizon.

Images suddenly crowded her brain, and she found herself talking about the first time she'd tried on a bikini, at her friend Kim's house when she was thirteen, about watching the sun quietly falling behind the ocean every night, and then about her first serious crush, on a ratty-haired surfer and high school dropout who was ten years older than her. Jackson squeezed her, pressing her against his ribs, nodding at everything she said. God, she felt like she could tell this man *anything*.

Her hand was damp from holding his, but she didn't want to let go. She wanted his perspiration. She pictured it leaking into her pores, dispersing into her bloodstream. She wanted to become a part of him, like the setting sun melting into the earth. This man she barely knew!

Janice sometimes wondered if she should steer clear of relationships altogether. She'd wondered it for years. Her whole family was bad at love. Her mom was on her third marriage, and Janice felt confident this latest one wasn't going to last either. Her father had also recently married for a third time—mom had been number two. Her dad had cheated on her mother with a lady named Candice, who owned a flower shop in the business district. He probably cheated on his new wife with Candy as well. Janice's older sister, Laurie, only dated scumbags. One of them—Scott, the law student—had hit on Janice when she was still in high school. He had insisted that he and Laurie had an open relationship, which was news to Laurie when Janice mentioned it. And then there was Janice herself. Who left home at barely eighteen and threw away a chance to go to college. All for Oscar Alphonse

Desario, who her mother had pegged as a loser after listening to his show for all of fifteen minutes. Were the Littlepaughs simply destined to live in misery with those they professed to love? Janice gripped Jackson's hand harder. Maybe it would take someone totally out of left field to break the family curse. Maybe the problem was that the Littlepaughs only got down and dirty with people just like them: pig-headed, selfish people who thought relentlessly of themselves. Jackson didn't seem to be that way at all.

Watching her feet moving in perfect sync with Jackson's, she wondered if this feeling in the pit of her stomach qualified as love at first sight. She'd thought the same thing when she met King, but that was different. She knew him from the radio. For months his husky voice had been the last thing she heard before she went to sleep. He'd confided secrets to her and told her tales out of school, long before they ever met. But this man—Jackson Dupre—hadn't existed until an hour ago. If she'd seen him on the street, she'd never have given him a second look. Worse, she would have pretended she didn't see him at all. Their meeting was a fluke, an aberration. And it might just change her life. She felt like it already had.

King had made her feel this way once, she reminded herself, trying to cool her ardor, worried that she was on the edge of losing control. She had felt the same bang inside of her with King. She remembered it vividly. She had been convinced, without conscious thought, that everything in her life up to that point had been an electric thread carrying her to him. Oscar Desario, the king of love, had her face in his hands, and he turned and moved slowly down the hall of the apartment he rented on Jones Street, leaving one hand behind on her cheek until his arm reached its limit and the palm released with a tiny pop of suction. The fingers grazed her bottom lip and then they were gone, too, trailing the rest of King down the hall. She followed, of course. He never had any doubt that she would, and neither did she. She walked down the hallway as if hypnotized, every part of her body tingling, the core of her on fire.

She was eighteen years old and she was innocent. Actually innocent. She thought about that now and couldn't believe it. There were plenty of boys in high school who would have loved to put their hands all over her, but she had been too scared. She couldn't even look them in the eye—how could she let them reach under her shirt, put their lips on hers?

She remembered touching the knob of King's bedroom door, which stood half-open. She had been in the apartment once before, earlier in the week, and she had looked in the bedroom after using the toilet. She had pushed the door open and saw the double bed in the corner, the expensive stereo system on the shelf above it, the framed posters for *Hair*, his radio show, and the Who, his favorite band. A photograph of a pretty blond girl stood on the top of the cheap, chipped dresser. She didn't dare ask who the girl was; she hoped it was his sister.

She stepped into the room for the second time knowing exactly what was going to happen. This time she didn't see the posters or the blond girl in the frame or the expensive stereo. She saw only King Desario, naked, standing in front of his bed. He had just pushed his underwear off his hips. It had dropped to his feet, and he flung it with his toes. It flipped in the air before parachuting to the floor near a half-full laundry basket. She looked at him, at all of him. She'd never seen a naked man in the flesh before. She stared at the hard, bumpy ribbon of his abs, before her gaze continued farther down. "Here I am," she said, feeling a blob of sweat drop out of her right armpit and roll down her side.

She wasn't sweating now, out in the open air, the tang of salt water in her nose. She wasn't nervous. She'd had sex with two men other than King in the past year—sordid, unsatisfying, cheater's sex, one-offs both times, just to prove she could do it with someone else. One of them was her boss, with his bad breath huffing in her ear as he leaned back in his leather executive chair. The other had been Larry, the resort's travel agent, who always called her *darling*, never her given name. But it would be different with Jackson, she told herself. This time she was in the clear. She'd broken up with King. Left him on the side of the road. She could enjoy herself and her body's sensations with whoever she wanted, whenever she wanted. She could do *anything*. The world was hers. Light-headed, from drink or her liberation or both, she stumbled, and Jackson caught her like she weighed nothing at all. She rolled in his arms. She couldn't ever remember being so happy.

She didn't hear the man at first, but she felt Jackson stiffen.

"Yeah, you," the voice said, rough and rural. She didn't have to see the man to know what he looked like. He would have a square head with reddish-blond hair cut tight to the skull. He would have soft, girly lips, like a retard or Mick Jagger. He would be strong, but his muscle already would be halfway turned to fat. He played football in high school—he was a star—but that was a long time ago. He would be wearing Bermuda shorts with white socks and a too-tight white undershirt.

"Let that lady go," the man said.

Janice felt herself swing upright. Jackson placed her on her feet, steadied her with a hand, and stepped away from her. Janice could now see who was addressing them. It wasn't just some redneck with a hard-on. It was a man in a dark uniform—a cop.

"Yes, sir," Jackson said. "There's no problem, officer."

Janice, confused by what was happening, heard something strange in Jackson's voice. Fear.

"Put your hands on your head," the officer said.

"What's going on here?" Janice heard herself say. She felt fear take hold of her, too. All at once she had to pee.

"Quiet, Miss," the cop said, holding out his left hand like a stop sign.

"Did we do something wrong?" she said.

The cop's face swiveled to her, the eyes narrowing in anger and—there was no other possibility—hate. "Do not speak, ma'am," he said.

Janice realized that the cop's right hand was on his holster. She brought her hands up to her face, and she noticed there was another man behind the cop, another police officer.

Jackson raised his hands over his head.

"Get down on the ground now," the cop in the front said. Jackson glanced at Janice.

"What did he do?" Janice said. She realized she was crying. "Did he do something?"

Jackson eased onto his knees. The second officer stepped forward and shoved him down by the head, pressed his face into the pavement.

"Please tell me what's happening," Janice said, really crying now. She began to hyperventilate. She ducked her head forward. She reached into her pocket, felt nothing, and remembered she had finished off the canister. *Shit!* She couldn't let herself have an attack. She squatted and took deep, ragged breaths in between sobs. She balled her fists and pushed them into her chest as hard as she could. She stayed there, eyes closed, concentrating on her breathing. A tickle in her throat bobbed, threatening to rise up and take over, but it didn't. She'd beaten it, headed it off. She wiped at her face, swallowed, and stood.

The policemen—and Jackson—were gone.

She spun around, looking in every direction. She could see only two people, one of the couples that had been kissing by the water. They watched her with concerned eyes but said nothing.

"Where'd they go?" she asked.

The woman glanced at her man, back to Janice, and pointed toward the hotel above them.

Janice realized what she must look like to these people: eyes bugged out, smeared makeup, hair helter-skelter. Jesus, she thought, what difference did that make? She raced along the path toward the hotel, bounded up the stairs, and wheeled around the corner. She stopped, out of breath, and saw a police cruiser idling in the hotel's car turnaround. She spotted Jackson in the back seat, his head dropped forward. A cop, a different one, almost obscenely fat, was opening the front passenger door, starting to lower himself into the seat. Janice looked around for the two officers who'd arrested Jackson, but she didn't see them. They must be foot patrol, she thought. They must have called a car just to take Jackson away and now they were back on the waterfront, looking for someone else to hassle, maybe looking for her. Janice hustled toward the vehicle. She could hear the engine revving.

"Wait! Wait!" she called out, watching the cruiser bend from the cop's weight. She grabbed hold of the door before he could pull it shut.

The officer, startled, looked up. "Step away from the car, ma'am," he said.

"Please . . . please . . ." She didn't know what to say. "Can you tell me what he did?"

The cop looked up at her with his small, watery eyes. Janice understood the look immediately: he knew who she was, and he felt pity for her. The man blinked heavily, then flicked his head at the back of the car, at Jackson. "Someone like this . . ." he said. "You have to be careful. Some men want to take advantage of a pretty girl like yourself."

Janice felt her face get hot. "Excuse me?"

"Let this be a lesson," he said.

"But . . . what's going to happen to him?"

The cop shrugged. "Night in jail. 'Les you want to come down and make a statement."

Janice gawped at him, and he shrugged again. "You should consider yourself lucky," he said, easing the door shut.

Janice couldn't believe what she had just heard. This cop thought she was a whore. He thought Jackson was planning to bed her and maybe rob her, that he didn't care about her at all. This fat bastard cop who probably couldn't find his pecker with a magnifying glass. She wanted to spit in his fat goddamn face.

"Walter Lame?"

Janice turned. She found Jackson peering at her through the car's back window, his eyes like saucers.

"What?" she said, putting a hand to the glass as the car began to pull away from the curb. Had they beaten him? Was he incoherent?

"What's your last name?" he shouted through the window.

Janice saw the fat officer turn around in his seat, no doubt to tell Jackson to pipe down. The car angled toward the driveway and gained speed. My God, she thought, panicked. He really does like me.

"Littlepaugh!" she yelled. She started to jog after the cruiser. "L-i-t-t . . ." The car rolled out of the turnaround and headed down the driveway. She couldn't tell if Jackson was looking at her through the back window. The vehicle slipped from view.

CHAPTER TWENTY-FIVE

They gathered in clumps on the sidewalk. One small group clasped hands when the corpses were finally brought out. Alice Krendel's bare right leg had fallen free of the plastic covering. There was a dark bruise on her kneecap. Everyone stared, unable to look away as they knew they should. One man raised his hands to the sky, to the heavens, and began to loudly chant as the deputies put Alice's body into the back of the vehicle. Once the bodies had been driven away, none of the gawkers wanted to be there anymore, standing around with nothing to say to one another. But they couldn't bring themselves to leave.

Around them, the little downtown was returning to normal. Other than the gaggle on the sidewalk, few people knew what had happened at the bank. Most of Mammoth View's citizens were happy to be home after a panicked day driving around Bakersfield or Los Angeles. Cruising down Main Street in their pickups and station wagons and Continentals, they honked their horns at neighbors and waved. Winnie raised her hand reflexively at the sound as she stepped into the street, but she couldn't match Arlen Thomas's smile as he rolled past in his Dodge. How rude he must think I am, she told herself. She turned at Third, heading for Main. She had assumed she needed to be alone after her ordeal, but she discovered she couldn't bear it. The silence in the house had pressed against her ears, the lack of movement in the rooms made her flinch every time she looked up. She hoped Angelo's was open. She'd sit at the bar, by herself but surrounded by the soft, comforting murmur of other people's conversations. She flinched as a bird or a bat swooped down from a rooftop. It shot across the street and disappeared under an eave. Ahead, near the bank, dulled human reflexes tried to keep up with the creature, swiveling to follow it. The movement made Winnie realize something was up. She spotted Frank Durr, Ben and Sharon Langely, and a dozen more, all gathered as a group. Some of them held hands, comforting each other. Winnie's stomach dropped. Could they know what had happened to her?

She stopped and took stock. She was wearing bell-bottomed jeans and a white T-shirt with an image of Tweety Bird on the chest. Hair pulled back into a ponytail. No makeup. She'd go on anyway, she decided. Deflect their questions, accept their concern but tell them it wasn't as bad as they'd heard. She'd confront Marco tomorrow about why he'd told everyone.

"Winnie, it's so awful," Sharon Langely said, taking Winnie's hands in hers.

Winnie started to dismiss Sharon's concerns, but the words stuck in her chest. Panic seized her, followed by a strange, discombobulated feeling. No one else was looking at her. Ben had glanced away, his eyes flicking over his shoulder. He always looked angry, she thought. Deep creases streaked horizontally from the corners of his eyes, demarcating his face into two halves, the lid and the container. With a jolt, Winnie realized this gathering wasn't because of her.

"What's happened?" she asked.

Tears bubbled in Sharon's eyes. Her round, middle-aged face shone in the streetlight. "There's been a bank robbery," she said. "You haven't talked to Johnny? Alice Krendel is dead . . ."

"Oh, no," Winnie said.

". . . and the bank manager. Mister—I don't know. What is his name, Ben?"

Ben swung his head around. He shrugged.

A pounding rhythm filled Winnie's head. Her eyes lost focus, and she gripped Sharon's hands to steady herself. "Was it the Johnsons?"

"That bastard Melvin Johnson is no good," Ben said, the hatred filling his pupils. "The other one's a dummy. The chief and your husband are after them. But you must know that."

"Yes, yes," she said. "I didn't know about this, though. Dear God."

Dead, Winnie thought. Sweet Alice Krendel was dead. Alice Krendel, who could never hurt a fly, who couldn't even look at you straight on.

"Oh, darling girl," Sharon said, grabbing Winnie by the shoulders and pulling her into a motherly hug. "He was just trying to protect you. He doesn't want you to know there's such evil in the world."

"If you watch the evening news, you can be under no illusions about that," Ben said.

Winnie stepped back from Sharon's embrace. She didn't want to ask for details, but she wanted to know. She wanted to know what the Johnsons were capable of doing, what she had just barely avoided. What had they done to poor Alice before putting her out of her misery?

"I'm not feeling well," Winnie said. "I shouldn't have come out."

"Of course, dear. Of course. We'll walk you home, won't we, Ben?"

Ben looked up. "Yes, sure."

"Thank you, but I'm fine on my own. It's just a few blocks."

"Let's us walk with you—you can't be too careful," Sharon said.

"No, no, thank you. Really. The Johnsons are long gone. I'm fine."

"You never can be sure."

"We should let her be, if that's what she wants," Ben said. He put his hand on his wife's forearm.

Winnie smiled, thanked them again. She turned and headed back the way she had come. She bypassed Third, deciding to take the long way around. She wasn't afraid. She felt confident the Johnsons were indeed long gone—and that Johnny and the chief would track them down. Johnny was a stud, she thought. He understood human nature; he understood the way people thought when they were panicking. He'd find them. He'd make them pay.

She wondered if she'd have to testify at the trial. They'd punched her smack in the face and dragged her away, thrown her in the trunk of a car. Those were serious crimes. They hadn't succeeded in raping her, so maybe there'd be no need to bring that up. You couldn't prove something that hadn't actually happened; it wouldn't be allowed in court. She didn't want her parents to know that the dumb one had torn her blouse and yanked her pants down. That he'd been so excited he'd snorted like a pig. She couldn't help thinking about what would have happened if the chief hadn't arrived. How much would she have fought? Could she have fought him off?

The road rose as she headed out of downtown, and she leaned into it. The pressure in her knees vibrated up her legs. Houses stutter-stepped up the hill with her, close together. People sometimes opened their windows to talk to their next-door neighbors—it was considered perfectly normal. Most of the front doors along this block weren't even locked, she knew. Nobody worried about crime here, at least not during the off-season. That's how it was in a town where everybody knew everybody.

When she and Johnny moved to Mammoth View, she figured he would soon grow bored and would want to move on, that he'd find a position in a police department in a real city, a place with culture. But now, quite suddenly, things had gotten interesting for him. And, to her surprise, she realized she didn't want to leave—or at least she wasn't entirely sure about it. She'd grown to like Mammoth View. What was so wrong with the slow pace of life here? This was a good place to raise a child. She stretched her hands over her head, reaching for the sky. Trees—the forest—rose behind the houses like a huge barrier, as if the town was walled off from the rest of the world. If only that were so. It really was beautiful here. The most beautiful place she'd ever been.

At the top of the rise, she turned and looked back over the little downtown. The rooftops spiked and dipped under the blue-black sky. Beyond, Winnie's eyes caught a flash, a speck in the moonlight. She squinted, trying to make out what she was seeing. Was it two specks? She searched for the hiking trail that fell from the mountain like a waterfall and circled Mammoth View, but it was difficult in the darkness, with only the moonlight to guide her. The muscles in her stomach clenched. The Johnson brothers had sneaked back into the town. They were coming for her. Fear sucked the air out of her lungs. She couldn't feel her legs, couldn't say for sure her feet were planted on the ground.

She squatted and put her face in her hands. She was seeing things, phantoms, she told herself. Take a deep breath. Deep goddamn breaths. She crossed herself. Forgive me, Father. She wiped tears from the corners of her eyes and flung them into the dark. She stood and took a deep breath. The Johnsons were miles away, out in the forest running for their lives. Johnny was after them. She had nothing to worry about. Those creeps didn't even know her name.

She started to walk. She decided this was a good example of why her parents should have had another child. She'd longed for an older sister throughout her adolescence—a confident, popular girl who would ease Winnie's way with teachers and give her advice about boys. She longed for one even more in adulthood. She needed someone—a woman—she could trust absolutely. A sister would answer the phone and wouldn't be angry with her no matter how late she called. A sister would soothe her when she began to cry and know just what to say. Winnie would be able to unburden herself to a sibling. Her sister would understand what she was feeling right now, would tell her it was perfectly normal, that she'd been through a terrible trauma and she was okay.

On cue, a tear fell out of her eye and bounced down her face. She let it roll all the way to her jaw. No use crying over spilt milk, her father used to say to her, but Winnie didn't agree. Spilt milk, a bad grade, a lost love, a missed opportunity—the only things worth crying over were the things you couldn't change.

She'd almost gone all the way with a boy long before she met Johnny. Dear me! Why was she thinking of that now? Gus Mannarino. The beginning of her sophomore year. He had used his finger on her until she'd screamed out involuntarily, screamed in ecstasy and fear and shame. Winnie stopped in her tracks, the night air hanging heavy on her. She squeezed her fists into her eyes. He was the RA in the dorm next to hers. A tall, skinny kid with a cloud of bouncy black curls. She and Danielle met him in the shared laundry room. He brought a six-pack to their room later, and the three of them had cracked open the suds and talked about their classes and Creedence Clearwater Revival. When Dannie left for choral practice, it was just the two of them, smiling at each other from opposite ends of her bed. The next day she had no idea how things had gotten so hot and heavy, but she remembered vividly the effort it took to ask him to stop. It took everything she had. He had stopped at once, smiling at her the whole time as he put his shoes on. When he closed the door behind him, Winnie sat there alone, physically drained, feeling herself leaking onto her bedspread, wondering where her underwear had gone. She expected him to call her for a date in a day or two, or to stop by again with more beer, but he never did. In the months that followed she saw him every once in a while, walking into or out of his building. One time, she spotted him with a girl, a short, stocky, black-haired girl with a bowl haircut. If he noticed Winnie watching them, he didn't give any indication.

She trudged on, cresting the top of the incline and falling gawkily into the descent. The houses here were all two stories, clapboard, with winking eaves and gaudy wraparound porches that chased the sunlight through the day. She and Johnny rented one of the smaller houses in the neighborhood. It was poorly constructed, put together seemingly without the aid of architectural plans. At the top of the stairs to the second floor, Johnny had to duck or he'd hit his head on the ceiling. Half the time he still forgot. Catching sight of the house, Winnie reached under her shirt and cupped her belly. They would have to move, of course. Those stairs were too steep, too dangerous, for a toddler.

Winnie rubbed her stomach some more, tried to gauge if it was rounder—bigger—than normal. She didn't think so. It had always pooched out a bit, a soft and smooth mound. If she'd had her heart set on being a Playboy centerfold she would have had to do something about that, work with a medicine ball or whatever, but Johnny seemed to like her just as she was. She tried to picture herself with a huge, pregnant belly. The roll and bounce of it, her breasts swollen and her face flushed. The thought of it made her smile.

She was still pure, she thought. There was still only Johnny, her first time being on their wedding night as God intended, on that hard, narrow hotel bed overlooking the Columbia River Gorge. Today had been close with that man—Gordon. Gordon Johnson. But not as close as with Gus Mannarino, and she'd never counted that, either. Close only counted in horseshoes, she thought. Her father said that one, too; he said it all the time. He was full of stupid sayings.

She hopped up the step to the front door, walked in, and locked the door behind her, the first time she'd locked it in weeks. She checked every room, every closet and window. She looked behind the shower curtain in the bathroom and left the curtain pulled back, the tub exposed. She noted that from the hallway she could see the empty tub in the bathroom mirror. She sat in the living room, looked out on the dark, empty street, and breathed. The phone lay on the table next to her, within easy reach. The front window was cracked open, allowing the night air to infuse the room, to insinuate itself along her bare arms and ankles.

The baby inside of her was so quiet and still that Winnie

strained to believe it was really in there. She slipped her hands under the shirt again, felt the warmth coming off her flesh. Her belly *was* rounder, she decided. The baby was in there, all right, sleeping safely—while its father was miles away, deep in the forest, unreachable.

Who would she call if the Johnsons came banging through the door? Winnie stewed on that for a minute. She didn't want to have to call anybody. She should be able to look after herself, to protect her child on her own. Johnny kept a gun in his bedside table, under his men's magazines. Winnie went into the bedroom, kneeled down, and pulled open the drawer. She hefted the revolver in her right hand and managed to heave open the chamber. Empty. She looked around; there were no bullets in the drawer. Where would he keep the ammunition? She peered at the closed closet door where his extra uniforms hung but decided not to open it. She placed the gun back where she found it, put the latest magazine on top. The girl on the cover leered lasciviously, daring Winnie to admire her cleavage. She ignored the girl, closed the drawer.

Back in the front room, she stared out the window. Maybe she should learn karate, she thought. She felt herself nodding. Yes, there had to be classes she could take in Bakersfield. She imagined herself flying through the air like Bruce Lee. If he could do it, so could she. She leaned back and kicked out with her right foot. The movement felt good. She was still limber; she could get her leg shoulder-high without any effort at all. She'd go to the library in the morning, ask for the Bakersfield phone book. The thought of doing it, of making a call to a dojo and signing up for a class, sent a satisfying jolt through her. She loved Johnny, but she wanted to take care of herself.

CHAPTER TWENTY-SIX

The car door swung open and creaked on its hinges. Tori hid behind her hair.

"Come on, now, hon. Come out of there."

Tori closed her eyes and pretended not to hear. She had pretended for the whole five hours she'd been in the car, except for when she needed to pee or was hungry.

The woman sighed. "You're acting like a little baby. You're not a baby. You're seven years old."

"I'm not seven," Tori said.

The woman waited, and Tori waited.

"You're going to like it better if you get out on your own," the woman said.

They went through this same routine when they stopped for lunch, and the woman was right. Tori pushed herself off the seat and stepped down from the car. The air in Phoenix was cool and heavy. She didn't like what she saw. The world looked like it had been erased, leaving only the dull shadow of what should be there. Her feet wobbled on the gravel that filled the driveway. The front yard was barren, a moonscape except for a green-brown stump here and there, a stone pathway cutting through it. The adobe house was short and bent, a house for the old lady in the shoe.

"This is grandma's house?" Tori asked.

"Yes, it is," the woman said.

"Where's my grandma?"

"I'm your grandmother," the woman said, indignant. "I told you that."

Tori stared at a window along the side of the house; it was the only window with any light coming from it. She turned and looked up at the woman. "Yeah, but you're not my grandmother. My grandmother lives on Bear Road."

"That's your other grandmother, dear. That's your daddy's mother. I'm your mother's mother."

"My mother's dead," Tori said.

The woman kneeled and took Tori's shoulders in her hands. "I know that, dear. It's very sad."

"So you can't be my grandmother."

The woman stood up and snatched Tori's hand. "Come on, let's go inside."

Inside was where they kept all the color in Phoenix. Red walls gave over to blue walls and then yellow walls. Green curtains hung in the living room. The room where they put her suitcase also had green curtains, along with a tightly made single bed, a small desk, a drawing board and a set of shelves. Tori started to cry. She blinked to make them disappear, but that only forced them down her face.

"Oh, dear," the woman said. She moved around Tori, into the room, and grabbed a picture frame from the desk. Tori saw the picture before the woman pressed it to her hip. Her mother. *That isn't why I'm crying*, she wanted to say. She saw pictures of her dead mother every day.

"This is a nice room, don't you think?" the woman said.

"Yes."

"All right then. I'm glad we can agree on something." The suitcase was on the bed, and the woman unzipped it and began to search the front pocket.

"When's my dad coming?"

The woman glanced over her shoulder to offer a disapproving look before returning to what she was doing. "Your father," she said, "isn't welcome here."

Standing in the doorway, Tori watched the woman rifle through her clothes, and in her mind she watched her father looking through the house for her, calling out her name. She squeezed her hands into fists. More than anything she wanted to run, and so she did. She bolted from the room, tore down the hallway, yanked open the front door. She'd so surprised the woman that as she ran past the room's window, out in the street, Tori saw that she was still in there, looking around the door toward the hallway. Was the woman calling her name? Tori didn't hear anything. She raced to the corner, turned, and kept going.

She could do that same thing right now, she thought. Just take off running. The men would be so shocked that they wouldn't do anything. They'd know right away they couldn't catch her, that no one could catch her. She looked over her shoulder. Gordon was still clutching the gun in his hand. He spun it on his finger like a Wild West gunfighter. She looked over the other shoulder: The meaner one, Melvin, plodded on, mumbling to himself, his shirt still balled up in his hand and pressed against his head. The shirt was soaked in blood. Tori had a headache that she attributed to the crash, but at least she wasn't bleeding. She watched Melvin's belly shake and bounce with every step. She studied the intricate weaving of hair that flowed around his navel and swept upward to overwhelm his chest. Her father had hair along the stomach and chest, but Melvin's was another four or five levels of magnitude. Tori wondered if that meant the man's family had evolved less from the apes, that he had more physical strength and less intelligence. Melvin adjusted the shirt and muttered something.

The woman did catch up to her, of course. Tori remembered it with the pure clarity of a nightmare. The woman pulled the car alongside her about three blocks from the house, rolled down the passenger-side window, and ordered her to get in. Tori kept walking, her head down. Tears started to fall from her eyes in skittering dribbles, and she swiped at her nose with a forearm.

"Do you want to be in big trouble, young lady?" the woman barked.

Who was she talking to? Tori wondered. She marched on. Her breathing had begun to sputter. She coughed on the snot rolling down her throat, stumbled over her own feet as she tried to squeeze off the tears with some mighty blinking.

The car sped ahead of her, pulled to the curb, and the woman got out. The woman grabbed her by the arm and pulled. Tori let herself go slack, and she fell, swinging on the woman's arm like Tarzan in the jungle. Her heels scraped the asphalt, and the woman grunted in surprise and effort. The woman stabilized herself, took hold of Tori under both arms, and dragged her. Tori offered no resistance and said nothing. She gazed up at the blue, cloudless sky. A pick-up truck jangled toward them and slowed, the driver giving them a good long look. The woman shifted, humped Tori's weight to her right arm, and waved at the pick-up with the other one. The truck accelerated, made a lazy right turn at the end of the block.

Back at the house, Tori sat at a small table in the kitchen nook, unspeaking, for hours. The woman didn't give her a glass of milk or graham crackers or anything. An old man walked through a couple of times. He didn't say anything to her. The third time he came through he put a Scrabble board on the table. He didn't ask her if she wanted to play. He turned and left the room. She dropped her head back, closed her eyes, and began to count. She counted and counted until she lost track. She was thinking about starting over when she heard a thump on the door. She opened her eyes and saw that it was dark outside. A few minutes later, Billy stepped into the kitchen and smiled at Tori.

"Hey, kid," he said.

"Hi."

"You want to go home?"

Tori started to cry. "Yes."

"Okay, let's go."

Tori put her hands to her eyes and pushed to hold off more tears. The pain as she pressed her fingers against her eyeballs felt strangely satisfying. She glanced over her shoulder again at Gordon. He was walking with his head down, trying to ignore the other one's cursing, probably because he knew it was directed at him. The other one, Melvin, had turned around in his seat to tell Gordon to trust him, and that was why he had lost control of the car. The vehicle had barely missed ramming a tree, glanced it instead, and ended up on the shoulder of the road, turned all the way around and with two wheels off the ground. Gordon somehow hadn't been injured at all and pulled Tori out through the window. Melvin managed to get the front door open and stepped free of the wreck. He had banged against something when the Eldorado swung around. Blood oozed down the side of his head, dripped off the back of his ear.

The three of them had shuffled down an incline, pushed into the woods and started walking, even though they could barely see more than a few feet in front of them. Melvin had been through all of this more than once over the past hour. He made Tori stay a couple of steps ahead of them so they could keep an eye on her in the moonlight as the two men bickered over the car crash.

It was a warm evening but shivers raced through Tori's body, making it difficult to breathe. She understood what was happening. Fear was making her system shut down. She knew what these two men were going to do to her. They were going to beat her and rape her, and probably leave her in the woods to die. The thought of it made her retch and she bent forward. Her legs felt like logs, and she feared they were going to stop working altogether and she'd fall over. She pictured the men kicking her in the stomach and the head, yelling at her to get up. She straightened herself, sensing that they had also stopped and were watching her carefully. She thought again about making a break for it, but she wasn't sure she was capable. And she wasn't sure it would matter. Gordon held the pistol in his right hand; he continued to twirl it on his index finger, three revolutions forward and then three back. Tori was staring at it out of the corner of her eye when it whipped up and exploded. Stunned, Tori threw herself at the ground. She landed on her stomach and knees, and the pain of the landing made her jerk into a fetal position.

"Yes, sir! I got it!" Gordon yelled. "You see that thing spin? It was just like that dog!" He cackled, high and loud.

"Goddamn it, Gordon, what's the matter with you?" Melvin was brandishing the sopping shirt at his brother like a lightning bolt.

Gordon turned toward his brother, confused and defensive. "I'm just trying to have some fun. Everything's so serious."

Melvin threw his shirt at him in strangled fury. It fluttered in the air and fell well short of its intended target. "We crashed the car—which was your goddamn fault—and we're on the run from the law. So, yeah, I don't want to hear any knock-knock jokes right now."

Gordon bit down on his left hand, pouting.

"You, Missy," Melvin snapped. "Go pick that thing up."

Tori did a double take. "Me? Pick what up?"

"The possum. The *possum*."

Tori followed Melvin's pointing finger and spotted a dead animal smashed against a tree. It looked like a huge rat. She looked away, and the movement made her dizzy. "I can't."

"Oh, yes, you can."

"What do you want me to do with it?" she finally said.

Melvin sighed in irritation. "Pick. It. Up."

Gordon raised the gun. "Go on, pick it up. *Missy*."

Tori stepped over to the opossum and kneeled down. The animal had been hit above its back legs, paralyzing it, but it was still alive, curled in on itself. Its black eyes jumped helplessly. Smoke from the wound, or mist from the night, hovered around its head. Tori's heart clanged in her chest, her hands shook. She just wanted to be a normal girl, she thought. She wanted to have a normal father. And a boyfriend and a proper first kiss. She started to reach out for the animal, but an invisible barrier—her revulsion—stopped her. She lost her balance, screeched in panic, and fell backward, wrenching her spine. Shoving off with her feet, she violently pushed herself away from the opossum as if it were attacking her.

"Goddamn it," Melvin said. He marched over to the animal, noted that it was still breathing, and stepped down on its neck. He picked it up by the tail and held it in front of Tori's face. "This is dinner, Missy, and now you ain't getting any of it."

That was fine by her. Tori got to her feet, looked at Melvin and the opossum, and then at Gordon and the gun. There had to be a way to make this all go away, she thought. She shut her eyes and started counting.

"Go on, get moving," Melvin said, and gave her a push with an open palm.

They walked for another forty minutes until they came upon a fallen tree, and Melvin decided they'd found the right place to settle for the night. He tossed the animal corpse on the ground and indicated that Tori should sit on the tree trunk. Tori sat as commanded and hugged herself, squeezing her knees together so hard she felt it in her throat. Melvin sat down next to her.

"What do you think, Missy? These accommodations not as good as you're used to? Far as I'm concerned, it's the Taj Mahal. Because the law is after us, but it doesn't matter. Because there's no law out here. Except the law of the jungle. You heard of that?"

Tori nodded.

"No laws!" Melvin suddenly cried out, thumping his chest. He rubbed her shoulder, just to show her he could, and stood up. "*I'm* the law. You got that?" He moved away from her, unzipping his pants. He started peeing as he was walking away.

Gordon seemed to sense Tori needed comforting. He sat next to her, right where Melvin had been sitting. "You're going to be one of us," he whispered. "You'll learn." Melvin heard the whispering, zipped up, and marched back to them. He stepped up close to Tori, squatted, and put his hands on her, kneaded her flesh, her most private places. Tori closed her eyes, forced herself not to scream. Gordon stared like a hungry dog, and Melvin kept it up until he could tell his brother was in distress.

He let go of Tori and stood up. "We'll find you a girl," he told Gordon. "But not this one. You got that?"

Tori screamed—she couldn't help it—as Melvin's knees buckled. Melvin disappeared from Tori's line of vision. He was on the ground, with another man on top of him, arms flailing. It was King! King had come out of nowhere, hitting Melvin under the ribcage with his head and shoulder. Now Melvin yelled, too— "Ahhhhh!"—as he tried to orient himself and figure out what had happened. Gordon turned toward the noise, confused, and raised the pistol. Without even thinking, Tori swung her elbow, catching Gordon in the cheek. He fell backward off the tree trunk and dropped the gun. Tori leapt and grabbed it.

Gordon sat up and put his arms out at his sides, as if he were pretending to be an airplane. He looked at her, this time without any lust. Tori leveled the gun and dropped into a crouch.

She thought about being at the shooting range with her father, both of them wearing those heavily cushioned earmuffs. "Yes!" her father barked whenever she hit the mark, causing a feeling of pride and happiness to course through her. She was doing this for him, shooting at these paper targets because he needed her to be strong for him—for *them*. Because all they had was each other. He never said that, but he didn't have to. She knew. Who else would do this for him? Who else would save his life? Who else expected her to? They rehearsed what she would do if more men came to the door asking for him. The gun was always the last resort, for DEFCON 1 only, but it was there in the desk drawer, always loaded, ready to go.

The pistol shook in her hands. She considered her technique: she had both hands on the handle, arms locked, crouched as if about to sit in a straight-back chair. It didn't matter. Her hands shook. The gun shook. This was nothing like being at the shooting range. She was having trouble breathing. She was having trouble holding her arms up. She couldn't do it, she realized. She couldn't shoot this man, no matter what he was going to do to her. No matter what he had already done. She just couldn't do it. She backed up, stutter-stepped. She took in the scene, trying to figure out what was happening. King was on top of Melvin, but it didn't look like that was going to last.

She reeled then, like a planet knocked out of orbit. Gordon had whacked her and was now scrambling in the dirt. He was going for the gun. She'd dropped it as she crashed to the ground.

"Run!" King yelled at her. "Go, go, go!"

Tori staggered to her feet as Gordon grabbed onto the gun. Without even thinking she thrust her right foot up and out, just like she remembered the blond guy in the movie *Breaker! Breaker!* doing, putting everything she had into the kick. Gordon flailed backward, his free hand grabbing at the air for balance. She couldn't believe she did that! She watched in wonderment as Gordon fell. The sounds over by the tree trunk snapped her out of her self-pride. She wheeled around and spotted Melvin and King. Melvin had flipped King over and was trying to get a good punch at him. Tori kicked again, this time like a field-goal kicker. She caught Melvin in the forehead. He thrashed like a hooked shark, and King twisted his torso, trying to extricate himself from Melvin's limbs. Tori followed his eyes to Gordon, who was upright again, gun still in hand. The gun went off, cracking across the sky like timpani just as Melvin hit King with a roundhouse right.

Tori, blinded by a flash of panic, took off as if reacting to a mechanical rabbit. She crashed into a tree, fought to stay upright, and kept running. Her shoulder throbbed, the panic pulled on her legs like an undertow. The trees and the sky—everywhere she looked—shook out of control. She realized she was on her knees, and so she scrabbled with her hands, digging her nails into the earth, forcing herself upright, forcing her legs to move again. Had Gordon shot King? Was he going to shoot *her*?

Tori stumbled into a clearing. She recognized where she was. She had run through here every morning for the past two weeks. She could find her way with her eyes closed. She closed her eyes and picked up the pace. She felt the wind whipping around her, its coolness gliding over her skin. Her legs loosened up, her arms pumped. Muscle memory kicked in. She made it to the other side in no time at all and ducked into a stand of trees. She was the fastest girl in the world, she told herself. Faster than Mary Decker could ever hope to be. Faster than Wilma Rudolph. Faster than the Kalenjin.

Except she could hear Gordon behind her. Crashing through the woods like a wildebeest. This mountain man in his lumberjack boots was *gaining* on her. How was that possible?

Tori felt her throat closing up. Her stomach bounced in panic, and she tasted bile in the back of her mouth. She forced her left knee higher with her next stride. She pulled her shoulders back. She knew she needed perfect form to survive; she needed to be perfect. Sure, Gordon was bigger than her—yes, he was much stronger. But she was lithe; she was as light as air. No way he could match her in a foot race. No one could. She was Flash! She was Mercury! She pictured herself turning into the home stretch at the Olympics. Mary Decker was a step behind and kicking for the finish, now two strides behind, now four. It was all in the mind, Coach Berman told her. Success was mental, not physical. It was all about belief. Tori dug deep, deeper than she ever had before. Her mind jumped, unbidden, to her first full day at Spritle's, her first group run with the girls. For five miles she bounded along in the middle of the pack, nice and easy, her confidence growing—expanding, exploding—until she felt invincible. She *belonged* here; she was just like these girls, these beautiful gazelles. She even allowed herself to enjoy the scenery: the trees across the valley stacked in perfect order, the distant mountains with their white tops, the blue-gray sky that swirled up and up to infinity. "New girl. You okay?" Mary Bowen said.

"Yes," Tori huffed, grateful for the concern. "Doing fine."

"You sure?" Mary asked again, her voice reverberating with the pounding of her feet.

"Yes. Thank you."

"Let's see about that." Mary took off, her shoes rudely throwing dirt high in the air. The others had started to move away too, right on cue. Shocked, Tori picked up her pace as well, but the gazelles stayed ahead—and kept extending their lead. Breath banged in Tori's throat; her legs refused to pump. Gravity held her like a wet coat. She wondered, terrified, if she could find her way back to the camp on her own.

A hand grabbed her shoulder and immediately lost the grip. She couldn't believe it; Gordon had caught her. Tori tried to turn on the afterburners, but her legs ached. They had begun to go numb. She wobbled, and the hand grabbed again, this time snagging a tricep. Tori screamed, and her stomach collapsed, caving in on itself like a coal-mine disaster. She lost her balance and threw her arms out to save herself from crashing into a tree. The hand grabbed again as she tumbled forward, all momentum gone, but she fought on, swinging her body violently to break free.

"Whoa! Whoa! It's okay. It's me!"

Tori recognized the voice. It was King, not Gordon. Tori pulled up, came to a stop. A shiver ran through her body. Her extremities tingled with relief. She gagged and felt the burn in her throat. She and King leaned into each other, hands on knees, sucking air.

"You were really moving," he said between huffs of breath. "If you hadn't fallen back there . . ."

"I'm a runner," she said.

King nodded, still struggling to control his breathing. "I ran the four-hundred meters in high school. Almost went to State my senior year."

"That's pretty good." Tori silently thanked God he was a runner too. She wouldn't have to kill herself now.

King stood up, looked back the way they had come. "Maybe this isn't the time to stroll down memory lane. You hear that?"

Tori cocked her head. A rustling? Voices? She couldn't be sure.

"Those hillbillies don't look like they can move too swiftly," King said. "But they've got a gun." He turned to Tori. "Can you run some more?"

Tori nodded.

"Okay. Follow me."

King led Tori to the south, away from the mountain, heading downhill. The landscape dropped gently but consistently. King jogged this way and that through the thin pines, trying to save his knees, before he finally found what he was looking for: a path that weaved down the mountain, one hairpin turn spinning into another, like a packed-dirt version of San Francisco's Lombard Street. He knew it would eventually flatten out and connect with a paved path that stretched past the Krendel orchard, crossed a stream, and circled downtown Mammoth View before continuing on to Kingsburg.

Kristi Sasaki had told him about her mountain jogging route, and he'd gone out to the path a couple of times in hopes of running into her so he could impress her with his health-consciousness and see where that led. He heard Tori bounding down the path after him, her breath bouncing with the angle of the slope. He gazed at the treetops rolling out below them. If memory served, it was about two miles into town. He slowed, pacing himself, confident the hillbillies were far away and would never find them. The two of them ran in silence for a while before the forest opened up and spat out a subdivision.

King came out on a narrow private road that fronted one and two-car garages. Turning a corner onto a residential street, he and Tori hustled past dark, featureless adobe houses. The night air had the unmistakable feel of moisture in it, cool and heavy. He guessed they were about a mile from his house, maybe a little more. Tori came up beside him. The girl was the real deal, King could tell. He watched her pass him. She'd been holding herself back all the way into the town but she couldn't do it anymore. At the end of the next block, King had to guide her by grunting for her attention and pointing. King wanted to take the lead again, to be the man, but by this time he was straining, wiped out.

He ignored the dark houses on each side of the road, the

curtained windows and the emptiness beyond them. The town was still vacant, a ghost town. He tried not to think about it. He needed to focus his mind only on the task before him, on the process and mechanics of running.

He zeroed in on the soles of the girl's shoes kicking up at him. She was a machine, he thought. This was how an android would run. Her buttocks rolled like an axial ball bearing, tilting into turns and then righting themselves into perfect alignment. King was transfixed—he could admit it, even if she was a teenager—but his physical limitations, his straining lungs and pounding heart, kept him from truly appreciating the sight. He now decided that the girl wasn't a piece of machinery. That was too cold, too analytical. No, she was a magical creature, a griffin or something, her feet barely touching the ground. A sudden pain jolted through his body. He stumbled, and his arms flew up, cartwheeling wildly.

"Hey," he croaked. "Hey—stop." Falling into an awkward, peacock-like stroll, he put his hands on his hips and gulped air. Sweat streamed down his face.

Tori jogged back to him, her breathing even and calm. She didn't seem to notice his distress.

King hunched over, leaned his elbows against his knees. He looked up at her, embarrassed by his huffing. What he found surprised him. The girl's face was starting to break apart right in front of him. She was going to *cry*.

King stood up, took a deep breath, and let the air whistle up through his windpipe. This was his chance to impress her, he thought, and then he immediately shook the thought away. A wave of shame rolled over him, the fear that he was a perv. He had to save this girl. That's what he was feeling, right?

He decided it was. They wouldn't go back to his house. And he wouldn't ditch her and get out of town, either. "I just realized there's a better way," he said. "Follow me." He crossed the street, trotted to the end of the block, and headed east at a slow pace. After putting a few more rural-suburban blocks behind him, he reached the still-empty Route 23. He jogged across it, Tori a step behind. He paused at East Hills Road, crouching at a row of hedges, and looked across at Second Avenue.

"What do you see?" the girl said, her voice low and anxious.

"The police are open for business," King said. "So all order hasn't collapsed."

Tori peered over the hedges. The lights blazed inside the squat building, the little downtown rising behind it. A man appeared in the front window. The badge on his chest glimmered.

King looked into Tori's face. "You okay?"

Tori nodded. "Yes."

"They'll be able to reach your father for you."

Tori nodded again. King rose and started across the street, Tori following.

They stepped into the police station, looked around. A man wearing a trooper hat and a beige uniform listened to the phone. Another in army fatigues stared at a map on the desk. King smirked to himself. Reinforcements had arrived, better late than never.

"Excuse me," King said.

The army man looked up. "Yes?"

"This girl. She's lost. She needs help finding her father."

The army man moved around the desk, levered a smile onto his face. "What's your name, sweetie?"

"Tori," she said. "Victoria Lane."

"Come on over here and have a seat. You want some pop?"

"Yes, thank you," Tori said, sitting where he'd indicated.

The soldier, heading for the soda machine, stopped in front of King. "Where'd you find her?"

"Uh, Dawes Street. She was . . . upset."

"Of course. Thanks for bringing her in. We're asking citizens to stay indoors for the time being. You live nearby?"

"Just a few blocks."

"Okay, good." He continued across the room.

King almost made it out of the building, but a voice— "Hey!"—stopped him. King recognized the voice, thought about bolting, turned instead.

Sheriff Davis had come out from the back. "You're the disc jockey," he said.

"Sorry?"

"Don't play dumb with me, son."

King let his head drop in defeat. "Yes, sir," he said.

CHAPTER TWENTY-SEVEN

Billy gripped the phone so hard his hand cramped.

"Sir," the voice said over the line. "Would you like me to repeat that?"

Billy replaced the phone in its cradle. The only message was from the Mammoth View Police. They had his daughter, Victoria, and he should call and ask for Officer Barea. Billy's hands were clammy, and he wiped them on his pants. He wondered what she did. Jesus, would she pick this day of all days to shoplift a record? His mind raced: who could go up there for him and bail her out? Who did he know that he could trust? Then it hit him. He called the service back and asked the woman to read him the message again. They had Victoria, that was all, no mention of charges. He shook out his hands and cracked his neck in an attempt to relax. They might have her for safekeeping, he realized. It was chaos in that little town. God only knew what was going on up there. He thought back to Spritle's Racers. Maybe he hadn't seen her because she wasn't there. She could have walked away from the camp. That would be just like her, he thought. Doing things her own way, looking for her own solutions, refusing to do what the authorities told her to do. He smiled to himself. She was her father's daughter. He took down the police department's phone number and hung up.

He flipped through the yellow pages on the table next to the bed. He called the Hilton, asked about rates and room security. He disconnected the line and started dialing again. He stopped when he noticed the waste bin. It was right next to the bed. Red, stringy flecks hung from the lip. He peered inside. A blob of vomit sat dully at the bottom of the can. Jesus. He'd woken up, puked, and fallen right back to sleep. Didn't remember any of it. He started dialing, and when the ringing cut out, he asked for Officer Barea. After a short conversation, he hung up and went into the bathroom to throw back some mouthwash. He checked out of the motel and drove to the Hilton.

The man at the desk, the same one he'd spoken to on the phone, had a thin, pencil-eraser face cut in two by a fat mustache. His eyes turned angry when he smiled. Billy was carrying the bag full of money, folded in half, but he still managed to look quasi-respectable. He asked for a room high up. He requested that the room receive no cleaning or turndown service. He paid for three nights upfront, cash.

Taking the key, he turned and surveyed the lobby. The overheard lights were all on, even at this late hour, which only highlighted the emptiness. Thick green carpeting rolled around faux-marble columns. Down two shallow steps lay a sitting room; a couch and two leather chairs wavered at the far end of his focus. He crossed to the elevators and punched the button, which caused the nearest set of doors to spasm open. The car stopped on the third floor, and a barefooted woman in a purple polka-dot chemise and black pajama bottoms stepped on, yawned extravagantly, and pressed the button for the fourth floor. She flinched at the sight of Billy, then quickly collected herself. She threw her shoulders back and smiled at him. "The icemaker on my floor isn't working," she said. It was a throaty, metallic voice, sexy but as false as her heavily made-up face. Billy noted that she wasn't carrying an ice bucket.

"You in town on business?"

She smiled again, pleased to have provoked interest. "Why,

yes, I am. Big meeting, big client. The whole team is here." She rolled her eyes.

She had to be mid-thirties, Billy thought, possibly more without the makeup. He guessed a divorcee. An executive assistant to some asshole.

"What's that?" she said, eyeing the big bag in his arm.

"My life's savings."

She barked out a laugh, spackling the elevator doors with spittle. "Oh, you're a funny one," the woman said.

Billy was warming to her. "How much longer you here?" he asked.

The door opened and she stepped out, half-turning back to him. "Tomorrow's our last night." She offered a conspiratorial smile. "Well, I'm right here." She pointed to the first door in the hallway. Billy nodded as the elevator doors closed.

Billy was feeling surprisingly good all at once. He replayed the woman's seal-like laugh. She reminded him of someone. He searched his memory. Right, the girl outside the bookstore last year. Jennifer . . . Jane . . . something like that. Same laugh. Same hair. Billy still had the W.I.N. button—Whip Inflation Now—that she was giving out to people. It was in an old Folgers container on his bedside table. He had promised her he would wear it if she'd have a drink with him, and of course she wore hers, too, right next to her heart, until he pulled the blouse over her head and plopped her down on his bed.

Billy couldn't believe it had been more than a year since that day. President Ford's anti-inflation campaign had failed miserably, just as everyone knew it would, despite all the free buttons. Nobody could afford to save any money. That's why decent men turned to crime. That's why Jennifer/Jane couldn't find a real job.

The elevator eased to a stop and he stepped out. The woman—the executive assistant to the asshole—hadn't told him her name, he realized. He kept walking. It didn't matter; he'd remember which room was hers. Smiling, he now realized he was looking forward to returning to Stockton tomorrow. That was all it took—a woman's throaty laugh.

He strode down the hallway until he found Room 720. He opened the door, placed the Do Not Disturb sign on the outside door handle, and then went straight to the safe in the closet. The bag wouldn't fit in it, so he put the contents inside one stack at a time until it was full. He still had some left, mostly loose paper bills, so he wrapped the bag into a small bundle and stepped into the bathroom. He opened the cabinet under the sink, kneeled down, and jammed the bag between the pipe and the back corner. He peered in, checked from every angle, and decided it was good enough. Even if a cleaning lady did come in here, she was unlikely to see the bag.

This was definitely better than taking the money back to Mammoth View with him. Safer. Safe was his middle name. It was the reason he'd never been in the can. Becky's death had made him careful, which, in his world, made him unusual. Billy understood how easy it was to get cocky. When you're running cons, pulling jobs—you're the one in charge. You plan it out, step by step. So after it works a few times, you start to think nothing can go wrong, that you're the puppet master. All you have to do is follow your list, scratch through each item when it's done, and carry on to the next one.

The real world, of course, didn't work that way. Unexpected problems cropped up, people proved untrustworthy, you made mistakes. A real pro—and Billy thought of himself as a real pro—expected the unforeseen, and so he could adjust on the fly. Like his daughter ending up at the police station in the town where he'd just pulled the biggest heist of his career. Maybe he should have been able to see that possibility, but he didn't. It didn't matter. He wasn't fazed. Not much, anyway. And he figured it out. He felt confident it was all going to work out just fine.

He took Highway 99 south out of the city. After all those hours on the tiny, two-lane 120, fighting that goddamn truck, the 99 felt huge, like he was cruising through outer space. He guessed it would be past dawn by the time he collected Tori and they made it home to Bakersfield, and that was assuming he had no trouble with Officer Barea.

The radio babbled news: Reggie Jackson struck out three times today and was now on track to set a season record for whiffs. Something about the CIA conducting mind-control experiments. California's snowpack was at an all-time low. Billy's breath stuck in his throat when he heard the voice say ". . . town of Mammoth View in the southern Sierra. Three are dead and a panic ensued after . . ." He punched the button, cutting off the report.

Billy took a deep breath and slowed the car. He tried to anticipate how this new piece of information—a piece that was highly predictable—could go wrong for him. Who might have spotted him in Mammoth View and made something of it? He came up empty. There might be roadblocks coming out of the town, but since he didn't have any of the money on him, he wasn't worried about that. He banished the radio report from his mind.

Once he put Stockton's industrial district behind him, the drive became pleasant. Collections of trees and bushes along the sides of the road were interspersed with open stretches that offered expansive views of farmland. He found the perfect rows of crops fascinating. To him, it looked like some higher form of life had designed them. Humans didn't create such perfection. He watched the hills that rolled along the horizon. This was pretty country, he decided. People thought of Los Angeles and San Francisco as California, but this was the real California, the breadbasket of America. Los Angeles only existed because it had stolen the Central Valley's water. He'd seen *Chinatown* a second time—on his own, at a matinee—so he could understand what exactly it was trying to say. The first time he saw it, Tori asked him afterward what Faye Dunaway meant at the end, when Jack Nicholson was slapping her, and Billy didn't have an answer. He still wasn't sure.

He noted the sign for the Sierra National Forest and swung into the exit. Coming out of the turn, he accelerated. He hated the idea that he was driving back into Mammoth View—right back into his own crime scene—but he was in a good mood anyway. He liked Jack Nicholson. The man had style. And he felt confident he could brazen it out at the Mammoth View police department.

He also was happy that he'd be with Tori soon. He could admit that to himself. She was a good kid. A pain in the ass sometimes, but smart and talented. It wasn't just Becky's genes; he'd had something to do with it. He'd raised the girl. Guided her. He enjoyed spending time with his daughter. He loved the rare Bakersfield night when it rained—always a deluge, the gutters clattering, windows keening with the wind. Because Tori couldn't sleep with the noise and the worries it brought. She would sit up with him, talking about the Dodgers and the Los Angeles Strings, matching him drink for drink, hers being iced tea or hot chocolate.

If she went to college, he realized, he'd be alone. He thought about that. He had no friends, an occupational necessity. Friends expected you to have a story, a history they could delve into like the card-catalog files at the library. You could keep things from your child much easier than from a friend.

He tapped the brake to bring the car down to the speed limit. He wondered how Tori had done at the running camp, if she really was as good as her high school coach said she was. Billy marveled at how smooth she was at full sprint; she looked more natural running than walking. In the meet against San Pedro, the first time he'd ever seen her really doing her thing, she'd come around the final turn in fifth or sixth place. He could tell she was going to win going away. Everyone else looked like they were being lashed, but Tori's face offered only determination. It was the first time he'd made it to a meet, and she wanted to win for him. That's what she said afterward. He was very proud. Being able to run like the wind came in handy in his line of work. He'd had to hoof it a lot of times, from property owners and security guards. He ran pretty good, too, though nothing like his daughter.

He gazed out the side window at the mountains on the horizon. He had no sense of their actual size, which bothered him, and he quickly turned his eyes back to the road. He was going to be a better father, he decided. Spend more time with Tori. It was important to him. He started to tell himself he was going to give up the criminal life for her, but he stopped the thought. Now he was just being sentimental. What would he do, bag groceries like that fifty-year-old retard at the Pac 'N Go? Besides, life was good just as it was. It amazed him how easy the bank job had been. Maybe this was the secret: little towns, just like Dillinger did it in the 1930s.

He reached for the radio. The newsman had said three people were dead. The other two must have been from the fire at the city warehouse. He had picked the site because he figured there wouldn't be anyone there early in the morning, and there definitely wasn't anyone there when Sam struck the match. The dead men could be firefighters, he thought. They'd be volunteers in such a small town, and so they'd be incompetent. Whatever the case, the report sat in his stomach like bad meat. He regretted the fire. They didn't need it; they had enough diversions already. He considered finding out who the victims were and anonymously sending their families some cash. He should probably do the same for the bank manager, he thought. He regretted that, too.

He turned the dial on the radio. He didn't want to think about the bank manager. He didn't want to think about his poor impulse control, about how he'd taken a man's life and wrecked a family. He'd already begun to wall it off, to squeeze it into the part of the brain left over from caveman days, the part that felt nothing and remembered nothing. He'd found he could fit a lot of shit in there. He kept rolling the dial until it alighted on a high-pitched voice and stopped, thinking it was a Johnnie Ray song. "My woman takes me higher, my woman keeps me warm . . ." Nope— not Johnnie Ray. He rolled the dial some more. "Captivating, stimulating, she said you sexy lady . . ." Nope—Black music. He rolled again. Wait. There. He inched it backward until the static blinked out. Dino. He patted the dashboard. Good dog. He preferred the jazzier, lesser-known Sinatra version of the song, but you couldn't complain about Dino. Billy joined in: "*The world still is the same, you never change it. As sure as the stars shine above. You're nobody 'til somebody loves you. So find yourself somebody to love.*"

Tapping his foot to the rhythm, suddenly happy, he turned his mind to Tori. Being able to run like that—like a bat out of hell—there were no two ways about it, it was a definite plus in his line of work. He was warming to the idea of getting her into the business with him rather than sending her to college. What she'd been through today—the cop on the phone made it sound like it was traumatic but that she was okay. The man called her brave. Billy smiled to himself. Of course she was. She was Billy Lane's girl. Nerves of steel.

The Chevelle's engine groaned as it began to climb toward Mammoth View. He couldn't believe that a town existed so far up in the mountains, in the middle of nowhere. A whole town, with shops and a barber and a police force—all so that rich people could come along in the wintertime and go skiing. What a country, he thought.

CHAPTER TWENTY-EIGHT

Melvin couldn't get up. It took too much energy, and he needed all that he had left for his brain. There were too many problems to work out, too many possibilities—so many that he didn't want to get started. Besides, his right eye throbbed. The pulsing headache made him feel swollen and sick. His tongue had no place to go: it crowded his teeth, lolled at the top of his throat. He looked up. Gordon had his hand out, offering to pull him to his feet. Melvin ignored him. He'd already decided, he didn't want to get up. He couldn't face the hard miles they had to put in tonight. He watched an endless chain gang of ants marching out from under the log and circling around it. The ants had a purpose, Melvin thought. They had each other. He only had his brother.

Melvin couldn't see an easy solution. Not without the car or a hostage. They were going to have to walk into the mountains. There, he'd admitted it. They were going to be Mountain Men. He hoisted himself to his feet and brushed off the underside of his pants. Homer wouldn't have hesitated to head into the mountains. He loved his weeklong hunting rambles through the Sierras. Melvin, when he was twelve or thirteen, asked to go with him, and the old man had laughed in his face.

"I bet the girl hasn't gone far," Gordon said. "She'll get lost and walk right back to us."

"Forget the girl."

Gordon looked up like he'd been slapped. "Why?"

"We've got bigger problems."

"Like what?"

Melvin started walking east, into the black night. The moon had fallen behind the mountain, blotting out the world. Melvin kept a hand in front of his face, in case a tree jumped out at him. Gordon fell in behind him and matched his stride. They had a cousin outside Bishop in Inyo County—Bobby Lee. They'd have to hide out at his place before getting a car and heading for Mexico. On foot, they could get to Bobby Lee's place in about three days, maybe four, assuming they could find food and water. Melvin couldn't stand Bobby Lee. The last time he saw him was at Homer's funeral. The guy finished every sentence with "baby." *Hey, Melvin, baby! This is a tough day, baby. Real tough, baby.* Bobby crated dates for a living, but he liked to talk like a hippie. Melvin wanted to tell him his hair wasn't long enough to be a hippie. And that he was too fat. Hippies weren't fat.

He figured the sheriff might not find the car until the morning. That would give them a good head start. He and Gordon might be coming up on Red Mountain by then. It'd be like finding a needle in a haystack for the police. The forest there was deep and thick. They'd be so far gone it'd be like they never existed. The cops might not find the girl and her boyfriend either. Gordon was actually right about something; it was easy to get turned around out here if you didn't know what you were doing. You get tired and woozy, and pretty soon you just lie down and go to sleep.

Melvin wondered if they'd get blamed if the girl died of exposure. Everybody always cared a lot more if it's a girl that dies. *Damn it, we didn't do anything*, he complained to himself. He figured they shouldn't be on the run at all. They didn't kill those two in the bank. And the girl and her boyfriend attacked *them*, not the other way around. They should turn around, march into Mammoth View, and file a police report. He and Gordon were the victims.

Melvin didn't turn around. He continued to head east, away from Mammoth View. That girl was something, he had to admit. A thoroughbred. Almost as tall as him, long goddamn legs. Think of the son she could produce for him: a real ballplayer, a natural centerfielder. Joltin' Joe! He thought about his Padres tryout, the three girls behind the backstop, their chanting and laughing. *Hey, hey, batter, swing! Hey, hey, batter—suh-wehhng!* They were having fun out there. He was trying to achieve something, trying to *be* someone, and these chippies were messing around, messing him up. He had cut them a look after his second swinging miss, and they laughed and clapped.

God, he remembered them so clearly. The one in the center had a round face with bright eyes that caught the sunlight. The girl next to her, the one closest to the dugout, was sexier, round everywhere except the face, her Padres T-shirt a size too small. She grinned at him, and it tipped directly into a leer. The girl on the other side was indistinct, lost behind her cap and windbreaker. Melvin dug deep into the batter's box. He didn't even see the next pitch; he'd lost his concentration. Despite his disappointment in his performance and theirs, he still looked for the girls when he walked into the parking lot at the end of the day. He figured they were there for a good time with a ball player, but there was no one waiting except family members: hard-eyed fathers and trembling mothers and sullen younger siblings.

"You okay, Melvin?"

"Yeah. Why?"

"I don't know. You look kind of peaked."

"How would you know? You can't see anything out here."

Melvin could feel his brother trying to not get mad. "I can see fine," Gordon said. "Clear night."

Melvin stopped. The forest floor had given way to an upward slope, and he'd lost his breath. He craned his neck and blinked vigorously. The land shook off all signs of life as it rose. No trees, no bushes: the first hint that the desert was out there at the horizon, spreading its tentacles, pushing further into the woods every year. He could see the sky now, and his vision cleared for a moment. It was a beautiful night. He leaned forward and put his hands on his knees. His head throbbed harder, be-bopping over his face and into his throat. And now he felt his foot again. He wondered if it had started bleeding.

"Melvin?"

Melvin hawked up a wad and spat. It hit the dirt in front of him. He stared at it, studied it. Some blood from his foot seemed to have gotten in there. He straightened up. "I've got to take a dump."

"Right now?"

"If bears can crap in the woods, so can I."

"Well, all right."

"Stay here, relax. I'll be back in a minute." Melvin returned to the forest. He pushed on a tree to propel himself forward, held out both hands as the darkness fell. He kept walking until the woods closed around him, sealing him in. He worked at his belt, but instead of pulling down his pants and squatting, he sat down. He needed to rest. He worried that Gordon wouldn't be able to make it all the way to Inyo County. Gordon had never gone into the badlands with Homer. He'd never really been an outdoorsman, except for that one year he did Boy Scouts. They'd be skirting the edge of Death Valley on the second day, so it was going to be hot as hell. They would have to hit all of the lakes along the way, drink as much as they could. He dropped flat on his back and let out a long breath. They should walk all night and hole up somewhere during the day, that was the smart way to do it. But he was pretty tired right now, and you had to listen to your body. He closed his eyes, and his breathing slowed. His head kept pounding, but flat on his back, the pounding spread evenly through his body, drumming him into a comfortable reverie. His whole body jerked as his bowels evacuated, but he didn't notice.

King waited for one of them to start playing Good Cop.

"Come on, Oscar. The more you say now, the better it will be for you. You could be looking at real time for this."

King, seated in a fold-out chair, looked across the dented metal table at Sheriff Davis. The sweat that had dried on his skin felt like it had been reanimated. "Jail time? For what?"

"Inducing a public panic is no joke, Mr. Desario," said the deputy who was pacing behind the sheriff.

"It's *War of the Worlds*," King said. "I didn't expect any of this to happen."

"What do you mean, war of the worlds?" the deputy asked.

King threw his hands up. Why didn't they get it? "The novel. The novel!" he exclaimed, stunned by the deputy's blank look. "H.G. Wells. *The Time Machine? The Island of Doctor Moreau?* Come on, H.G. Wells." King's breath caught in his throat, and he coughed. Sheriff Davis put his hands in front of him, palms down. *Calm yourself, kid*, the hands said. King noticed the deputy wasn't making the same gesture. Instead, his right hand was on his gun. Only then did King realize he had stood up.

King sat back down. He ran trembling fingers through his hair.

The deputy, a beefy young guy with a thick mustache, put his hands on the table. He leaned into the suspect. "You were reading a story?"

"Yeah, the Mercury Theatre adaptation. Everyone reads H. G. Wells in school. How can doing it on the radio be a crime?"

"When it makes people grab their guns and run for the hills, it's a crime," the deputy said.

King closed his eyes. His head pounded; he could feel his lungs straining against his chest. He was in trouble here, he knew that. But it wasn't the trouble he'd thought he was in.

"What are you smiling about, Oscar?" the sheriff asked. He was a small man, wiry, with a boxy face. Leaning on an elbow across the table from King, he affected casualness, as if this interrogation was nothing, the case was all wrapped up, and he was just dotting i's and crossing t's.

King tried to pull his face into a grimace, the appropriate look for this situation, but he couldn't manage it. The grin wouldn't be denied. He put his hand over his mouth.

"Let us in on the joke," Sheriff Davis said. "We like a good joke."

King took his hand away from his mouth. The sheriff seemed like a decent man. He might understand. "It was a radio show. The Mercury Theatre did it in 1938, like I said. It created a panic just like this. But that was years ago. Not so many people were literate. There was no TV. You know how good I had to be to do the same thing today?"

"To do what?"

"Start another panic," King said. "Did Orson Welles go to jail for his show?"

"Who?" the deputy asked. "Achy Wells?"

"Orson Welles," the sheriff said. "The sell-no-wine-before-it's-time guy. The actor."

The deputy caressed his mustache. He had no idea what either of them was talking about. "You're one up on Orson Welles then," he said to King.

Yeah, King thought. I'm better than Orson Welles. Better than a guy who has an Academy Award on his mantel. He couldn't wipe the smile off his face. He'd watched the TV movie about the panic a couple of years ago—that had put the idea in his head. Paul Shenar played Welles. *The Night That Panicked America*—that was the title. He remembered that nothing about the Mercury radio hysteria had seemed plausible in the movie, but now King had proved it. He hadn't really believed he could do it, but he had. People had actually freaked out and evacuated the town. He was still smiling even as the deputy clapped on the handcuffs.

When they brought him out for booking, he spotted Tori at the front desk. A man stood with her, nodding at a policeman. The man signed something on a clipboard, and the officer took it and moved away. King blanched when he realized who the man was.

Billy. King mentally shook himself to clear his vision. Yep, still Billy Lane. *Billy* was Tori's father? Tori spotted King. She stood up straight, smiled, and started to raise her arm in greeting. Her mouth fell into a surprised O when she saw the handcuffs. Billy turned then, following his daughter's gaze. He froze at the sight.

"Dad, what's going on?" Tori said. "That's the man who saved me. He's the one."

King, continuing across the room, watched Tori's mouth move. Another wave of happiness rolled over him, better than the one during the interrogation. She was coming to his defense! She liked him; she respected him. A feeling of power followed, surging through his torso. He gave no indication that he recognized Billy. As the sheriff and the deputy guided him toward a back room, he casually raised his hands as if to scratch an itch. He put an index finger to the side of his nose and tapped, making eye contact with Billy. *You're safe.* King was no snitch. Especially when the cops were clueless. He thought about the other girl, Alice Krendel, who helped set all of this in motion. He thought about how she gave up the morning routine and the vault code so easily. He didn't even have to bed her. A make-out session in the park behind the bank, his hand up under her bra—that was all it took. She was desperate for it—desperate for anything he would give her. King smiled to himself. He sniffed at his fingers, as if he could still smell Alice on it. He felt on top of the world.

Billy followed King's progress until the DJ and the two lawmen had disappeared into the booking room.

Tori saw the look from King, too, the swipe at the nose, and immediately understood it. "We should go, Dad," she said.

Billy started to respond, but the front door swung open behind them. The Mammoth View police chief—a gaudy patch on his shoulder identified him—and another Mammoth View officer pushed into the building. They stopped, scanned the room, and clocked an unfamiliar cop—the state policeman who had been helping Billy.

"Where the hell is Marco?" the chief said.

The state policeman had turned away and didn't respond.

The Mammoth View officer with the chief noticed another cop, a sheriff's deputy, in the back room. "I'll get this thing moving," he told the chief. The officer headed for the deputy in the back. "Hey," he called out, "we found the suspects' car wrapped around a tree on Minaret Road."

The chief had nodded at his subordinate, but he didn't seem interested in what was going to happen next. His look was inward, deep into unexplored space. He took hold of the badge on his shirt and carefully unhooked it. He smoothed out his shirt; with the other hand he squeezed the badge as if crushing it. Looking up, he noticed Billy and Tori. He gave them the once over.

Billy put his arm around Tori's shoulder as he offered the chief an appreciative smile. "I heard about the bank," he said, probing. "I have a safe-deposit box there."

The chief looked like he needed to spit. "Well, you'll have to check with the bank when it reopens."

"Of course. Of course. Thank you." Billy steered Tori to the door, pulled it open.

Once they were outside and by themselves, Tori looked up at her father. "Dad, you know King?"

"Yeah, we go back."

"What's going to happen to him?"

Billy patted his daughter's head. He was impressed that she picked up on King's signal in there. "Don't worry. He'll be fine. He'll come by the house in a few days, say hello."

The Chevelle sat in the space right in front of the building. Billy ushered her inside it and closed the door behind her. "Nice wheels, huh?"

"I like it," Tori said.

Stepping around to the other side of the car, he looked out at the horizon. The stars glimmered in the sky like Christmas decorations. He read the small metal sign that stood in front of the Chevelle: "Reserved For Police Vehicles." Billy inhaled the evening air. He liked it up here in the mountains. It smelled fresh and pure. Like freedom.

ACKNOWLEDGMENTS

Jana Good, my editor, believed in this book from the very start. Her encouragement, insight and attention to detail have made it immeasurably better. I'd also like to thank Kayla Church, Dayna Anderson, and everyone else at Amberjack Publishing who helped make *Mammoth* happen.

I must offer a hat tip to Jeff Guinn, Michael Meggison, and Derek Zeller, my close friends who always support my efforts. And, of course, endless thanks to my wife, Deborah King, for making this book—and my life—so much better.

ABOUT THE AUTHOR

Douglas Perry is the author of two critically acclaimed nonfiction books: *The Girls of Murder City: Fame, Lust, and the Beautiful Killers Who Inspired Chicago* and *Eliot Ness: The Rise and Fall of an American Hero*. He lives in Portland, Oregon.